CATCHING A COWGIRL

CALLAHANS OF COPPER CREEK BOOK 6

NATALIE DEAN

DEDICATION

I'd like to dedicate this book to YOU! All of my wonderful readers that have been following my stories over the years.

We're embarking on another new journey through Copper Creek. I hope you enjoy these stories as much as you've loved the Baker brothers!

Thank you to my biggest fans.... There's a lot of you! Jess, Bernie, Wren, Judy, Sherry, Vicci, Phyllis, Debbie, Indra, Jennifer, Carol, Jeanette, Margaret, Paul, and I know there's more I didn't list. But thank you all!

And I can't leave out my wonderful mother, son, sister, and Auntie. I love you all, and thank you for helping me make this happen.

Most of all, I thank God for blessing me on this endeavor.

AND... I've got a special team of advance readers who are always so helpful in pointing out any last minute corrections that need to be made. I'm so thankful to those of you who are so helpful!

ALSO BY NATALIE DEAN

CONTEMPORARY ROMANCE

Copper Creek Romances

BAKER BROTHERS OF COPPER CREEK

Copper Creek Romances Series 1

Cowboys & Protective Ways

Cowboys & Crushes

Cowboys & Christmas Kisses

Cowboys & Broken Hearts

Cowboys & Second Chances

Cowboys & Wedding Woes

Cowboys' Mom Finds Love

CALLAHANS OF COPPER CREEK

Copper Creek Romances Series 2

Making a Cowgirl

Marrying a Cowgirl

Christmas with a Cowgirl

Trusting a Cowgirl

Dating a Cowgirl

Catching a Cowgirl

Loving a Cowgirl

Marrying a Cowboy

KEAGANS OF COPPER CREEK

Copper Creek Romances Series 3

Some Cowboys are Off-Limits

Some Cowgirls Love Single Dads

Some Cowboys are Infuriating

Some Cowboys Don't Like City Girls

Some Cowboys Heal Broken Hearts

Some Cowgirls are Worth Protecting

Some Cowboys are Just Friends

Some Cowboys Fall for Hidden Stars

Some Cowboys Come Home for Christmas

Some Cowboys Brave the Flames

Some Cowboys Fight for Love

PALMERS OF COPPER CREEK

Copper Creek Romances Series 4

Mateo & Nicole

Sophia & Cameron

Roman & Olivia

Camilla & Dallas

Isabelle & Jason

Marcus & Wynter

Miller Family Saga

BROTHERS OF MILLER RANCH

Miller Family Saga Series 1

Her Second Chance Cowboy

Saving Her Cowboy

Her Rival Cowboy

Her Fake-Fiance Cowboy Protector

Taming Her Cowboy Billionaire

BROTHERS OF MILLER RANCH SERIES BUNDLE

MILLER BROTHERS OF TEXAS

Miller Family Saga Series 2

The New Cowboy at Miller Ranch

Humbling Her Cowboy

In Debt to the Cowboy

The Cowboy Falls for the Veterinarian

Almost Fired by the Cowboy

Faking a Date with Her Cowboy Boss

MILLER BROTHERS OF TEXAS SERIES BUNDLE

BRIDES OF MILLER RANCH, N.M.

Miller Family Saga Series 3

Cowgirl Fallin' for the Single Dad

Cowgirl Fallin' for the Ranch Hand

Cowgirl Fallin' for the Neighbor

Cowgirl Fallin' for the Miller Brother

Cowgirl Fallin' for Her Best Friend's Brother

Cowboy Fallin' in Love Again

BRIDES OF MILLER RANCH, N.M. SERIES BUNDLE

~

Though I try to keep this list updated in each book, you may also visit my website nataliedeanbooks.com for the most up to date information on my book list.

CONTENTS

1

Shane

This couldn't be happening. Not now. Why was it that when one thing went wrong, everything else followed like a couple of baby ducks after their mother? Shane raked a hand through his mussed hair as he stood in the hallway in front of his closed office door. On the other side of that fancy mahogany barrier, his two least favorite cousins were probably scheming at this very moment.

His hands curled into tight fists at his sides. He didn't know how they had managed to track him down. Marc and Madeline weren't the brightest members of his family. Shane's jaw was so tight it ached. He couldn't deal with their shenanigans tonight. His nerves were already frayed, and he was barely holding everything together.

It wasn't just the restaurant opening without one of his chefs. It wasn't the fact that his heart had been stomped on by a lovely woman only a few months ago. Nor was it the arrival of his cousins reminding him exactly why he'd decided to settle down in the middle of nowhere.

No. It was all of the above, and he didn't have the patience to deal with any of it.

Maybe if he hid out in the kitchen, his cousins would get the hint and leave. They were part of the Owens family tree, after all. Their patience was bound to run out eventually.

He took a step backward, ready to make his escape, when he bumped into someone. A soft gasp burst behind him and he spun to find Eloise Callahan staring at him.

"I'm so sorry," she murmured, her voice just above a whisper. "I was just about to head out when I realized my phone was missing."

Shane glowered.

She stilled. "Is something wrong?"

"You didn't by chance let one of my cousins borrow it, did you?"

Slowly, she nodded. "Madeline was hoping she could use it to look something up. I must have forgotten to get it back from her."

"Yeah," he muttered, "it must have slipped your mind." He spun around and stalked toward the door. Madeline was up to her old ways already. Not even thirty minutes here, and she was stealing from the locals. He heard Eloise's footsteps and he stopped suddenly, only to feel her collide with him.

She gasped again. "I'm so sorry."

"Stay here."

"Pardon?"

Shane faced her, taking care to keep his voice level so he didn't startle her or make her feel like she was the one in trouble. She didn't deserve to be roped into any of this. In fact, if he could get her to leave and not come back until he had safely forced his family to vacate the state, he'd prefer that above all else. "I'm going to have a word with my cousins—in private. If you wouldn't mind waiting out here while I do that, I'll return your phone to you."

She thumbed over her shoulder. "Would you mind if I go visit my sister?"

"That would be fine." Actually, it would be perfect. If she could stay away from his office, he'd be able to have the conversation he needed in order to get them to leave.

Eloise offered him a small, shy smile, and for a moment he was taken aback. She was definitely related to her older sister. Some of the Callahans resembled their father, but Brielle and Eloise must have resembled their mother more.

He had to give his head a sharp shake to clear it before getting back on track. "I'll come find you."

She nodded. "Okay. Thanks."

Shane watched her go until she turned the corner and was out of sight. He let out an irritated sigh and faced the office door again. Calm. He needed to stay calm. Marc and Madeline always fed off his fury. The ironic thing was that they used to be the only things that made him react that way.

Now, his attitude was far more volatile—which probably had something to do with a certain Miss Callahan.

He couldn't think about how Brielle had hurt him. Right now, he needed a clear head so he could see through his cousins' lies.

Shane pushed his way into the office to find Marc seated in his office chair with his crossed ankles resting on the desk. Madeline perched on the edge of his desk, studying her nails. They had been speaking quietly when he'd opened the door, but their conversation died off the moment they saw him.

And just like he'd expected, they smiled at him like the crocodiles they were.

These two were not to be trusted.

"Hey, cousin!" Madeline sang. She gestured around his office. "You've gotten all fancy—just like Gramps."

He stood just inside his office, his back to the door. These two were predators, willing to tear into his throat at a moment's notice. "What do you want?"

Madeline and Marc exchanged glances, then laughed.

This was their game. They made a mockery of him any chance they got.

Madeline hopped off the edge of the desk. "What? Can't we come drop in and visit our cousin on the night of his big restaurant opening?" She trailed a well-manicured fingernail down his suit jacket.

He brushed her off with a swipe of his hand. "No. You can't." He didn't think it was possible, but her lower lip puckered even further.

"Why not?" she whined. "Didn't you miss us?"

Shane stepped away from her so he could get a better look at Marc. "I want you two to leave. Tonight."

"But we just got here." Marc had his arms crossed, and by the stubborn look on his face, he wasn't planning on listening to anything Shane had to say. "Ever since Gramps died and left us all that money, you've kinda just turned your back on us. I thought we were family."

Shane's eyes narrowed. "Grandfather didn't leave you two anything. He left it all to me." He shifted his focus to Madeline. "I gave you each enough money to last a lifetime if you spent it wisely so you would leave me in peace."

Both of his cousins reacted the same way. They rolled their eyes and scoffed at his statement.

"If you'll recall, I also gave you his loft apartment in the city. Heaven only knows why you've decided to come all the way out here." He had his own suspicions, but he prayed he was wrong. There was only one good reason why Marc and Madeline would leave the comfort of the city.

They needed more money.

Well, they weren't going to get anything from him. He'd invested and tied up most of his liquid assets to a point where he wouldn't have access to them for another quarter. They were going to be plum out of luck if they thought they'd get one dime from him.

"So? Why are you *really* here?" Shane asked.

Madeline glanced at Marc, and he nodded. She let out a sigh and her soft, high-pitched voice flattened into what Shane was used to. "Fine. We wanted to see what you were doing with your share of the money. We're almost out."

"You're *almost out*." Shane hated how he'd managed to hit the nail on the head. He made a show of looking around the office. "Where are the hidden cameras. They're here somewhere, right? You're pulling my leg."

His cousins were less than amused. Their expressions didn't change one bit as they stared him down. Marc's feet dropped to the floor with a resounding thud and he stood up. "We only have one mil left."

Shane's brows shot up and his eyes darted from one to the other. "Please tell me that you *each* have that much." He smacked his forehead with his hand. "Geez. I gave you each five million. How did you manage to blow through that in just a few years?"

They glanced at one another, and Madeline shrugged before she dug a compact mirror and lipstick out of her purse. "Really? You judge us when you took ten million. That was hardly fair, was it? You weren't even related to him by *blood*. You didn't deserve any of it."

A sharp pang sliced through him. Whenever Madeline had a chance, she reminded him that he hadn't been wanted. His parents had adopted him, then passed away before he'd turned ten. Their grandfather was all he'd had left, and now he was gone, too. His jaw tightened and he spoke through gritted teeth.

"Grandfather left me the whole estate. I didn't have to give you a dime."

Madeline finished pressing her lips together, then shot him a withering look. "You turned him against us, and you know it. If you hadn't given us anything, we would have taken you to court."

This was the exact reason he'd come to Copper Creek. He'd needed to get away from the poisonous lifestyle his cousins led. His arm jerked outward, and he pointed toward the door. "Out."

They stared at him with blank expressions, unmoving.

"I mean it. You're not getting anything more from me, and you're not welcome in Copper Creek. I want you two to catch a bus and head back home."

Madeline pouted as she strode toward him. "Now, is that any way to treat your family?" She peered over her shoulder toward her brother. "We actually really like it here. That Eloise lady was really sweet and Marc thinks he might be in love."

Shane bristled. "You leave that young woman alone. She didn't do anything to you."

Madeline's eyes narrowed and her bright red lips curled into a sly smile. "Do you have a *thing* for her?"

He glowered at his cousin. Right family, wrong daughter. But he wasn't about to give these two any of that information. Somehow, they always found his weak spot, and that was when his life went downhill. A muscle in his cheek twitched.

Her lips puckered to the side, and she tilted her head slightly. "No, I don't think he likes Eloise, Marc. But there's something about her that gets him all riled up." She reached forward and patted his cheek. "Don't worry, cousin. I'll figure it out. We have plenty of time. Heck, we saw a ranch for sale on the way out here. Maybe we could be neighbors." She shot a look over her shoulder toward her brother. "Come on, Marc. We need to check into our hotel so we can get settled." She winked at Shane as she brushed past him. "I'll see you later, cousin."

Marc followed on her heels, smirking at Shane as if they'd won some great battle.

And maybe they had.

The second they were out of the room, Shane grabbed a glass decanter and launched it at the wall. Glass shattered and the amber liquid trickled to the ground. He didn't drink—never could stomach the stuff—but there were some clients who appreciated a nice bourbon. Now, they'd have to be happy with a seltzer water.

Shane breathed heavily, his hands clutched in fists at his sides. His vision was a blur, and he had a hard time recalling why he'd ended up at his office in the first place.

Eloise's phone!

He let out a curse and spun around. Madeline had stolen Eloise's phone for whatever reason. With his luck, she'd already be long gone. His steps slowed as he made it into a more crowded area of the country club. Who was he kidding? He doubted he'd be able to get it back.

Shane raked two hands through his hair. He was a ball of nervous energy, and all he really wanted to do was go for a walk —or a run.

But he couldn't. He had a restaurant opening, two cousins who wanted nothing more than to bring him misery, and a woman who was expecting him to return her phone within the next few minutes.

Why did they have to show up tonight of all nights? Maybe it was for the best that Brielle wasn't interested anymore. The last thing he needed was for his cousins to latch on to someone they thought he valued. There was no telling what they might do.

He straightened his shoulders and headed for the restaurant. Before he made it five steps into the waiting area, someone tapped him on the shoulder. Shane glanced toward one of the kitchen staff but continued his stride. "What is it?" he demanded. Could this night get any worse?

"Sir?"

Shane spun around. One more thing was all it would take to break the camel's back. It almost looked like the cook was trembling in his boots. Being intimidating wasn't one of Shane's normal personality traits. He'd never liked being that kind of boss, but at this moment in time maybe that was what he had to be. "Spit it out. I have a restaurant to oversee."

"We're short-staffed. Penelope just went into labor. She's on her way to the hospital now." The poor guy shrank back slightly as if Shane were the type to strike him down. The thought was laughable. If he had that reputation, his cousins wouldn't be hounding him so much.

Pinching the bridge of his nose, Shane attempted to draw out any sort of solution he could find in the recesses of his mind, but there was none. He literally had nothing left to give in this moment.

"Eloise is a really good cook," came a female voice.

Shane stiffened. Even above the quiet roar of the quickly filling restaurant, he could hear Faye's voice. If they hadn't arrived moments earlier with news of their new engagement, he wouldn't have been able to place it. Actually, if he hadn't dated Brielle for a time, he wouldn't have even bothered facing her.

Faye grinned while Eloise dug her elbow into her sister's side. "Seriously. Out of all of us, Eloise is the best cook. We all avoid the kitchen as much as we can just so she'll give in and make supper."

Eloise gasped. "Faye! I'm not a chef."

"But you *can* cook." Shane didn't know what possessed him to accept this recommendation without another thought. He hadn't tasted Eloise's cooking, so he had no idea if Faye was just telling him what he wanted to hear. On top of that, he needed more time to figure out what to do about Marc and Madeline, along with the missing phone.

Eloise blushed a deep red. "I enjoy cooking, but I don't think I'm going to be good enough to help out in your kitchen."

"All we really need is an extra pair of hands." The cook behind him jumped into the conversation, his voice hopeful. "It would be more helpful than you know."

Shane studied Eloise. He hadn't heard much about her from Brielle. Granted, Brielle didn't like talking about her sisters much at all. She preferred to keep her family life tucked away. If he'd been paying attention, he would have noticed that was a big red flag. She wasn't serious about dating at all.

He shook off the depressing thought. There were far more important things to worry about—a cook being number one on his list. Eloise shifted in her seat, and this time, Faye was the one to nudge her.

Shane had no other options. All he could do was pray Eloise was as good as Faye insisted she was. "Would you mind? I'll make it worth your while."

She glanced at her sister, then brought her gaze up to meet his. "Okay, but I'm not making any promises."

2

Eloise

Eloise couldn't believe she'd actually agreed to cook… for Shane Owens, no less. Okay, so she wasn't exactly cooking for Shane. She was cooking for several actual customers who'd come to this restaurant to be wowed by the local millionaire.

She didn't know if he actually had that kind of wealth, but she'd heard the stories. As she stared at the back of his head while they made their way toward the rear of the restaurant, she couldn't help but let her thoughts wander.

Shane was the wealthiest man in town. He kept to himself, which was why it was so strange to find out he had family visiting. Did Brielle know them? They seemed nice enough, if not a bit more curious than the average local.

One thing she noticed right away was how different they were from their cousin. Every time she'd interacted with Shane, it had been—stiff. That was the only way to describe it. He seemed far too serious. Or grumpy. Perhaps he was a little bit of both.

He pushed through a set of heavy, metal double doors, and immediately she was swamped by sights, sounds, and smells so delicious she had to pause to take it all in.

Shane grasped her by the elbow, successfully putting a stop to her wandering eye. He led her toward the back of the kitchen, where there appeared to be an office for whoever was the manager of the kitchen. He gestured toward a chair, then stood in the doorway that led back to the busy kitchen. His hands were clasped behind his back, and he looked more like one of those military guys in front of the European palace.

Eloise took the seat he'd pointed out but couldn't get comfortable. It wasn't that the chair was plastic; it was more the situation she'd found herself in. If she wanted to slip out and go back into the main part of the restaurant, she wasn't quite sure Shane would allow it.

She cleared her throat, but he didn't face her. "Shane—Mr. Owens?"

He glanced over his shoulder toward her.

"Is there something we're waiting for?"

Shane nodded. "Yes, I'm sorry. I'm a little distracted tonight."

She offered an understanding smile. "That's to be expected, right? With everything that's going on?"

His dark gaze didn't change. In fact, he stared at her like she knew something she wasn't supposed to. Eloise tore her gaze away from him. Either he was having a terrible night, or he didn't like her all that much.

Shane heaved a sigh. "We're waiting for my head chef. He needs to know what you're capable of before he assigns you to start cooking. The last thing I need is for you to get burned or chop off a finger."

Her eyes flitted up to meet his, but she found he had turned away from her again. "With all due respect, I've been in a kitchen most of my life. I think I can handle not getting hurt for one night."

He shifted his weight but didn't face her. "If it's all the same to you, I'd like to cover my bases. There's already too many things going—" He cut himself off and peeked at her again. "By the way, I couldn't retrieve your phone. Are you sure my cousin borrowed it?"

Eloise frowned. "I suppose it might have dropped between the seats. I'll double-check after everything gets settled here."

His grim expression only made her feel more self-conscious. It was like he expected her to apologize for something she had no idea she'd done wrong. Before she could ask him if she had in fact done something to offend him, the man they must have been waiting for hustled into the kitchen. "Mr. Owens. What do you need, sir? As you can tell, we're already incredibly busy and we're short—" His gaze swept over Eloise, then he froze.

"That's why I'm here," Shane said. "Eloise has some experience in the kitchen. She's going to help out this evening until we can find a replacement for Penelope."

Eloise's eyes darted from the cook to Shane and back. She couldn't tell if the chef was pleased or upset by this executive decision.

The man stepped toward her, and she scrambled to her feet. He held out his hand. "I'm Chef Gabriel. Can you tell me more about the experience you have with cooking?"

She glanced at Shane to find him slipping from the office area. Holding up a finger, she gave him an apologetic smile. "One moment, please." Eloise tossed her jacket on the chair where she'd been sitting, hoping that was enough to let the chef know she'd be returning to the room in a minute. Then she darted out of the office, following Shane as he wove between those working in his restaurant. She would have called out to him, but her voice stuck in her throat. Instead, she placed her hand on his shoulder.

Shane spun around to face her. His eyes raked up and down her body briefly before he tilted his head toward the office. "Did Chef Gabriel say something?"

"What? No. We haven't had enough time to say anything. But you're just going to leave like that?"

He stared at her with confusion. "Was there more to discuss?"

"Of course there is. I can't just start working for you without being officially hired. I haven't agreed to terms. What if something were to happen to me? Would I be covered by your insurance? And there's the matter of pay."

Shane appraised her, and a sense of intrigue and maybe some amusement flickered in his eyes. "You think I would let you work here if I thought there was any concern with liability?"

She stilled. He made an excellent point. Since the moment he'd arrived in Copper Creek, he had made a name for himself. He'd managed to buy one of the largest properties on the outskirts of the town and turn it into a thriving business that catered not only to the locals but brought in people from out of state.

Somehow, Shane had even managed to impress those who lived in this small town, and he had made several friends which was no small feat. Only a smart man could do that.

As much as she fought it, Eloise couldn't stop the blush that crept up the back of her neck. She looked away, squirming under his stare. "I'm happy to help. But I'm not going to just go along without covering my bases first."

"How does one hundred sound?"

Her eyes flitted up to meet his. It was six now. If she worked until midnight, that was a little over fifteen an hour—not bad for kitchen help. She nodded. "I can do a hundred for the night, but if you're going to want me to continue helping out—"

"That's an hour, Miss Callahan."

She nearly choked, and her head had to catch up with what he'd said before she could bring herself to utter one stammered word. "*What*?"

"This is last minute, and you're being thrown into a situation you weren't planning on. I need the help desperately, and I have no time to negotiate."

"You can't possibly afford—"

"Don't offend me with what you think I can afford. Now, if this conversation satisfies your concerns, you can stop by my office at the end of the night and I'll cut you your check." His eyes darted behind her, and she followed them to find Chef Gabriel standing with his arms crossed and an irritated look on his face. When she glanced back to Shane, he was walking away.

Despite her head having a hard time catching up, her legs didn't seem to suffer from the same problem. She wheeled around, heading straight for the chef. "I can do just about anything you tell me to if I have instructions."

Gabriel lifted a brow. "I can't be your babysitter."

"You won't have to be. I can handle most dishes. Just tell me what to make." Her voice held more confidence than she felt on the inside. She still couldn't believe how she'd managed to get roped into this whole thing. Right about now, she would have been heading home to fix herself something small before snuggling up with a good book.

Gabriel jerked his chin toward the kitchen. "I'm going to start you on plating. It's a two-person job, and Hannah can keep an eye on you." He took a few steps without another word, leaving Eloise wondering if she was meant to follow him or go track down whoever this Hannah was. But then he stopped and faced her. "Well? Are you coming?"

She lurched forward. Of course he wanted her to follow him.

He gestured vaguely toward a row of lockers just outside the office. "You can find an apron over there. Are you wearing comfortable shoes? You'll be on your feet all night." His eyes dropped lower, and when they settled on her footwear, she tapped the heels of her boots together. "I work in these all day. They'll be fine."

Gabriel sighed. "I knew I would be sorry when Shane convinced me to move out here."

Eloise blinked a few times. Wait a minute. Did Gabriel know Shane from before he moved here? Or was he head-hunted? She didn't have enough time to dwell on her theories because Gabriel had already managed to slip around a corner. If she didn't pay attention, she'd get lost. It was time to get her head on straight so she could show Shane she wasn't just some dumb cowgirl who didn't know her way around a kitchen. He'd given her a shot. This could be the beginning of a new adventure for her.

Over the next six hours Eloise did her best to hold her own. What started out as simple became chaotic as the dinner rush hit. The chef shouted orders and received resounding comments from his staff. While it put her on edge, there was something thrilling about being in the center of all this chaos. She was part of something big that was happening, and she'd never felt so alive.

She was beginning to understand why so many of her sisters had opted to find jobs away from home. Being ordered around in a clean kitchen surrounded by mouthwatering food was one hundred times better than stepping over mounds of manure.

Eloise wiped her forehead with the back of her hand before she whisked the dish she'd put together over to the counter for the waitress to pick up.

"Callahan, we need another chef's salad."

"Right away, Chef." Eloise spun around, nearly colliding with someone—not just someone—Shane. She peered up at him and murmured, "Sorry." Then she darted around him and headed for the walk-in refrigerator. It made sense that she'd nearly bump into Shane. The kitchen was a well-oiled machine, but one that didn't account for the addition of a person who normally wasn't hanging around. It was strange how often she could hurry toward another part of the kitchen without any concern she'd get in someone's way—almost like she wasn't in a kitchen at all. They were like a herd of wild horses flowing and moving as one.

She retrieved the fixings for the chef's salad and hurried back to her station. She knew this one by heart, granted it wasn't all that difficult, but she was proud of how quickly she could fulfill her duty.

Her eyes swept through the kitchen, and it wasn't until they locked with Shane's that she realized she'd been looking for him. She couldn't put her finger on just why she was so interested in finding him, but it was probably because she wanted to make sure he saw she was worth what he was paying her. Eloise dragged her gaze away from him and focused once more on the food.

A snort left her chest as she placed the salad on the counter with a flourish. No one was worth being paid one hundred dollars per hour—definitely not her.

One moment she was running a forgotten platter out to a table that had been waiting for their food, and the next she was leaning against a counter with Hannah. The restaurant had slowed down, and they had already done a lot of the clean-up.

Hannah grinned at Eloise. "You're pretty good at this stuff. You can't tell me you haven't done it before."

Eloise bit down on her lower lip, fighting a smile. "Truly, I haven't. I mean, I love to cook at home, but I've never been in a restaurant setting."

Hannah's eyes widened. "That's crazy. You for sure have a natural talent."

Glancing away, Eloise warmed at the compliment. "Thanks."

"Maybe you should ask about staying on. Since Penelope had her baby, she won't be back for at least six weeks."

"You really think so?" Eloise glanced around the kitchen envisioning what it might be like to work here for more than one day. The whole environment gave her such a high. The thought was both thrilling and terrifying all at once.

Hannah nudged her. "I *know* so." They'd only met a few hours before and already she felt like a close friend.

Eloise shrugged. "Maybe I'll talk to Mr. Owens when our shift is over."

"You totally should."

"Hannah, Eloise, we need some cheesecakes plated."

"Yes, Chef," they said in unison. They glanced at one another and then laughed, earning a sharp look from Gabriel. This only brought on more quiet giggles. Perhaps she wasn't ready to work for such a serious chef.

Then again, Shane wasn't the epitome of a happy-go-lucky guy either. She didn't know if she could work with people who couldn't lighten up every so often. Besides the pay, the only perks of working here would be the change of scenery and finding a friend in Hannah.

When the last customer had finally ordered their dessert, the kitchen staff closed up shop. Waiters and waitresses worked on wiping down tables and cleaning the restaurant. Eloise followed Hannah toward the lockers. She leaned her shoulder against one of the metal doors, contemplating their conversation. "How long have you been working here?"

Hannah laughed. "Is that a trick question? This restaurant just opened."

Eloise rolled her eyes. "Well, you weren't hired yesterday."

Her new friend glanced at her. "Okay, that's true." She tilted her head. "I guess we have all been helping out here and there for the past month or so."

"And you like working for Mr. Owens?"

"Shane? Oh, yeah. He's great." Hannah dug into her locker, focused intently on whatever she was trying to retrieve.

"Really? He seems a little too—"

Someone behind Eloise cleared their throat, and Hannah's eyes shot to a spot over her shoulder. Eloise's eyes widened and warmth bloomed in her cheeks. Even without looking, she knew Shane was behind her.

3

Shane

Shane had been on the wrong side of eavesdropping before, and he wasn't sure he wanted to hear what Eloise was going to say about him. After the day he'd had, he didn't need any more negativity.

Hannah gaped at him, then ducked back into her locker as if the small metal box would hold her. Eloise looked absolutely mortified, which he couldn't deny gave him a small amount of pleasure.

He had his hands shoved into his pockets and he jutted his chin in the direction of the exit. "I'm available right now for our meeting."

She nodded. "Just let me gather my things. I think I left my coat in the office." She moved toward him, then stopped short. "Excuse me."

Shane stepped back, allowing her to pass him. He shot a quick look in Hannah's direction. "How was the first night?"

"Oh, it was great. I can't think of anything that went wrong. Chef Gabriel is amazing to work with."

He nodded. That was what he needed to hear. Of course, he knew that Gabriel would pull off a miracle. That was the reason he'd hired the guy. It didn't hurt that they had a history back home. The man was one of the only guys Shane could trust. Gabriel had never lied to him in the entire time they'd known one another.

Hannah shut the locker door and then took a step closer to him. She kept her voice low and her words short. "If you're looking to hire someone to replace Penelope even temporarily, I'd say Eloise would make a good choice." She straightened and a wide smile spilled across her face as she turned toward Eloise, who'd emerged from the office. "You have my number, right?"

Eloise nodded. "Yep. We should definitely get together sometime."

"Definitely." Hannah met Shane's eyes once more, then ducked away from them as if she was worried she'd said something to get herself in trouble.

He might have been in a bad mood lately, but he wasn't *scary*. At least he didn't think so.

Shane stretched out his arm toward the exit. "Ladies first."

Eloise stepped forward and led the way. She appeared to be less confident than she'd been when she'd demanded to know the terms of their arrangement. He'd thrown her off guard. Good. It was healthy for those who worked for him to have a strong sense of respect. He was still the boss, after all. And just because his cousins didn't know how to treat someone like him didn't mean others should follow suit.

When they reached his office, he opted to keep the door open in case Gabriel needed him. He walked past Eloise, who chose to remain standing for some reason. Shane pulled open his desk drawer and retrieved a small leather book. He flipped it open and scribbled out her name and the amount of six-hundred dollars.

The check ripped cleanly from the notebook, and he wandered around the edge of the desk before holding it out to her.

She looked down at it and then lifted her eyes to meet his. "That's too much. I only worked for five and a half hours this evening."

Shane didn't move. "You're correct. However, I'm not going to shortchange you for leaving thirty minutes earlier than expected."

Her gaze cut to the check, then back up to meet his before she reached to take it from him. "I was wondering something."

He headed around his desk and pulled out the chair before sitting down. This conversation had already taken a strange turn. He'd expected her to take the money and leave. Based on what he'd overheard from her conversation with Hannah, she wasn't quite sure about working here, which suited him just fine.

Faye might have been okay with her big sister taking a job at the new restaurant, but Brielle might not appreciate him getting close to one of her sisters.

Okay, that was a stretch. He didn't know *what* Brielle cared about at this point. It was possible she wouldn't mind at all. Shane swallowed down those intrusive thoughts about his ex and met Eloise's eyes once more. "What did you need?"

"It's not about what I need... it's about what you need."

He arched a brow. First of all, he didn't need anything from her. He already had too much on his plate. Secondly, he wasn't one hundred percent sure she was safe from the likes of his cousins. The farther she remained from his restaurant, the better. "And what is it you think I might need?"

"Help."

"*Help*," he drawled with disdain. "You think I need help."

She nodded, though she appeared even less confident, which was quite a feat.

Shane steepled his fingers at his lips. "And just why do you believe that?"

"Because you…" Her cheeks flushed. "You needed the additional help tonight—"

"Tonight was the grand opening. I fully expect everything will level out. And I didn't fire Penelope. She will return as soon as she is able. I'm sure we can handle everything for the next few weeks."

"But—"

He rose to his feet. "With all due respect, I was up against a wall tonight. I needed to fill a position and fill it fast. I only accepted your help because of that fact and that fact alone. You were overpaid for the menial job you were asked to complete."

She sucked in sharply and her eyes dropped to the floor. For a moment guilt swirled around him, knocking into organs he'd never felt before. Then he reminded himself that his cousins never gave up easily and Eloise would be far safer at home with her father and certain sisters. "Don't get me wrong. I fully appreciate your help with tonight. Everything went smoothly—exactly according to plan… well, after we found out about Penelope. I just don't have a need for more kitchen staff." He turned his attention to his computer if only to quell the growing guilt that continued making a home in his gut.

More than that, he didn't have any room for another Callahan. If he counted correctly, he had at least three or four working for him. More if he included those who were getting married to men who worked for him. One more Callahan was just asking for trouble—especially with his cousins snooping around.

If Madeline got wind that the Callahans were one of the wealthier families in this part of the state, then there would be no stopping the destruction that would follow. She had no regard for decorum. All she wanted was money. She should have stayed in California where she had more victims to choose from.

His eyes flitted up to meet hers, and he was surprised to find she didn't look at all as upset as he'd expected. Though she was staring at the check in her hands thoughtfully. Shaking her head, she slapped the piece of paper on his desk. "I don't want it."

Shane choked as he inhaled sharply. He coughed in an attempt to clear the irritation and sat up straighter. "What?"

She shrugged. "I don't want this. I would wager that I don't need it as much as you probably think I do. Tonight was fun. It was different."

He leaned forward, pushing the check across the table with his finger. "I'm sorry, I can't accept that explanation. For legal reasons, among others—"

"Call me a volunteer then. I'm not taking the money, especially for such a *menial* job. Thanks for the offer, though." She turned before he could make sense of what had just happened. His thoughts were ping-ponging around in his skull, refusing to allow him to grasp onto even one of them.

From the moment she'd stood up to him before the shift to the way she'd just thrown his money back in his face, he just didn't understand what she was trying to do. Was she manipulating him into hiring her?

No, that didn't make sense either. And why would she want to work in the kitchen when she was practically raised in the saddle? That was one thing he knew. After observing the way Dianna and Grace could handle his horses, he had no doubt all of the Callahans were just as prolific with the four-legged animals. Asking Eloise to work in the kitchen would be like asking a pilot to take a desk job. It just wasn't a good idea.

But as he stared at the space she had previously occupied, he couldn't help wondering if she was disappointed he'd turned down her request.

Just as quickly as that thought appeared, he shoved it aside. He picked up the check. "Why are Callahan women so obstinately stubborn?" he muttered.

A FEW DAYS PASSED, and while certain things had sorted themselves out, there were still several issues he had to deal with. His cousins were still in town, lurking somewhere. He knew better than to believe they would grow tired so early. He was just waiting for the other shoe to drop.

The kitchen staff was still burning the candle at both ends. It shouldn't have been this hard to find a replacement for Penelope. He was already short-staffed as it was, which only made her absence felt more.

Shane had thrown Eloise's check in his drawer, expecting that she'd return with her tail between her legs and tell him she'd actually like the money. He wouldn't fault her for it. From what he understood, her father wasn't the kind of man that doted on his daughters in the way that his wealth would suggest. He raised hard-working women.

His gaze locked onto the check, and he almost contemplated calling Eloise to see if she'd like to work out something temporary. But he wasn't that desperate, right?

He shoved the drawer closed and got back to his job. Everything would work out. It always did. He didn't need to worry about staffing because Penelope would return. And maybe he could get one of the bartenders to help pull some weight.

A knock rapped on his office door and he glanced up to find Gabriel standing with his hands clasped tightly in front of him. "Sir?"

Shane motioned for him to enter. "What do you need? Is everything set for tonight's dinner rush?"

"That's what I was going to speak to you about."

He glanced up from his computer screen and then sighed before turning his chair to give his friend his undivided attention. "Is there a problem?"

"Reservations are fully booked tonight. There are several large groups listed on our schedule. This will be a strain on the kitchen staff and the wait staff. You hired me to help you create the kind of dining experience that people go to the city for, and yet you don't give me the support I need."

Shane's defenses rose immediately. "You know as well as I do that this place is a small town. It's hard to fill positions without head-hunting out of town."

"I do know that. What happened to Eloise? I thought you had decided to hire her. Even if you hired her temporarily, it would be better than not having that position filled."

That was before he realized just how much he needed to protect people like Eloise from his cousins. One night offered very little risk. Having her here when they could show up was a completely different matter. He didn't want to give them any excuse to speak to her.

"Shane," Gabriel said more firmly. "We need at least one more person on staff. If you can't provide that for me, then we need to close for the night."

He scoffed. "Closing an entire restaurant because one person needs to be on staff? Do you even hear yourself?"

"It's either that, or you need to be the one to weed out our reservation list. I don't know how you'd do it, but I wouldn't want to be the one to explain to anyone why they didn't get a table when their friends did."

Shane sighed. Gabriel made a good point. The town was too close. Someone was bound to notice, and the older generation of women were bound to talk about it—gossiping about who might be considered favorites.

He dragged a hand down his face. "And you're sure you can't make it work with those you have on the schedule tonight? Is there anyone who can pull a double? Can we offer overtime to anyone?"

"If you ask me, you might have pushed the opening of this restaurant too soon."

Shane bit back a retort. The restaurant was a new venture—a way to continue growing his small empire like his grandfather had. This restaurant was really an ode to that man. Truth be told, Shane didn't know the first thing about running a restaurant. He was better at the therapeutic service business.

"But to answer your question, there is no one else who can fill in tonight. You need to hire at least five more people, but we could make do with one more until then." Gabriel lifted his arm, pulled aside his sleeve, and checked the time. "I'll need to know within the hour. We have prep work to do. I'd rather not waste any food for this evening's meals if I don't have to." He gave Shane a meaningful look. "If Eloise can return, she'd be my first choice. She was a quick learner, and she had no problem following orders."

Gabriel headed out the door, leaving Shane to mull over what he'd said. Marc and Madeline hadn't made an appearance since that first night. The probability that they would cross paths with Eloise coming or going wasn't high. And in the meantime, he could keep an eye on Eloise from here.

Something deep down inside him seemed to shy away from where he was going with this thought process. That part of him continued to insist this was a bad idea. If only Marc and Madeline hadn't managed to cross paths with Eloise. Then none of this would be an issue.

He groaned, settling back in his seat. This was the exact definition of being between a rock and a hard place.

Shane picked up his phone, then let out a curse. Of course.

She didn't have her phone. He wasn't sure what her family's house number was. The only one he felt he could try would be Brielle unless he chose to drive out there in person and hope she was home. Both options made him feel absolutely sick to his stomach.

The latter would be better. At least then, he wouldn't have to speak to Brielle.

4

"That guy is giving your phone back today, right?"

Eloise glanced up at Brielle and then back to the buttons she was working on. "Yeah. He wanted to take me to lunch and apologize for his sister forgetting to give it back." She flashed her sister a smile. "He seems pretty nice. I think it will be fun."

Through the mirror, she could see Brielle watching her from her vantage point in the doorway. She leaned her shoulder against the door jamb. "And how did you meet him again?"

"I guess he's Shane's cousin?"

Brielle's brows furrowed. "Are you sure? Shane said he didn't have family."

Eloise shrugged. "They definitely knew each other. And Madeline called Shane her cousin."

"I don't get it. Why would Shane lie about his family?" Brielle wandered into the room and took a seat on the edge of Eloise's bed.

Letting out a soft laugh, Eloise spun to face her sister. "How many times have you been caught not telling the guys you date about your family?"

Her sister held up a finger. "*That's* different. I don't *lie*. I just omit things I would rather they don't know. Besides, it's not like the guys I've dated *don't* know stuff. If they've been in Copper Creek for more than a year, they pretty much know our whole family history, thanks to the people who gossip about us in town. I mean, seriously. Don't they have anything better to talk about?"

Eloise shook her head with amusement as she faced the mirror and fiddled with her hair. "I guess our family is just a little more interesting than most of the others." She peeked at her sister over her shoulder. "And it's not like you don't give them plenty to talk about. How many guys have you gone on dates with since Dad lifted his restrictions?"

"Actually, I've gone on less than when they were in place."

"That can't be true."

This time Brielle laughed. "It is *so* true. Dating when it was against the rules was exciting because I didn't want to get caught. Now that I get to do it out in the open, the spark just isn't there. The guys have all gotten so *bland*. I need a palate cleanser or something."

Eloise faced her sister again and crossed her arms. "Somehow I don't think you're going to get that when you've been dating anything that moves since you were fourteen."

Brielle rolled her eyes. "You don't know that. You're way younger than me."

"Five years isn't that much. And seeing as we're the only two single people left, I have a feeling we're going to be considered the outcasts until we fall in line and find a guy like the rest of them."

They gave each other a look and laughed.

Eloise wandered toward her dresser. "As if that would happen. Honestly, I'm more interested in finding my place right now. I feel like everyone has their role to play, and I'm the last one standing. You help Adeline with the ranch, and you've got those other projects with the Keagans. Constance has her vet thing. Dianna and Grace work out at the equine therapy center. And Faye is trying to convince Dad to let her teach kids how to ride. I'm the only one who... doesn't have anything."

"You help out at the ranch," Brielle insisted. "And you don't have to have a *thing*. There's a lot to do to keep this place running. If you want to take on more responsibility here, then I'm more than happy to share my workload with you."

The only problem with Brielle's suggestion was that it made Eloise feel even more trapped. She didn't want to stick around just because there was nothing else for her to do. She wanted a dream—a passion. She wanted to do something more with her life than just be a cowgirl.

Those cowgirl roots ran deep, and she knew she'd always want to be around the animals. She just wanted to find something that fulfilled the part of her that longed to belong to something different than what she'd been exposed to all her life.

Shane's restaurant had been tempting, but by the end of her conversation with him, she knew better than to believe it was where she was meant to be. She didn't have the experience, and it didn't appear that Shane could tolerate her.

Eloise's eyes flitted to Brielle and found her staring. She hadn't told Brielle what she'd been up to that night. She'd only mentioned running into Faye and Adam and then spending time with a new friend. Shane was a touchy subject.

"What?" Brielle demanded.

Eloise shook her head. "Nothing."

"That look *isn't* nothing. This is really bothering you, isn't it?"

Forcing a smile, Eloise lifted a shoulder. "I don't know. I love it here. But I don't want to *work* here for the rest of my life. This is my home." She let out a sigh. "I bet that doesn't make any sense, does it?"

"Not really."

Eloise laughed. "Thanks for that. Now I feel like I don't know what I'm talking about."

Brielle still stared at Eloise, making her feel even more put on the spot. She fidgeted, then looked away. "Do you think Marc will be like his cousin?"

The room seemed to grow colder by a few degrees. "I still don't think Shane has cousins."

Despite her attempt to hold it back, Eloise snorted.

"What? I dated the guy longer than I'd dated anyone except—"

Eloise shot a curious look toward her sister. "Except who?"

Brielle sliced her hand through the air indifferently. "It doesn't matter. It was in high school. Anyway, Shane was the other serious guy. I think I knew him as well as anyone. He insisted he didn't have family and that was why he moved out here. So if he's got cousins, then he's more of a jerk than anyone realizes."

"I'm sure he's not a jerk. A little grumpy and prone to brooding maybe."

Once again, silence filled the air.

"Why do you say that?"

"Say what?"

Brielle got up from the bed and crossed the room. "How would you know if he was brooding? Whenever he's in public, he's pretty happy. He doesn't show that other side of himself very often. He says it makes him feel weak."

Chills crawled up Eloise's spine. That was strange. The more she thought about it, Brielle was right about one thing. He'd been pretty happy before she'd shown up with his cousins in tow. After that, she'd only been alone with him.

She released a breath and faced Brielle once more. "I don't know. I guess he was really stressed out about the restaurant opening a few days ago."

Brielle pressed her lips together as if trying to decide whether or not she should push the subject. Finally, she moved away. "I'm curious to hear Marc's side of things. I'm beginning to wonder if I ever really knew Shane like I thought I did."

"Does it matter?"

Brielle shot Eloise a sharp look.

"I mean, you broke up with Shane a while back. You didn't break up because he was dishonest."

"Yeah, well it's starting to sound like maybe that *should* have been the reason."

Eloise scrambled to smooth over the edges of this conversation. Brielle was starting to get worked up over this, and Eloise didn't know how far she would take it. "Then be grateful things didn't end on bad terms. You knew you weren't going to work it out. Maybe your gut was telling you that he wasn't any good for you."

Brielle didn't speak right away. She crossed her arms, tilted her head then sighed. "Yeah. Maybe you're right." Then she moved closer and pointed a finger at Eloise. "But you should be careful. We don't know who Marc is, just like we probably don't know who the real Shane is. One or both of them could be bad news. I'd stay as far away from them as you possibly can."

Eloise let out a nervous laugh. "I'm sure they're both just fine. And it's not like I'm going to start dating the guy. I just want my phone back. Getting lunch doesn't mean we're *together*."

"Just be careful. There are a lot of bad people out there. Take it from me."

IT WAS PROBABLY a good thing that Eloise had opted not to give Marc her address—though if he really wanted it, he could probably ask anyone in town. But after her conversation with Brielle, Eloise was a lot more on edge.

She was leaning against Faye's truck as she waited in the diner's parking lot. Sal's was the perfect place to meet a stranger and exchange her phone. It was a public place, and she could count on any of the local cowboys to come to her rescue if anything were to happen.

Those thoughts needed to vacate. The more she contemplated the possibility that Marc was dangerous, the more antsy she became. She really shouldn't have let Brielle get into her head like that. She shouldn't be this nervous; he was Shane's cousin, after all. She'd picked them up when they were having car trouble. Then again, he'd had his sister with him.

Eloise shoved her hands into her pockets and heaved a sigh. She should probably just head inside and wait for Marc in there. At least then she could get something to drink. Just as she was about to walk toward the door, a car pulled up. Marc got out of the back seat and waved to the driver. Whoever it was, waved back. Marc's eyes found hers and he smiled wide.

"Hey!" Marc jogged toward her. "Thanks for seeing me."

"Well, you were holding my phone hostage, so…" She offered a small smile. He was just as she remembered him. There wasn't anything about him that stirred trepidation.

"Right. Here." He held out her phone with a sheepish grin. "We didn't try to break into it or anything."

"Thanks? I guess?" She tucked her phone into her purse. "It doesn't have a lock on it or anything. All the security measures are on the specific apps."

"Oh. Well maybe you should change that. There are some

pretty scary people out there who could do some damage." He flashed her a smile and a dimple appeared on his chin. His square jaw, dark eyes, and dark hair reminded her of a movie star. He was fit and wore nice clothes—definitely a city boy.

She tilted her head, studying him. Was *everyone* concerned about how bad the world had gotten? Perhaps she'd been far too sheltered. Maybe she shouldn't be so willing to trust people at their word. Maybe she shouldn't allow herself to find him attractive, either.

Marc jerked his head toward the diner. "You hungry?"

"Absolutely." She stepped away from her sister's truck, and he fell into step beside her. His hand gently touched the small of her back, and almost immediately, her heart leaped into her chest. It wasn't an unpleasant experience, but it was definitely unexpected.

He pulled open the door to the diner and gestured for her to head in first. His manners were impeccable. She couldn't help the small smile that touched her lips as they were led to their table.

Much like Brielle, she'd been spending a lot of her free time going on dates with various guys. She had no interest in settling down right away because she was having too much fun. Marc might be the next guy she gave her attention to, but like she told Brielle, she wasn't going to date long-term any time soon.

He sat across from her, smiling as he reached for his menu. "So you're a local, right?"

"And you're not," she said pointedly.

Marc chuckled. "Nothing gets past you." He glanced down at the menu, then lifted his gaze to meet hers. "Do you like living in such a small town?"

"I don't know if it's that small. We have a lot going for us here. Your cousin has been drawing a lot of activity with his business ventures. Is that something you like to do as well?"

He shrugged. "I dabble in some stuff here and there, but nothing like Shane. He's a workhorse." He snapped his finger, placing his menu on the table. "That ranch we passed when you took us to the club. My sister and I made an offer on it." Her wide eyes must have been something else because he let out a laugh. "*What*? Are outsiders not welcome? Your town seemed to accept Shane pretty fast."

Eloise's face filled with heat. "It's not that. I'm just surprised you were so quick to make an offer when you barely know the place." Her eyes swept over his body. "And no offense, but you don't seem like the type to want to run a ranch."

"No offense taken." He laughed again, and the sound of it was so infectious she didn't even bother fighting the smile that appeared on her lips. Marc closed his menu, then rested one elbow on the table and his chin in his hand. "Well, it's always been the plan to reunite with our cousin. And he's intent on staying here no matter how hard we tried to convince him to return to the city." He shrugged. "So, I guess you're stuck with me." He winked at her, and before she could respond, the waitress arrived.

"Hey, I'm Hope and I'm going to be serving you today. What can I get for you?" Her eyes landed on Eloise and her smile widened. "Eloise, I didn't recognize you for a minute." Hope shifted her focus to Marc, then back. "Do you already know what you want or will you need some more time to think on it?"

Marc held his menu out to Hope. "I'll have the all-American burger and a Coke."

"You got it, hun. And you?" She turned, then winked at Eloise before mouthing the word "cute."

Eloise gave a short shake of her head, then held out her own menu. "I'll have the same."

"Fries good for both of you?"

"Yes," they said in unison.

Hope nodded. "Coming right up."

Marc waited until she was gone to speak again. "And I don't think I'll ever get used to that."

"What?" Eloise turned, peering across the restaurant to where Hope was placing the order with the cook.

"A town where everyone knows your name. You're like a full-blown sitcom out here."

She snickered. "Yeah, I suppose you're right about that."

5

Shane trudged up the steps to the Callahan residence, hating the way it made him feel. Brielle had demanded he never step foot on her family's property. She insisted that he wouldn't be welcome even though her father was allowing all her sisters the flexibility to date whomever they wanted. It didn't matter that on their very first date, he'd come here with his friend Tristan to take her and her younger sister on a date. Brielle simply didn't want her father to see them together.

At first, he didn't care. A new relationship was bound to have certain quirks, and he was willing to do what she wanted. But the more they snuck around, the more he realized she wasn't going to change.

Hopefully, she wouldn't be home, and he could meet with Eloise to apologize for being too hasty in his decision a few days ago. They'd have a short chat, and he'd see her tonight when she showed up to work in the kitchen.

That was how things were supposed to go.

Only when he knocked on the door it opened to reveal the one person he would have given anything not to see.

Brielle's eyes narrowed the moment they landed on him. She stood in the doorway, her forearm resting against the doorjamb and her lips pursed together. "I told you, Shane. I'm not interested in dating anymore. We're not a good fit."

"That's not what I'm here for."

"I mean, it's been how long... Wait, what?"

He rubbed the back of his neck and looked away. "I need to see your sister."

"Over my dead body."

Shane let out a dry laugh. "What exactly do you think I'm up to? Dianna and Grace work for me."

"And they're not here. You know that because *you've* scheduled them."

She made a good point, but this was still regarding business, not pleasure. "I'm actually here to see Eloise."

Brielle tossed back her head and let out a derisive laugh. "Isn't that something. I was going to talk to you about that. When were you going to tell me you lied about having family?"

His brows creased, then immediately they shot upward. Of course Brielle would hear about this. Both Faye and Eloise had seen his interaction with Marc and Madeline.

"See? I knew it! You lied about your family."

"It's not what you think, Brielle. Just... can I speak with Eloise? She helped me out at the restaurant on opening night and the chef is adamant we still need her help."

She let out a groan. "You have got to be kidding me. What is *with* you? Can't find anyone to work for you that isn't a Callahan? You have to keep pulling from my family?"

Shane pinched the bridge of his nose. So much for ending

things amicably. *She* was the one who broke up with him. What did she have to be so upset about? "Look, I'm not offering her a permanent position. I'm asking for a favor. That's all. She's the one who asked if she could continue working with me." When he glanced back in Brielle's direction, she was glowering at him.

"You refused her help?"

He muttered a curse under his breath. "For heaven's sake, Brielle. You can be mad at me for hiring her or you can be mad at me for not hiring her. It can't be both."

She snapped her mouth shut and her face flushed with color.

"Will you please go get her for me? I just need to see if she can help out this evening and then I will get out of your hair."

Brielle crossed her arms, then shook her head.

"Why not?" he demanded in exasperation. "I'd call her phone but—"

"Your *cousin* has it."

His jaw tightened. She was upset about what she perceived to be a lie. Technically he *did* have family, but none he had wanted to tell her about. Every family had that one member who was considered the black sheep. Well, in a herd of black sheep, Shane was the one that didn't belong. His family were all undeserving criminals that only ever wanted to take from his grandfather. "Yeah. My cousin has it," he muttered bitterly.

"Not anymore. Though I don't know if Eloise would answer a call from you at this point. She didn't seem all that happy this morning when we were talking. I had a feeling something was up, but I never dreamed it was because *you* did something."

His heart stuttered. "What do you mean, not anymore?"

"I can't believe you thought it was okay to use her like that. You should know better."

"Brielle!"

She jumped. "*What?*"

"Where *is* she?"

"Eloise is on a date. Why?"

It took everything in his power to keep his voice level. This couldn't be happening. He prayed Marc wasn't doing what Shane knew deep down he was capable of. "Please tell me she's with some cowboy from town."

Brielle's eyes narrowed. "I don't think that's any of your business."

"It's every bit my business if I—" He snapped his mouth shut. Who was he kidding? He knew better than to assume Marc wasn't involved. Eloise had her phone, and she was now on a date. It all added up, and there was no denying any of it. "I'm only going to ask you this once. Where did they go?"

"Honestly, Shane. You're acting like a jealous boyfriend, and you aren't even dating my sister."

He was just about to throw his hands in the air and go hunting for the two of them when he heard the sound of a vehicle coming along the drive leading to the property. Shane turned toward the noise.

"Looks like you're not going to have to worry about tracking her down. She's back." Brielle set her steely gaze on him and let out a big sigh. "Just don't do anything stupid." She flipped her hair and headed inside, shutting the door behind her.

Shane stared after her, dumbfounded. Was there a full moon last night? What could have caused Brielle to act like this? He thought he'd been the one who was broken up about their failed attempt at a relationship. Brielle was the one to insist they call it quits.

He shook his head before he headed down the steps and toward Eloise. The second she saw him, it was as if someone had pushed the slow-motion button. She climbed down from the truck and shut the door, then stood there unmoving.

Eloise glanced toward the house and then back to him. "You didn't talk to Brielle, did you?"

Shane glanced over his shoulder toward the house. "Actually, I did."

She sucked in sharply with a grimace. "How did *that* go?"

"Not well. Wait…" He returned his focus to her. There were so many questions he had, the answers to which probably wouldn't make him happy. Rather than go down that rabbit hole, Shane forced himself to focus. "I need to talk to you about something."

"You do?" She stepped away from the truck, her hands in her back pockets. "Is this about the restaurant?"

"No. Yes. There are a few things I think we should discuss." How on earth was he supposed to explain about his cousin? Was it possible he was overreacting? Marc wasn't with her. Maybe his interest was benign? Shane took a deep breath, prepared to just jump in and tell her what was going on when they were interrupted.

"Eloise!"

Her head whipped toward the person calling her name.

He let out a groan, drawing her focus momentarily.

A young man in a cowboy hat hurried toward them. "I'm so glad you're back. Some of the goats got out. You know they only listen to you." The cowboy briefly looked to Shane. "I'm sorry, are you busy?"

Eloise glanced at Shane. "We were just talking. I can come get the goats. You don't mind, Shane, do you?"

"Well—"

"You can come with me if you like." She didn't even bother waiting for him to answer before she followed the cowboy.

Shane's arms dangled listlessly at his sides. If he didn't get back to tell Gabriel that Eloise would be available to help, then the restaurant would be closed for the evening. And if he didn't tell her about Marc, then there could be bigger consequences.

He let out another groan and charged after her. He just needed to wait for her cowboy friend to leave them alone and he would bite the bullet and tell her everything.

Well, maybe not everything. He didn't need her sharing some of the sordid details with Brielle. At this rate, he didn't know how much she would tell her sister as it was. The fewer people who knew about his family's problems, the better.

They entered the barn, and the cowboy led a horse from a stall. "Bandit was just about to get some exercise. You can take him to round up the goats." His gaze cut to Shane. "You riding with her?"

"Riding?" His voice cracked. He was in a suit. What made this guy think that would be a good idea?

"Sure. Get him Bella. She'll be easy on him," Eloise answered the cowboy.

Shane scoffed. "I don't need a horse to go easy on me—"

She patted his forearm. "Trust me, you will want Bella."

So he was doing this. A trip out to the Callahan ranch that was supposed to be just an invitation to return to the restaurant had turned into him nearly tracking her down to save her from Marc, and now he was getting on a horse.

The cowboy brought another horse toward him and held out the reins. "I have to bring in a few horses from the corral. You got this?"

"Of course. You said the goats are in the southern pasture?" Eloise asked.

He nodded. "Thanks, Eloise. I appreciate it."

Eloise nodded toward the door. "You coming?"

Clarity hit him over the head hard. He shook his head and held out the reins toward her. "No. I'm not."

"Okay?" Eloise accepted the rope.

"I only came to ask you if your offer still stands. We need the extra help at the restaurant, and Gabriel was impressed... with you."

She didn't respond. He couldn't tell at all what she thought about that. At this point, he didn't know if he wanted to find out. Based on the reaction he'd gotten from Brielle, he'd overstayed his welcome. If she wasn't going to answer him, he might as well cut his losses and head back to the club to break the news to Gabriel.

"Good luck... with the goats," he muttered.

Shane pushed past her and headed for the door. He couldn't believe he'd almost gone along with her to retrieve some animals out in a pasture. He had work to do.

"Shane!"

He froze just as his foot touched the earth outside. Slowly, Shane turned to face Eloise as she headed toward him, leading two horses behind her.

"Is this a permanent position?"

Shane had no clue how to answer that. One word would be all it took to mess up what was already proving to be a terrible day. "I don't know."

Eloise pressed her lips together firmly then she heaved a sigh. "I liked helping out in the kitchen."

"I'm aware." Even he could hear the flat tone of his voice. The arrival of his cousins had done a number on him. If he couldn't find a way to get rid of them, his attitude—and more importantly, his business—would suffer. "Gabriel mentioned that we're already understaffed. I suppose if you show him your worth, he might take you on... permanently. Just don't mention it if you're not sure. I'd rather not get his hopes up, if you know what I mean."

She nodded. "Sure."

"Does that mean you'll be there tonight?"

"I'll be there," she confirmed. "Same time?"

He lifted his wrist and checked his watch. "I believe they start prep work about two hours before dinner starts. You've got about three hours before you'd need to arrive."

She nodded again, and he started toward his car.

Shane couldn't even enjoy the relief he felt from taking care of this particular issue because there were so many more pressing matters to attend to. Stopping on a dime, he spun to face her. "Brielle didn't seem too pleased about you working for me. I'm assuming that has something to do with the way we left things?"

Eloise shrugged. "I don't know. I think she regrets it."

"Regrets dating me or regrets breaking up?" He held up a hand. "You know what? Don't answer that. I'm not interested in having my heart torn up a second time."

Her lips quirked upward. "For the record, I think she made a mistake."

His brows creased as his brain attempted to make sense of what she'd said. Her suggestion that Brielle should have stayed with him did strange things to him. He knew better than to toy with that idea. There was no going back. Why did people have that weakness? The past needed to stay hidden most of the time. He worked his jaw and gave her a short nod. "Thanks—for coming tonight."

Once again, Shane headed toward his car and then let out a sigh as he turned to face her. "As far as pay goes, you'll be offered the same wages as the others in the kitchen. You've proven yourself to have ingenuity and drive. Does that sound acceptable to you?"

"It does." Eloise's smile appeared fully this time. "I'll see you in a few hours."

"You might not. I don't... normally spend time in the kitchen. I typically oversee the restaurant where the guests are concerned."

"Right. Well then, if I don't see you, thank you. For the opportunity."

He gave her a sharp nod and finally made his escape. That was the most awkward conversation he'd had, and he still didn't bring up the problems with his cousins. There would be time for that later.

For now, he'd take care of one thing at a time.

6

Eloise

Eloise threw her arms around Hannah's neck and let out a laugh. "I guess I'm going to be hanging around a little longer."

"I love it! I'm so glad you're back." Hannah pulled back and smiled broadly. "This place has been insane the last couple of days. You missed so much."

Laughing, Eloise slipped an apron over her head. "I can't believe I've missed that much. What could have happened in the few days that I wasn't here?"

"Well, Shane hired a new dishwasher and the poor kid dropped a full bus bin on the floor. It completely shattered all the dishes."

Eloise's eyes grew wide. "You're kidding."

Hannah shook her head. "Then someone left the refrigerator door open and some of the food near the front went bad."

"Oh no! Was Gabriel furious?"

"Oh yeah. He's used to perfection, and he's dealing with having to train people to do what he wants them to. So if you want to be promoted, I'd make sure you follow all of his directions to a T."

A promotion? Eloise hadn't even considered staying through the end of the month, let alone trying to get a promotion. She'd had fun plating and preparing food with Hannah. But something long-term? That thought made her more nervous than she'd like to admit.

"Anyway, I'm just glad you're here so we can really get to know each other."

Eloise shut the locker where she'd placed her belongings, then pushed her hands into her pockets. "This will definitely be fun. And hey, I finally got my phone back, so now we can really get together when we're not working."

"Oh! That's great! You found it?"

She shook her head. "Actually, Shane's cousin had it all along. I guess they didn't realize it until they got unpacked." She bit back a grin, one that didn't go unnoticed by Hannah.

"Ooooh. I know that look."

Eloise laughed. "What look?"

"The look that says you might be interested in a guy." She nudged Eloise as they wandered toward the meal prep side of the kitchen. "Is this the guy who had your phone? Or is it someone else?"

"His name is Marc, and he seems really nice. Not to mention, since he's Shane's cousin—or at least I think he is—that should mean he's a pretty okay guy, right?"

"I guess so."

They reached the stainless-steel countertop where several vegetables were laid out in front of cutting boards.

"Looks like we're doing some chopping today." Hannah

grimaced. "I'll buy you a slice of cheesecake if you'll do the onions."

Eloise lifted a brow, and a teasing smile touched her lips. "You've been working in the food service industry for years and you still can't handle cutting onions?"

She made a face that was more comical than before, eliciting a laugh from Eloise. "I don't know what it is, but I can never make more than two cuts before those things make me bawl like a baby." Her lower lip puckered, and she held up her hands together. "Please?"

"Oh, alright. But how about we do lunch instead? The last thing I need right now is another dessert."

"*Girl*, everyone needs cheesecake. It's the stuff dreams are made of." Hannah picked up a knife and a head of lettuce. She was a breath of fresh air—someone who didn't know much about Eloise's family but didn't have to. She seemed content just to be Eloise's friend.

They worked side by side for the next two hours prepping the food for the salads and laughing about guys they'd dated. Eloise conveniently left out the part where her father had practically kept her locked away like a princess in a tower. Whenever she told that story, people got weird around her.

With Hannah, she felt she could just be herself.

Her thoughts shifted to earlier that afternoon when Shane had dropped in unexpectedly. He'd said he had a few things to discuss, but he'd only mentioned the one. For the life of her, she couldn't come up with any idea for what the other thing might be. She'd almost asked him about it before he left, but he was so antsy when he'd shown up she thought better of it.

She glanced over to Hannah, who was busy wrapping their bowls with plastic. "Shane seems grumpier lately, don't you think?"

Hannah glanced in her direction and shrugged. "I guess so. Why?"

"Do you know what happened? Is he dealing with something..." Eloise didn't know how to bring up that he might be dealing with his latest breakup without making it sound like she was interested in him.

Hannah's hands stilled. Her expression went from confused and thoughtful to realization mingling with a teasing smile. "Do you like him?"

"What? No. Of course not!"

Her voice took on a high-pitched quality as she mimicked Eloise. "*What? No! Of course not!*" She laughed, then faced Eloise with her hand on her hip. "You totally do. You have a crush on the boss."

"Seriously, I don't. He used to date my sister." Eloise realized her mistake the moment the words left her lips. She grimaced and looked away from her new friend. There would be no telling what might happen now. What if Hannah thought Shane only hired her because of his connection with the Callahan family?

Her cheeks flushed with warmth. There was no hiding her reaction to her own statement. She might as well hit this head-on. "They ended things amicably, but I can tell they've both been acting a little different—moody, maybe?"

"Do you think they still have a thing for each other?"

Eloise scrunched up her face as she considered this. Brielle hadn't really been dating lately. She didn't go out as often. It was as if she had lost her will to do so. Was it possible she still had feelings for Shane? "I don't know," she mumbled. "If they do, then they have no plans on doing anything about it. I can't even say for certain how serious it was. I only ever saw him come over to the house once."

Hannah started slicing some cucumbers. "That doesn't sound

like they were serious at all. Maybe something happened on their date."

"No, they were definitely more serious than it seemed. I guess he didn't tell her about his family."

Neither one of them spoke for a few minutes, lost in their own thoughts. Then Hannah shrugged. "Oh well. I don't even know why we're talking about Shane when I want to know more about his cousin." She winked, then laughed when Eloise made a face. "Come on. I don't have anyone in my life right now. I need to live vicariously through *someone*."

Eloise joined in on her laughter. "If it makes you feel any better, I don't think anything will come of it. Like I said, he was nice and all, but he didn't seem super interested in me. I think he just felt bad he had my phone."

"I don't know," her friend sang. "Sounds to me like he tried a little too hard to come up with any excuse to see you again."

"You think so?"

"I know so. That's what shy guys do."

Eloise bit back a smile. It wouldn't be the worst thing if Marc was interested. There was something about him that she was drawn to, though she couldn't figure out what it was. If he planned on staying put, maybe she'd have an excuse to continue seeing him.

That evening went much like the first one. There wasn't a lot of time for small talk due to Gabriel continuously barking orders at them. This kind of high-intensity work probably should have worn on her, but surprisingly she found she loved it.

"House salad!" someone called out.

"Got it!" she responded.

Gabriel stepped into her path. "No. Hannah can get it." He nodded toward her. "I'm going to put you on the soups. Geoffrey has to leave early."

Her eyes widened. "But aren't the soups made to order?"

"Each soup goes off a base. Then all you have to do is add the fixings and additional spices. Do you think you can handle that?" Gabriel set his firm gaze on her.

She squirmed under his stare, then nodded. "I can do it, Chef." Eloise wasn't sure, but she thought she caught a look of approval flicker across his face. He patted her shoulder, then brushed past her.

Eloise spun to watch him leave then her eyes dragged across the room toward the stockpots that sat on the stovetop. She took a deep breath and then let it out slowly. She could do this. It was just like cooking supper at home.

SHE BREEZED down the hall toward Shane's office. Who knew that she could get such a high from being in front of a pot on a stove? Everything had gone perfectly, and it was all she could do to keep from smiling like a complete idiot.

Just before she reached his office door, her phone buzzed in her pocket. Eloise pulled it out and stared at a number she didn't recognize. She glanced toward Shane's office and then opened the message.

UNKNOWN: *Hey*

ELOISE FROWNED. She couldn't think of anyone who might message her that she didn't already know. She'd put Hannah's number in her phone already. Before she could respond, they messaged again.

.   .   .

Unknown: It's Marc. I wanted to see you again.

Her silly grin returned and she stuck her phone in her pocket. She'd respond after her meeting with Shane. Eloise pushed through the door that had been left ajar, then stopped. Shane paced behind his desk, having not seen her yet. He spoke in a low, angry tone.

"I don't care how you do it. Back out *now*." Shane stopped, his back to Eloise. "I'm not going to let you stay here. Visiting me is one thing. Setting up shop so you can torment—" He turned just enough that she caught his eye. His gaze darkened. "This isn't up for discussion. You'll back out and head home." He broke eye contact and his voice lowered further. "I'll do no such thing." Shane's jaw tightened and he spun around, muttering something she couldn't hear.

He ripped the phone from his ear and chucked it across the room. It collided with a loveseat that sat against the wall. Without turning to face her, he muttered, "It's not polite to eavesdrop."

"I wasn't—that's not what..." The blush that filled her face was hotter than she could ever remember. "Sorry. I just came by so we could complete the paperwork you said you needed me to fill out. I can come another time."

"No. It's fine." He raked a hand through his hair and turned toward his desk. "You'll need to fill out a W9 and sign an NDA. There're some other forms that you'll need if you want your paychecks to be deposited automatically to your account." He opened a drawer and pulled out a manila folder. His eyes locked with hers and a chill swept down her spine. She couldn't tell if it was because he was so obviously upset about something or if it was something else entirely.

"Well? Are you going to take it?" he bit out.

Eloise lurched forward, taking the folder from his hand. "Sorry." She lifted it. "Do you want me to do it now?"

"That would be preferable."

"Oh, I just thought since it was so late..." By the look he gave her, she could tell he wasn't interested in what she had to say. He shifted his focus to some paperwork that sat on his desk. This had to be the most awkward situation she'd ever been in. Eloise cleared her throat, and he looked up. "Could I have a pen?"

Shane motioned toward a pen holder on his desk. "Be my guest."

She plucked one from the cup and settled into the chair that faced his desk. A few minutes later, her phone buzzed again. Eloise pulled it out and read another message from Marc.

Marc: You probably think I'm desperate now, but I don't care. When you get these messages, don't hold it against me. I'm available tomorrow for breakfast if you want to get a coffee.

She pressed her lips together and let out a soft laugh.

"Something funny?"

Her head snapped up and she found Shane staring at her. Shaking her head, she shoved the phone back into her pocket. "No, sir." A smile touched her lips once more. "It's actually your cousin. He wants to take me to breakfast tomorrow." Her eyes drifted to the clock on the wall. "I guess it's technically today."

"No."

Eloise's focus shifted to Shane again. "*No?*" She let out another laugh. "Are you seriously telling me I can't go on a date with your cousin?"

He got to his feet and placed his palms on the desk. There was a spark in his gaze that might have made a normal person shiver in their boots, but she wasn't going to let him intimidate her. Even still, she was careful not to elicit further fury as he pinned her beneath his stare. "That's what I'm saying. You're not going on a date with my cousin."

This time her laugh was louder, and it seemed to fill the entire room. "You're joking."

"I'm not."

Her smile faded from her face. "*Excuse* me?"

"I forbid you to see my cousin." He said it with such a serious tone she was momentarily thrown off.

She shot up out of her seat and shot a death glare at him. "You *forbid* me? I'm sorry. Where do you get off? Is this why Brielle hates you now? You have a serious problem if you think I'm just going to roll over and do whatever you tell me to. You're my boss, not my father, not my boyfriend. You can't tell me who I see or don't see during my personal time."

They seemed to be participating in a battle of wills. The way Shane refused to break eye contact made her wonder just what he had against her. Maybe he didn't want her dating his cousin because he was still hurt from Brielle's rejection.

Well, he should be upset if this was how he treated her sister. This was modern times. Men didn't have the power to control their women anymore. She lifted her chin and her eyes narrowed. "I don't know what you have against me, but you might as well let it go. If your cousin wants to go on a date with me, then I'm going to tell him yes."

He pushed away from his desk, then charged around it. She stiffened, though there was nowhere to escape due to the chair digging into the back of her legs. She had to stand her ground or risk toppling backward like an idiot.

Shane held up one finger as he towered over her. He opened his mouth, then he shut it. Finally, he shook his head and strode out of the office, leaving her alone.

Eloise sucked in sharply, gasping for breath her lungs had refused to offer her in that tense moment. Her wide eyes darted toward the door. She hadn't feared for her safety; that wasn't what this feeling was. She was fine, but she'd never seen someone so upset about something so benign.

Her thoughts shifted back to the conversation she'd had with Brielle about Shane and his lies. What if his dishonesty wasn't a lie for the sake of lying? What if he did it for a bigger reason? To protect something?

The papers in her hand slipped and fluttered to the floor. She dropped to gather them, then shot one more look toward the door. Good thing she was about done. She'd just leave them on his desk and let him deal with it.

Now she just had to deal with what was going on with Marc.

7

Shane

Shane should have known better than to hope that Marc and Madeline would keep to themselves. First, they decided to make an offer on the ranch that bordered his country club. Now Marc was making a play for one of the daughters of the wealthiest man in town besides himself.

This wasn't going to end well for anyone. They needed to be stopped. He didn't know what they had planned, but he wasn't going to let them take advantage of a single soul who lived in this town.

Already he could tell Eloise wasn't cut out to decipher the kind of person Marc was. She wasn't as shrewd as her older sister, and she was too kind to believe him if he were to tell her about their sordid past. There was no point in telling her about it because she'd probably just tell him he was manipulating her.

He let out a groan as he made it to his car and yanked the

door open. Madeline hadn't listened to him when he was on the phone with her. Perhaps Marc would. The guy was the weak link between them. If he got nervous enough, he might actually listen.

Shane shoved his key into the ignition and started up truck. If Madeline and Marc thought they could infiltrate this town and bring it to its knees, they had another thing coming. If Zeke got wind of just who was taking his daughter to breakfast, he would be livid. Marc might not live to see the next day.

A small smile crept onto Shane's face at that thought, but he immediately dismissed it. That wasn't who he was. Would this world be a better place without people like his cousins? Yes. Would he wish harm or death on them?

Probably not. Though they could use a little wake-up call. At some point they'd end up hurting the wrong people and they would suffer consequences they never knew existed. If they'd listen to reason, they'd avoid it for the next little while.

Shane drove along the dark road that led into town. There was one motel he was certain he'd find his family at. He didn't know what he was going to say to them, but he had to do something—*anything* to ensure they kept their distance.

He pulled into the parking lot of the biggest motel Copper Creek had to offer. It boasted three levels with big windows and an outdoor pool. Madeline probably hated it. There weren't any amenities she was used to, and the room service left much to be desired, as he'd found out when he'd moved to Copper Creek.

It was all part of the charm of living on the outskirts of anything. If they hadn't been lucky enough to run into Eloise, they might have grown tired of this place and left on their own accord.

Now, he had to get them to back out of that real estate deal and forget all about this place—a feat that was beginning to sound harder than starting up his business here when everyone had hated him.

Shane shut off the engine and climbed out of his car. If he had to guess, his cousins were staying on the top floor in the only suite this place offered. There was little chance the host would confirm his suspicions, so he went straight to the elevator as if he knew exactly what he was doing and who he was going to see.

Once on the third floor, he made a beeline for the room he'd once stayed in for a few nights. That was back when he thought he needed the bigger and better things in his life. Turned out he didn't need material things as much as he thought he did. What he really wanted was to make a change in people's lives some-how. But all he really knew in this moment was that Madeline and Marc needed to leave. There was absolutely no way they were going to grow and fit in with the sort of people who resided here.

His fist hit the door with three resounding thuds. Despite it being a little after midnight, the door swung open almost imme-diately. Madeline stood in the doorway, donned in a silk robe that came just above her knees. She didn't look the least bit surprised to see him, which had him wondering if Eloise had mentioned to Marc that Shane had run off.

He raked a hand through his hair, glowering at her and expecting her to make some snide comment about how he'd aged so much over the last few days.

Her eyes swept up and down his body and she smirked. "To what do I owe this pleasure?"

"I want you out of here, Madeline."

She rolled her eyes and moved back into the room. "I'm not going anywhere. We told you, we're here for the long haul—at least until you give us what is rightfully ours."

"What? You each want an additional million? Is that what

this is about?" He couldn't see her face, but with the way she snorted, he could tell she had no plans to listen to him.

"You think a million is going to make me happy? Geez, Shane. Have you gotten dumber since we were kids? How many times do you have to learn that when someone like me wants something, they get it? And if they know there is a way to keep that faucet running, they're going to try their hardest to make sure that happens." She peeked at him over her shoulder, then turned to face him fully as she leaned against the back of a sofa that sat in the middle of the largest room. "Why are you *really* here, Shane? I have never seen you so set on something before in my entire life. What triggered this response?" Her voice lowered. "Because I want to see if I can replicate it."

His hands formed fists at his sides. This town was his sanctuary from the outside world. It was the place he finally had to call his own—a place away from the drama and misdeeds of two very specific cousins.

Seeing her now, he knew he had little chance of getting rid of her, but there was one thing he couldn't deny. She wanted to toy with him, and she knew she was doing so successfully.

"I want you and Marc to pack up and leave. You have no idea what you're doing and how hard it will be to take care of that land."

She threw her head back and laughed. "I don't want the land. I could care less about that."

His brows furrowed. "You made an offer on it."

"So?"

"That's a binding contract. Once it gets past a specific point, you can't back out without financial repercussions."

"I'm not an idiot, Shane. I know how real estate listings work."

He stared at her, dumbfounded. What was her plan? How

was she planning to come out on top? "What are you trying to do?"

She shrugged. "I guess you'll just have to find out, huh?"

He dragged a hand down his face. "If it's money you want—"

"Oh, it's *so* much more than money." She pushed away from the couch and wandered toward him. "I'm just not going to tell you until I know I can get it." Her whispered words raised the hairs on the back of his neck, and he stifled a shiver. "Until then," she continued, "you can expect to see Marc and me hanging around. He's already grown quite attached to that cute little Eloise. I hear her family comes from money, too. Maybe we can all get our happily ever after."

Shane took a sudden step backward, his eyes blazing. "You're not getting a single thing. I won't let you ruin another life. You might as well get out of here and find someone else to manipulate."

She shrugged, moving toward the open door. Her hips swayed and she paused to look over her shoulder once more. "We'll see about that."

His blood practically boiled from his conversation with Madeline. The more he thought about it, the worse his head pounded.

How on earth was he supposed to protect people like the Callahans if he didn't know what Madeline had planned? He couldn't.

Shane should never have given them a dime from his inheritance. His adoptive grandfather knew what he was doing when he chose to write his ungrateful grandchildren and children out of his will. At least Madeline's parents had better sense than to come after Shane out in the country.

Unless they were on their way and this little visit was part of a much bigger plan.

He growled and slammed the door shut on his way out of the

motel. It was midnight, but he needed someone to talk to. He needed to get in the right headspace and stop being on the defensive. It was time to turn the tables and prevent whatever she had planned from coming to fruition.

A short drive later, he stood on the doorstep of Tristan's house. His friend had managed to make a home here in Copper Creek with his kid, and Shane couldn't be happier. Tristan belonged here. He made this place better. He was the level-headed kind of guy that Shane needed right now.

Shane stared at the door, hesitating. Tristan's kid would likely be asleep, and with his disposition, waking him would only elicit Tristan and Dianna's wrath. A phone call might be enough to rouse Tristan from bed. Then again, maybe this was a mistake and he needed to wait until morning.

He let out a sigh.

Waiting until morning meant that Marc would be on Eloise's doorstep and Shane would have one less night of planning. Would his friend understand this intrusion?

The door opened and Tristan stood on the porch with a hunting rifle in his hand. He was clad in a T-shirt and a pair of trunks. The look on his face said he wasn't against using his weapon until his eyes focused on Shane. They narrowed, then widened, and Tristan glanced back into the house before stepping out onto the porch and shutting the door.

"Shane? What in the world are you doing here? Do you have any idea what time it is?" Tristan hissed.

Grimacing, Shane stepped toward his friend, hoping he would understand once he heard what was going on. "I have a problem."

"What kind of problem?"

"The kind you met when we were in college."

Tristan's brows lifted immediately. "No."

"I'm telling you, this time it's even worse."

"What do they want?" Tristan whispered, though the hatred dripped from each word.

Shane gestured toward the steps. "You got a minute?"

Tristan glanced back at the door and then nodded. "But if Dianna wakes up, I can't promise she won't come out here and give you a tongue lashing."

"I don't doubt it." Shane dropped down onto the steps and let out a heavy breath. "I don't know what they want except what they've made clear in the past."

"Money," Tristan ground out.

"Yeah. But it's not just that. I don't know. It's like they want something *more*."

"You gave them ten million dollars. What more could they want?"

Shane lifted a brow as he gave Tristan a pointed look. "They always want more. You know that. Only this time, they're going at it in two ways." He wasn't sure he wanted to tell this part to Tristan. Seeing as he was married to Eloise's sister, he had no way of knowing how that family would react to him. He couldn't afford to receive Zeke's wrath, and he definitely didn't want to contend with his daughters. He took in a deep breath and let it out, but it did nothing to soothe the discontent he felt. "I need you to promise me you won't tell anyone."

"Sure, okay."

He faced Tristan fully. "I mean it. No one. Not a single person. Not even Dianna."

Tristan hesitated. "She's my wife, Shane. I can't just—"

"It's not forever. Just until I figure out a way to get them out of this town. The fewer who know about them, the better we'll be."

"You mean the better *you'll* be," Tristan corrected. "Look, Shane, if people are going to be at risk with them here—"

"They will *always* be at risk. You know how manipulative Madeline can be. Even when we know what they're capable of, they still manage to come out on top." Shane put his head into his hands and rested his elbows on his knees. "I don't know how, but I know I have to stop them from coming after me—and everyone here."

"How long?"

He peeked at his friend. "How long what?"

"How long do I need to keep this from my wife? Because I'm not going to give you a free pass indefinitely."

Hope flared within Shane. "Not long. Give me a few weeks. Two months at the most."

Tristan frowned. "That's a long time to keep a secret."

"I know. And I wouldn't be asking you if I didn't think it was important."

His friend seemed to contemplate what Shane had said for a moment before he gave him a sharp nod. "Fine. What do you know? Maybe I can help come up with a plan."

"That's what I was hoping." Shane tore his gaze away from Tristan. He couldn't bring himself to look his friend in the eye when he knew what this information would mean. "Right now, they've put an offer on a ranch."

Tristan let out a curse. "So they're planning on staying."

"Yeah. And Madeline is pushing Marc to court Eloise."

Tristan shot up from his seat. "Shane, you know I can't—"

Shane rose too, his hands held out as he tried to keep his friend calm. "I know, I know. They managed to find out about Zeke's wealth somehow. I think they might be trying to get close to her so she'll become some kind of way to get them more money. Madeline wouldn't tell me what she's doing, but that's about as close as I can figure." He could see the crimson color of Tristan's face even in the dim lighting. "I'm not going to let anything happen to Eloise. I just need to figure out a way to keep them apart."

Tristan paced in front of his door. "How could you ask me to promise not to tell Dianna? You know that she trumps our friendship, right? I need to tell her—"

"One month," Shane pleaded. "Dianna, Grace, and Eloise all work for me. Sean, too. They're good people—"

"Exactly. That's why you need to warn them."

"I thought for sure you would be the person who would understand. If we tell them, they get on Madeline's radar. You barely got out from her clutches unscathed. Think about what could happen."

Tristan worked his jaw, glowering at Shane. He had every right to be furious with him. Shane only prayed he'd be willing to go along with their original agreement.

"Just help me keep them apart—without alerting anyone—until I can convince Madeline to leave."

"I can't believe I'm going along with this," Tristan muttered. "You owe me."

"I know."

Tristan let out another sigh. "You know there is only one way to keep two people separate without telling anyone what is really going on, right?"

Shane frowned. "What's that?"

"You have to get closer to her than Marc can."

He shook his head. "I'm not going to manipulate her."

"What other option do you have? You know what's at stake here—what they're capable of doing."

"I'm not going to pretend—"

"You don't have to pretend. Just be there for her. You care about her, right? I assume so since you're not willing to let your cousins do something to hurt her."

"Yeah..."

"Well, hang around. Keep an eye on her. Make excuses to be with her. I don't know. Do *something* to make sure they're never alone."

Shane snorted. "How am I supposed to do that? I can't exactly crash their dates."

"Why not?"

He gaped at his friend. Technically, he was right. If that was the only way he could make this work, then that's what he'd do. He'd just have to figure out how to keep tabs on Marc without him knowing.

8

"I'm still not sold on this whole thing." Brielle stood in Eloise's doorway. It was as if she were trying to block Eloise from leaving altogether. "Are you sure he's not... you know..."

Eloise let out a laugh. "What exactly are you suggesting? That he's some serial killer? I assure you, he's absolutely harmless."

Brielle's dark look couldn't have been more humorous.

"Look, he took me to lunch, and he was a perfect gentleman." She pursed her lips to the side as her thoughts shifted to Shane's reaction. "There was *one* weird thing, though."

"What's that?"

"Shane didn't want me to go out with him."

Brielle stiffened. "See? If his own cousin doesn't want you to go out with him, then you shouldn't."

Eloise placed her hands on her hips and gave her sister a

pointed look. "I thought you weren't on team-Shane. What happened to thinking he was a liar?"

"That was before—well, that was before now. I don't know what it is, but I'm getting a bad feeling about Marc."

"You haven't even met him."

"I don't have to. There's something really weird about this, don't you think?"

Eloise shook her head. "You're the weird one. We'll be going to a public place. I'll be fine."

Her sister crossed her arms. "I'm being *serious*. I don't know what it is, but I don't think you should go out with him."

Eloise let out a groan. "I'm not *dating* him. We're just going out for breakfast or coffee. If you're so worried, maybe you should come with us."

Brielle gave her a disbelieving look. "I'm not going to be the third wheel on your date."

She shrugged. "Suit yourself. It could be fun. And you could ask him all the questions Shane never told you." Eloise saw it in Brielle's eyes. She was tempted by that idea even though she hadn't dated Shane for several months. That interest faded just as quickly.

"Nope. I'm not going. But I want you to give me access to your phone's location at all times. I don't want him dragging you off someplace to murder you before he dumps your body."

"Geez, Bri. That's a little morbid, don't you think?"

"He's an *outsider*. Until he proves himself, we should *all* treat him like a serial killer."

"For heaven's sake. You dated Shane. He was an outsider once."

"That was different," Brielle said.

Eloise sighed. "It really isn't. But do me a favor and refrain from saying any of this in front of him. I don't need him treating me differently. He's really sweet. And while I'm not *dating* him right now, maybe it could happen." She grinned. "You never know, right?" She pushed past Brielle and headed down the hall toward the door. She heard Brielle's footsteps behind her and smiled wider. Brielle might not be willing to go on their little date with them, but she wasn't about to let Marc take her little sister out without getting a good look at him.

At least she was consistent.

Just as she arrived at the front door to slip her jacket on, someone knocked. Eloise exchanged a look with Brielle. "Wow. He's really punctual, too. That's a plus, right?"

Brielle rolled her eyes and reached around Eloise for the doorknob. She pulled open the door, then let out a bark of laughter. "Are you sure you're going on a date with *Marc*?"

Eloise peered around the door to find Shane standing on the porch looking just as confused as she was. "Shane? What are you doing here?"

He rubbed the back of his neck, then shifted his focus to Brielle for just a moment. "I wanted to apologize for how I left things last night."

"It's fine." Eloise attempted to move around Brielle, but her sister's arm shot out to block her.

"What happened?" The edge in her voice was enough to make even Eloise flinch. If she knew the extent of what Shane had said and done, she wouldn't be standing here having this conversation. She'd be hunting down their father's shotgun.

Eloise darted beneath her sister's arm. "I told you. He didn't want me to go on a date with Marc."

"And why *is* that?"

Shane shifted his weight nervously. "That's actually something I wanted to talk to you about."

Eloise and Brielle stared at him, waiting for him to continue.

It wouldn't matter how hard Eloise tried; she'd never be able to come up with an excuse that made sense. She couldn't wait to hear what he had to say.

Shane continued to fidget. He glanced at Brielle and then back to Eloise. "Could we have a word—privately?"

"Not on your life." Brielle seethed. "Whatever you have to say to my sister, you can say to her in front of me."

"Bri," Eloise muttered with exasperation, "I'll be *fine*."

"I'm beginning to wonder if you know what that word even means." Brielle dragged her gaze to Eloise, then frowned. She was clearly not on board with leaving them alone, but she must have seen the determination on Eloise's face because she let out a resigned sigh. "I'll be inside if you need me."

The door slammed behind Eloise, causing her to flinch again. "Sorry."

He shook his head. "Don't worry about it."

She clasped her hands together, waiting expectantly for him to clear the air. She almost wanted to let him know that he'd better have a good reason for the way he'd reacted to her the other night. However, due to the fact that he'd come to her, she thought it better to let him take the lead in this conversation.

Shane shoved his hands into his pockets and then looked away. "I can't believe this is how I'm doing this."

"Me neither."

He shot a surprised look in her direction.

"You know... because of the way you left things last night." She bit back a smile. It was actually fun watching him squirm. She still cringed at their conversation. What he'd said to her was still burned into her memory. It had made falling asleep incredibly difficult.

Karma. That's what this was.

Shane broke eye contact, then he took a deep breath before releasing it. He let out a strained chuckle. "This wasn't how I wanted to do this." He met her gaze again, and she was taken aback by the way his eyes seemed to smolder.

"*Shane*." She laughed if only an attempt to ease the tension that only continued to grow. "Just spit it out. Marc is going to be here soon and—"

"I'm interested in you."

Eloise clamped her mouth shut. She couldn't possibly have heard him correctly. "I'm *sorry*, what?"

He took a step toward her, his head dipping a little and his voice lowering. "I find you... attractive."

Her throat closed up. If she didn't know any better, she would have thought her lungs had turned to stone. This wasn't happening. It couldn't be. She shook her head. "No, you don't."

"Pardon?" His voice was low and warm—too close.

She sucked in sharply, holding up a hand as she stepped back a fraction. "You can't. You were dating Brielle. This is just a ploy to get closer to her, isn't it? You still have a thing for her and you want to—"

"*No*," he bit out a little too sharply. "This has nothing to do with Brielle."

Eloise laughed. "Your tone of voice begs to differ."

He closed the distance between them. "I know you'll find this hard to believe, but it's completely true. I want to get to know you on a more... *personal* level. That's why I didn't want you to get too serious with Marc. The second I heard you were going to see him, I... got jealous." He shut his eyes tight, then his stiff shoulders relaxed and he peered at her. "I'm just asking you to give me a chance."

"What about Brielle?" That was probably the only thing that she shouldn't have said. She grimaced the moment the words escaped her lips.

Shane's attention shifted toward the door that Brielle had slammed. He turned a sad smile toward Eloise. "It's true that

Brielle was the one to break up with me, but we both knew it wasn't going to work out. I cared for her. I always will to a certain degree. But we've both gone our separate ways. I can't help who I'm attracted to. Besides, it's completely possible that nothing will come of this." He reached his hand toward hers, grazing her fingertips with his own but ultimately dropped it back to his side. "One date. That's all I want."

Eloise's mind was completely muddled. Normally she would have turned him down by now. She would have told him that she wasn't interested in dating her boss. Not only that but she wouldn't be caught dead dating her sister's ex.

What was she thinking? Was she actually considering his offer? No way. That wasn't who she was.

"I'm flattered, truly, but—"

A car pulled up to the house, and Eloise's attention was momentarily drawn toward it. Shane followed her focus, then let out a groan. Marc materialized out of the car and gave them both a little wave.

He headed toward them, a confident smile etched on his face. "Hey there, beautiful." His eyes swept over Shane. "Cousin."

Shane worked his jaw, stepping back to put distance between himself and Marc. Eloise's eyes locked with his when Marc pressed a soft kiss to her cheek. He slipped his arm around her waist to pull her closer to him, but the gesture felt foreign and forced. She stiffened, suddenly uncomfortable with the demonstration of his interest in her. It was only because she had an audience. If Shane wasn't here, she wouldn't mind his affection at all.

Marc released her, then crossed his arms. "What are you doing here? Madeline said you visited late last night. Everything okay?"

Shane's eyes didn't leave Eloise as he spoke. "Just peachy. She was telling me about your interest in the ranch property next to mine. I was giving her my advice."

A smile played at Marc's lips. "Always quick with the unsolicited advice." Marc nudged Eloise. "Shane here seems to consider himself the only smart investor in our family."

Eloise tucked a strand of hair behind her ear, shifting a step away from both of them. "Well, he's been quite successful in his personal and business investments. I'd say anyone would be grateful to get advice from him." It took everything in her power to tear her eyes away from Shane. His confession continued to run laps in her head.

The way they continued to size each other up was getting to her, and she didn't know how much longer she could take it. Eloise clapped her hands together. "Well, Marc and I are going to head out for breakfast or whatever he planned and—"

"Mind if I tag along?" Shane cut in. "I haven't had anything to eat yet, and we could catch up."

"I think that's a great idea."

All three of them turned to find Brielle standing in the now-open doorway. Her eyes were studying Marc, scanning him up and down. They flitted to Shane, then finally landed on Eloise. She didn't say anything, but Eloise had a feeling if she did, it would be to remind her about that *feeling* she had about the man she had never met.

Had they been alone, Eloise would have chewed her sister out. She had no intention of getting close to Shane. Three was a crowd, and she wanted to get to know *Marc* a little better. Before she could voice her opinion, Marc beat her to it.

"Sure. We could make it a double date."

Brielle held up both hands, her gaze immediately locking with Shane. "I'm involved with someone else."

Eloise gaped. This was news to her. Brielle was *dating*? No. She would have said something. This was an excuse to stay away from Shane. Eloise couldn't blame her for it either. But to refuse to tag along would make this breakfast nearly intolerable. Already Eloise felt stuck between a rock and a hard place.

Marc nodded. "Too bad. Maybe another time then." He turned toward Shane and Eloise, then motioned toward his car. "Ready to go?"

Shane offered her his arm. "May I?"

Eloise glanced from one to the other. This was ridiculous. She spun to face Brielle. "I'm taking your truck. Give me your keys."

Without a degree of hesitation, Brielle dug the truck keys from her pocket and held them out. A smile tugged at her lips, and she didn't break eye contact for even a second as she murmured, "Don't wreck it."

Though she didn't see them, Eloise could hear the men head down the porch steps and presumably toward their cars. At least they could take a hint.

"Yeah. Okay," Eloise muttered with exasperation. "I can't believe you did this."

"Me? What did I do?"

"You're a meddler. How about you start minding your own business and let the rest of us handle our lives on our own."

"Now, where's the fun in that?"

9

Shane

Shane couldn't believe the lengths he had to go to in order to shield Eloise from Madeline's nefarious plan —a plan he still didn't have a good idea of. The only thing that made sense at this point was that Marc was set on dating Eloise for her money.

There was only one problem with that. Out of all of the men who had ended up with a Callahan, Shane hadn't seen any of them profit from it. They were welcomed into this empire, and yet not a single man had taken advantage of it.

Well, except for Sean. His family had been struggling when he married Adeline. Only a few people were aware of that fact. He couldn't recall how he'd managed to get that information, but he'd made sure to keep it to himself.

Now, as he sat in a booth across from Eloise and Marc, he couldn't ignore how watching them made him sick to his stomach.

He probably should have just told her like Tristan had suggested.

But that thought only made the tightness in his chest worse. He couldn't afford to let his reputation take a hit right now. There were too many balls in the air at the moment.

Shane let out a sigh and tore his gaze away from the couple to look out the window.

Eloise hadn't accepted his offer to go on even one date. How was he supposed to pull her away from Marc when the guy exuded charm and wit?

This was a bad idea not just because of the deception, but because he was being outmaneuvered by such a slimeball.

He clenched his hands into fists in his lap. He had to up his game if he wanted any shot at coming out on top.

"Excuse me, I need to go to the ladies' room." Eloise stood. Her eyes landed on Shane briefly before she smiled at Marc. "I'll be right back."

Marc's smile dissolved off his face the second Eloise was out of range. Instead, he replaced it with something a bit more sinister. "What do you think you're doing? She's obviously not interested in you. She's here with me. She sat by me. You're wasting your time."

Shane leaned forward, punching his finger onto the table. "First of all, you're not going to get anywhere with her. Or did you not see her sister? Brielle is one of the most protective women I have ever met. She doesn't even let the men she dates meet her family."

Marc settled back in his seat, one brow lifting. The smirk he wore was one that made Shane's stomach churn. "So you dated her? Was she easier than this one? Somehow, I sense Eloise is one of those slow-burn kinds of women. Do you think she'll kiss me at the end of our date?" He frowned. "Probably not. But that Brielle, maybe she's more my speed."

Hot fire consumed Shane and his finger curled into his fist before he slammed it down on the table. "You leave her out of this."

Marc chuckled. "Madeline said we'd hit a nerve with this family. We just couldn't figure out why... until now." He leaned forward, his voice lowering to a whisper. "What do you think Madeline will say when she finds out the reason? Do you think she'll shift her focus to Brielle?"

Shane's fingernails dug into his palm. It took every ounce of control not to swing at his cousin. But they were in a public place, and if Eloise caught him in a scuffle with Marc, she'd never give him a chance. "You need to pack up and leave," he muttered through gritted teeth. "You're not going to win this one."

"That sure sounds like wishful thinking on your part," Marc chuckled. He leaned back again, crossing his arms against his chest. "No, I think I'm going to like it here. I think Madeline does too. The open spaces, the fresh air... I think she's finally figured out what she wants to do with you, and I can't say I hate the idea."

His whole body went stiff. Marc knew the plan. He was in on it. Of course he was. Gone were the days when Madeline would keep things on a need-to-know basis. She was still the brains of the outfit, but it appeared she was giving Marc a little more freedom in their schemes.

Shane's eyes narrowed. "What exactly is that?"

Marc laughed. "You think I'm going to tell you? Madeline would kill me for giving you anything you could use to stop her. This is bigger than you could ever imagine." He chuckled again. "I almost envy you because you get to sit back and enjoy the show."

His blood practically boiled. "Mark my words, if you even—"

"Everything okay?"

Shane snapped his mouth shut, his eyes darting up to meet

Eloise's as she stood beside the table with her hands on her hips. She sent an accusatory gaze in his direction. He gritted his teeth and settled back in his seat. So much for winning her over. Even if she only caught the last bit of that conversation, she wouldn't trust him. He wouldn't be surprised if she thought he was threatening Marc so he'd leave her alone.

Marc smiled widely at Eloise. "Better now that you're here, love."

Shane bristled. How could she not see that Marc was manipulating her? This wasn't boding well at all. He needed to do better—try harder—get her alone somehow.

As much as he hated to admit it, he needed to get into a different mindset. He needed to think more like Marc.

Worse.

He needed to think more like Madeline.

Shane's gaze swept over Eloise and his stomach churned. Not only would he be manipulating her, but he'd also be hurting the sister of a woman he had very much cared for. Brielle would rip out his throat if she knew what he was thinking of doing.

For Pete's sake! Why did Eloise have to be the one to pick up his cousins from the side of the road? Couldn't the universe throw him a bone?

Eloise scooted back onto the bench. She gave Shane a strange look, and he could just see the cogs in her mind whirring. She probably didn't even want him there.

Shane glanced at Marc, finding an obnoxious sneer on his face. Boy, how he hated his cousins more in this moment than he could ever recall in the past. Shane shot out of his seat, leaning over the table, his palms pressed flat on the surface. "I will see you at work tonight, Eloise."

She blinked, then nodded. "I suppose you will."

He stormed out of the restaurant, clenching and relaxing his hands. He needed a better plan. He needed a devious one.

Tristan wouldn't be any help. He couldn't think of anyone who had that kind of background that would help him take Marc down.

Shouldering through the door, he nearly collided with someone. When he got a better look at the man, recognition flitted through him. "Wade? I'm sorry."

The rugged cowboy sized him up with mild distaste. "Mr. Owens." His gaze drifted toward the restaurant and then back to Shane.

They stood frozen on the sidewalk, and Shane couldn't help but feel like the cowboy was sizing him up for some reason. It wasn't a secret that Wade Keagan was as hardheaded as they came. He wasn't exactly thrilled about the money that Shane had donated to his farm, but he should respect it.

Wade shoved his hands in his back pockets. "Well, then. Have a good day," he muttered. Wade moved to shoulder past him when an idea popped into Shane's mind.

Spinning around, Shane blurted, "Don't you have a criminal record?"

Wade froze. From behind, it wasn't hard to see every single muscle in his body tense. "*Excuse* me?"

Shane shrank back. That was probably the wrong way to start a friendship. "It's just that I have a need for that sort of background."

Wade turned to face him, his stone-like expression sending a chill through Shane's body. "You probably don't want to continue speaking if you know what's good for you."

Clearing his throat, Shane ventured closer to Wade. "In that restaurant, there's a guy who is on a date with a Callahan."

The cowboy's brows lifted marginally.

Shane attempted to clear his throat again, but the lump that had lodged there wasn't budging. "Eloise Callahan is in there with someone she shouldn't be. I don't want to alert anyone to his... past... but I need a way to get her away from him."

Wade snorted. "And you want me to do what? Kidnap her?"

Holding up both hands, Shane shook his head. "No. Of course not. But maybe you could pick a fight with him. Rough him up a bit."

Wade dragged a hand through the air. "You sound insane, you know that, right? I've got two weeks of probation left, and you want me to jeopardize it for someone I don't even know?"

"You're interested in Brielle."

The man's expression hardened again. "Where did you hear that?"

"Didn't have to hear it. She's been working out at your ranch. It's hard not to like someone who you spend so much time with, right?" Shane was making things up as he went. There was no guarantee that Wade had any such feelings. But based on the way the man was reacting, Shane had a pretty good idea. It could be as simple as a fondness, or it could have bled into a crush. Either way, he might take pity and actually do something about Marc. "Besides, I could make it worth your while."

Wade closed the distance between them, causing Shane to take a stumbled step backward. "I want to make it perfectly clear that Brielle is nothing more than a volunteer who has barely stepped foot on my property since you gave us that money. She's *nothing* to me. And I could care less about what happens to her or her sisters."

"Couldn't."

He stiffened. "*What*?"

"You *couldn't* care less." Shane snapped his mouth shut. "Not the time. I get it." He swallowed again. "Just pick a fight and I'll pay you."

"Why?" Wade's eyes narrowed. "You have a thing for Miss Callahan?"

Shane pressed his lips together firmly. "I... yes," he squeaked. "Yes, I do," he murmured more firmly. "And she's in there with my cousin. He's not a good guy, and I know she can do better."

This time Wade seemed to consider his offer. "And you just want me to scare him a little?"

Nodding, Shane gestured toward the restaurant. "Pick him up and push him up against a wall or something."

"How much?"

"Pardon?"

"How much are you going to pay me?"

"Whatever you want."

Wade's eyes narrowed. "Why couldn't you just pay your cousin? Seems like he might be the kind of guy who would take you up on that sort of thing based on how you described him."

"You make a good point," Shane let out a strained chuckle. "Except he's the kind of guy who will keep coming back for more."

"And what makes you think I won't do the same?"

Shane blinked. That was another good point. But there was just something different about Wade—something that Shane trusted. "Because you're a good man."

Wade's head reared back, the shock clearly written all over his face, but then he schooled his features. "Fine. I'll do it. Just this once."

Relief washed over Shane. "Thank you."

"I'm not doing it for you," he muttered. "And I don't want anything either. You gave my family enough money to keep our property. Call us even." He spun on his heel and headed straight for the restaurant.

Shane watched him until he disappeared inside, then hurried toward his car. He didn't want to be around when everything hit the fan.

"WHAT IN HEAVEN'S name did you *do*?"

Shane slammed his hand down on the paperwork that attempted to float away from the way Brielle stormed into his office. "I have no idea what you're talking about."

"That's a load of bull and you know it. What were you thinking?" She paced his office, adding more air circulation than was necessary. "Eloise is furious, you know."

"Is she as furious as you?"

Brielle stopped, glowering at him. "If you knew what was good for you, you'd shut your mouth right now."

Shane leaned back in his seat. He hadn't heard anything regarding the incident he had set up. Not a word from Madeline or Marc. He had almost expected to see them before he had a run-in with anyone else. The fact that Brielle was here surprised him more than he cared to admit. "Do you care to enlighten me?"

Her face turned bright red. "I just got a call from Annabel."

His brows creased. "I don't know who that is."

"Wade's *sister*. Does that ring a bell? What do you have to say for yourself?"

He knew better than to admit to anything. For all Brielle knew, Wade had issues with Marc that neither one of them were aware of.

Brielle let out an exaggerated groan. "Seriously? Nothing? I know you were behind this. Annabel had to bail her brother out of county lockup. Thank goodness Marc isn't pressing charges." She charged toward his desk and slammed her hands down on the surface. "Now, are you going to tell me what is going on? I *know* you. This isn't something you would do without a good reason."

Her bright eyes had always been able to take him off guard. Eloise's eyes were incredibly similar, but he'd forced himself to ignore that little fact. His jaw ached from how hard he clenched it. If Brielle found out about Marc, she'd do something drastic—even more so than he had. Shane had to keep her in the dark.

Slowly, he rose to his feet. "I have never gotten along with my cousins."

"Yeah. I figured," she snapped. "Wanna tell me why?"

"We just have... different views on certain things."

Brielle lifted one brow. "And why would it matter if he's interested in my sister?"

This was what he'd been expecting. Brielle was bound to come to certain conclusions. Inside, he cringed. She wasn't going to like this. "I'm interested in... her."

She stared at him for what felt like a full minute. Predator watching her prey.

He squirmed beneath her gaze.

Brielle shook her head sharply. "Liar."

Shane stiffened. "What? I can't be interested in your sister?"

Her bark of laughter almost wounded him. "First of all, you will never be allowed to date my sisters. This life that you offered —none of them would want it anyway. Second, no. You're not interested. Have you forgotten how close we got? I know you well enough to see who you're interested in—and you have zero chemistry with Eloise." She tilted her head. "That being said, I can't shake the feeling that as bad as you are for my sister, Marc is worse."

So he was right. Brielle could sense more than she was letting on.

Her gaze softened. "I'd be willing to call a truce—I'd even be willing to help you win her over."

He lifted a brow. "I find it hard to believe you'd allow her to fall for me only for me to break her heart."

Brielle waved a dismissive hand. "Don't get such a big head.

You just have to be more enticing than Marc. She doesn't have to fall in love with you."

Shane considered her words. That plan sounded a lot better than his—especially since he would have an ally on the inside without having to give her all the information. He held out his hand. "Deal."

She eyed his hand, then shook her head. "This doesn't mean anything. I'm helping my sister. We're still over." Pain flickered behind those large eyes of hers, and his heart went out to her. They just didn't work. They'd gotten in too many arguments. In the end, neither one of them could find happiness. He wanted to settle down, and she simply couldn't.

Brielle flipped her hair over her shoulder, then set her stern gaze on him. "If you hurt her…"

He held up both hands. "I get it."

"Okay. Pull out a piece of paper and start taking notes."

10

Eloise

*E*loise stood outside of Shane's office. Why couldn't she bring herself to knock? After what had happened today and last night, she didn't know how this conversation would go. All afternoon, she couldn't get what he'd said out of her head. His words ran through her mind on repeat.

I find you... attractive.

Putting aside that his statement had to have been the least alluring way to tell her he was interested, she couldn't shake the way his voice had sounded. There was an air of desperation to it.

Admittedly she'd never found desperation to be an attractive quality. She'd usually ignored the guys who showed even a hint of it.

So why was she hesitating right now? She fully planned on coming to his office to tell him to leave her be. They could have a professional relationship. That was all. That's how it had to be.

And if he refused?

That thought had also crossed her mind.

How could she come to work at the kitchen—a job she found she loved more than she'd anticipated—and be forced to see Shane knowing he wasn't going to let up? It seemed impossible.

Eloise took a deep breath, steeling herself for a conversation she didn't want to have. Then she lifted her hand and the door swung open.

Shane stared at her, startled. His tie had been loosened, hanging around his neck, and his hair was disheveled. He actually looked normal. Gone was the man who didn't quite fit in around here—the man in nice suits and shiny shoes.

Yes, he still wore his suit, but there was something different about him. She was thrown off guard enough that she couldn't find the words she'd been rehearsing in her head. Her throat closed up and her tongue felt heavy. Think! What was she going to say?

Right, she was going to say that he needed to stay out of whatever was happening between Marc and herself.

"You—" she started to say.

"Go on a date with me."

"What?"

Shane's eyes flashed with something she couldn't put a finger on. He shifted, shoving his hands into his pockets. His gaze focused on something behind her briefly before he continued. "Forgive me. This isn't the way things usually go for me."

Eloise placed a hand on her hip. "Oh, so you don't usually invite yourself into being a third wheel?" She bit back a smile. "Or send a cowboy into a restaurant to rough up your cousin?"

His eyes widened and his face flushed. "Brielle told you?"

She shook her head. "No, I figured it out all on my own. You left, then Wade appeared. Marc's a good guy. He's not pressing charges."

"But Wade was locked up in county—"

"You forget my godfather is the sheriff. He didn't take too kindly to Wade Keagan dragging my date out into the street to push him around a little." It was getting harder to fight the smile. Wait a minute. Wasn't she supposed to be telling him off? This felt an awful lot like they were flirting.

She schooled her features and crossed her arms. He wasn't going to get to her. This wasn't how this conversation was supposed to go. But before she could make that clear, he cut her off again.

"One date." His eyes pleaded with her, catching her off guard once more. "Please, Eloise."

"You keep saying that, but—"

"And you keep ignoring it. You haven't said you will or won't at this point. So let me ask you one thing. What's stopping you?"

She let out a laugh, but it sounded far more pathetic than she wanted it to. "*Why* wouldn't I want to go out with you? Well, let's see. You're my boss. You dated my sister. You set your guard dog on your cousin. Need I go on?"

Where she thought he might show a degree of clarity from her words, he demonstrated quite the opposite. "All of those reasons aren't good enough."

She stiffened. "What?" Another strangled laugh escaped her throat. "And who's the judge of that? You? Because from where I'm standing, they're absolutely acceptable reasons."

Shane shook his head and took a step toward her. His head dipped a little closer to hers. She could smell his cologne and almost feel his body heat. Their little shared moment had grown ten times more intimate as he lowered his voice huskily. "Not one of them is the reason that matters most."

"And what's that?" Her whisper was barely audible. Though there was nothing behind her and she had every capability of escaping if she truly wanted to, she found that she didn't. Eloise stood her ground for no other reason than the fact that he had intrigued her.

"You want to know what it would be like—to partake in something forbidden. There's a part of you that would relish the idea of receiving a kiss during a stolen moment. You might be intrigued with Marc, but there's an undeniable pull between us."

Eloise couldn't move. It was as if her feet had stopped working. It was getting harder to breathe, and she couldn't focus on anything except how hot her skin felt. Her head buzzed and her heart pounded.

Finally, she found the strength to utter, "And you want the same?"

He stared at her for what felt like a full minute. Then he took a step back. "No."

Just like that the air in her lungs—whatever had remained—whooshed out like she'd been punched in the gut. She wanted to be angry with him for taking her on this rollercoaster of emotions, for toying with her, but she couldn't. Eloise could only be angry with herself for allowing it to happen.

He turned his back, and she balled her hands into fists, making sure her voice would remain steady and professional.

"I would far prefer to court you in the light of day. I'd want you to care for me above anyone else—to think of only me and be grateful you had me. Dating someone under cover of darkness does not appeal to me." He glanced at her over his shoulder.

Chills rocketed through her body as another bout of whiplash accosted her. She blinked rapidly and her hands relaxed as she tried to wrap her head around what he'd just said.

Shane lifted his shoulders, then dropped them. "I can't expect you to feel the same way I do at this moment. I get it. I do. I've likely lost my shot at having anything with you—"

"Fine," she blurted.

Slowly he turned to face her.

She took a deep breath, then released it through pursed lips. "Fine, you can take me on a date. But I'm not going to agree to be your girlfriend. I'm still going to see Marc." She watched him carefully, expecting him to show some degree of disappointment, and she was right. It was small—shown only in the way his cheek twitched. She'd noticed that twitch when he'd come to her house earlier.

Man, that moment had seemed so long ago. Everything that had happened in the last twenty-four hours weighed on her as if she had experienced them over the course of a week. She felt utterly exhausted and yet surprisingly enthused over what might come next.

Shane shoved his hands into his pockets. "You're going to be late for your shift."

She glanced at the clock, then met his gaze once more. They hadn't decided on when their date would take place nor what they would be doing. She hated leaving things open-ended like this.

Eloise shifted, clutching her hands together in front of her before dropping her gaze to the floor. "Marc said he was going to be busy tomorrow with his sister and finalizing a few things regarding the ranch they purchased. I suppose we could go on our date then—if that works for you."

Shane pressed his lips together, and his brows pinched. "I have a business meeting in Texas. I'm not sure I'd be back in time..."

She hated how the disappointment swirled in her stomach, sending waves of nausea upward. Not even fifteen minutes earlier she was going to insist that he leave her and Marc alone. And now? There was that part of her that wanted to know what it was like to be taken on a date by Shane Owens.

He closed the distance between them. "Unless you'd like to come with me."

Her eyes widened.

"You'd likely want to bring a book or something to do while I have my meeting, but when we're done, we could get some dinner before we fly back home."

Was that hope she detected in his voice? She couldn't deny that the thought of him wanting to spend time with her so badly was incredibly attractive. She wasn't necessarily impressed with his money or his position in the community.

In fact, that was a con on her list. Both Shane and Marc had money. She'd seen the way it could ruin people. In her experience when priority was placed on money, then relationships lacked the thing that made them strong.

So far Marc and Shane had both kept their wealth out of the conversation—a fact that she had appreciated. This trip to Texas was the closest she was going to get to Shane flaunting his money on a date—but it wasn't really the trip that was the date.

Shane wanted to spend time with *her* so much that he was willing to invite her along.

It was flattering.

Eloise nodded. "Sure. I'll go with you."

He smiled at her. It wasn't a grim smile like the one he'd been wearing since he'd opened his restaurant. There was a hint of relief in it, but mostly it was genuine.

A small flutter of anticipation started in her stomach, and she scooted backward down the hall. "I guess I'll see you tomorrow?"

Shane nodded. "I'll pick you up at one."

She stopped. "One?"

Another nod. "The meeting is at four and the plane leaves at one-thirty."

"This is going to be an all-day sort of thing?"

Shane moved into the doorway, leaning his shoulder against the jamb. "Will that be a problem?"

Quickly, she shook her head. "It totally makes sense. I don't know why I was assuming that we'd be leaving in the evening. It's fine." She forced a smile, swallowing back her nerves. Offering him a small wave, she turned and strode in the direction of the kitchen.

This was just a date. Yes, they were going on a plane, but she could trust him. This was the guy who had dated Brielle, for heaven's sake.

Eloise stopped suddenly.

Brielle.

Oh no! What was she going to tell her sister? Brielle would be furious that she had accepted a date from her ex.

Then again...

Hadn't Brielle technically dated James before Constance did? Maybe she wouldn't be *that* mad?

Heat rippled through her body as she forced herself to take one step, then another. The way Brielle had been lately hadn't been the most predictable. Eloise didn't think it was possible, but Brielle was far moodier than she'd been before. She'd gone from the carefree older sister who wouldn't settle down if her life depended on it, to someone who seemed to despise the fact that she was one of the last ones standing.

Eloise didn't mind being one of the last. The pressure to get married was off her shoulders and she could date whomever she pleased.

Sorta.

Brielle still seemed to have something against Marc. And while she didn't seem to like Shane that much anymore, she could at least tolerate him.

Eloise shook her head. She needed to clear it—to get into the right mindset for work. Too much had happened in the last twenty-four hours, and she was ready for everything to return to normal.

She stepped into the kitchen, placed her apron around her

waist and stood by the counter she normally shared with Hannah. But instead of her new friend, there was someone else.

The young man offered her a small smile, then ducked under the counter to retrieve a few things.

"Where's Hannah?"

He glanced at her, surprised. "Oh. She called in sick. I'm Todd."

Well that was just great. Eloise could have used a friend to bounce ideas off. She didn't know how to tell her sister what was going on, nor how she was going to explain to Marc that she was now dating both of them—casual as it might be.

It was probably just as well. Hannah was likely to put her in her place and remind her that she needed to stop being such a pushover.

Eloise hadn't initially wanted to go on a date with Shane, after all. She'd wanted to put distance between them.

There had just been something about the way he looked and the way he acted toward her that had pulled her in. She couldn't explain it any better than that, which was probably a reason she could be grateful that Hannah wasn't around.

She'd go on this date with Shane and hopefully figure out what it all meant before she had to see her friend again. Then maybe she could explain why she had been so willing to do something so crazy.

11

Shane

Shane should have felt like a complete dirtbag. He'd done everything Brielle had told him to, right down to making himself look disheveled.

A decent person wouldn't stoop so low to manipulate a woman to go out with him. A good man would have found a way to convince her of his feelings.

And he felt like he was neither one of those.

He'd been desperate.

And yet, now that Eloise had agreed to see him, he couldn't deny that there was a little bit of light shining through the darkness of his heart. For whatever reason, he needed this—something to look forward to.

Was it wrong to play a part to get her to say yes?

Definitely.

But he had no intention of hurting her, no intention of making this permanent. And from the looks of it, Eloise felt the same. She was willing to keep this casual.

They would go on a date. They could remain friends after the fact. As long as he had a chance to show her what Marc's true intentions were, he'd be golden. Then Madeline wouldn't win and he could go back to the way things were.

There was only one problem with his plan.

Madeline didn't give up easily. Whatever she had in store for him would likely destroy him. He had to be ready for anything.

BEFORE SHANE COULD KNOCK on the door, Brielle opened it and stepped outside. He took a startled step backward and glanced over her shoulder toward the barrier that she'd kept between him and Eloise.

Brielle didn't smile, though her expression seemed less irritated than usual. "You're taking her to Texas?" she hissed.

Okay, so maybe she was just as irritated, but she wasn't showing it.

"I have a meeting."

"And you couldn't just take her out when you get back?" She pinched the bridge of her nose. "Seriously. What don't you get about her liking the underdog? She doesn't want a rich guy who can solve all her problems. Every guy she has ever dated has been on the bottom side of the economic scale."

"You guys have money."

Her eyes flashed. "That's probably why she doesn't care to date anyone who finds money important."

He still couldn't wrap his head around that little tidbit of information. "I don't get it. It's not like I'm buying her fancy gifts. I'm just—"

"Flying to another state in a private jet. Think about it."

"Oh."

Brielle rolled her eyes, then shot a look toward the house. "Look, I don't have much time. But if you're going to make this work, you're going to have to open up to her."

Shane stiffened. "What?"

"I *know*. You don't like opening up to anyone, not even me. For us, that worked. But for Eloise, she wants a connection. She doesn't care about money or things. She likes quality time, and she wants to feel like she's your whole world."

"I can't just tell her my past. That's part of the problem." He continued to grow antsy. This was just a first date. He shouldn't be expected to do any of that. "What happened to just having fun?"

Brielle gave him a pointed look. "You have to do both."

He felt like he was about to lose his mind. "I have to have fun and make her believe that I'm the kind of guy she has been waiting for her entire life."

"Bingo."

Shane worked his jaw. "Okay, so tell her about my past. Make her believe I am in love with her for any reason but money. Anything else?" He couldn't help the way he spoke through gritted teeth. Their date was shaping up to be more than he thought he could handle.

She clapped him on the shoulder. "Just don't fall in love with her."

He gave her a flat look, and she let out a laugh.

That laugh had once been the thing that brought him joy. He would have done anything to be the one to cause it. At least the memories of their relationship no longer hurt the same way they used to.

Brielle let out a sigh. "I'm sorry."

"For what?"

"That we didn't work out."

Shane shrugged. "It's fine. I've already hashed it out in my head more times than I care to admit. We just didn't work." He let out a harsh laugh. "Actually, besides the whole money thing, Eloise seems like she would be a better fit for me anyway."

"Don't you dare," Brielle muttered.

"Yeah, I know. I can't fall for her. Don't worry. I have zero interest in a relationship right now. Fake or otherwise. I'm only doing this until I can figure out a way to get rid of my cousins."

"You never told me about them, you know."

"For good reason."

Brielle tilted her head, her eyes drilling into him. He shifted his weight from one foot to the other and looked away.

"They're not even really my cousins." When he glanced back at her, he noted the confusion that filled her face. "I was adopted. They're not related to me by blood. They never treated me like family, so I never thought to tell you about them."

"Oh," she murmured softly. "Well, I guess that's something you could tell Eloise. Maybe then she might view Marc differently."

He held up his hands, shaking his head. "I can't tell her anything that would reveal—" He cut himself off when the door-knob rattled.

Both of them turned their attention to the noise, and Eloise made an appearance. Her eyes darted from Brielle to Shane, and then she sighed. "You're not telling him off, are you?"

Brielle glanced toward him, offering him a tight smile. "No. I think we've finally come to terms with what happened."

"Good." Eloise gave her sister a hug. "I'll be back late. Tell Dad not to wait up." She turned toward Shane, but behind her, Brielle gestured wildly to her arm.

It took everything in his wheelhouse not to roll his eyes. He was a gentleman. His parents and grandfather raised him as such. Of course he was going to offer Eloise his arm.

She grinned up at him as she accepted, and they headed down the steps toward his truck.

Her touch was gentle, and the warmth seeped through his suit coat almost immediately. A strange kind of shiver originated from where she held onto him, and it traveled up his arm into his chest.

He could do this—get close to her in a way he had never allowed himself to do with anyone else. He just had to plan ahead. She didn't need to know his life story. And telling her a little bit wouldn't make him weak. Just because he'd learned to keep a lot of that sort of thing to himself around his cousins didn't mean he had to do the same thing with Eloise. She'd probably see right through it anyway.

Shane opened the door, and she climbed inside. Between their drive to the airport and getting on the plane, their small talk was excruciating.

"So, what is your business meeting about?"

They had been up in the air for about twenty minutes of their two-hour flight. He shot a look in her direction, taking a break from the papers he was going over.

She gestured toward said papers. "I assume that's why you're enthralled with those documents instead of enjoying a conversation with me."

He flinched. Technically the flight and the meeting weren't part of the date. He should have been able to prepare for his meeting. But Eloise made a good point without even trying. "Yes, I'm preparing for my meeting. I have to look over the proposition they've sent." He tilted the paperwork. "They're suggesting a partnership where they are the sole providers of the horses I use at the equine therapy center I've started."

Eloise scooted closer to him, peering at the papers. "Why would you do that? Aren't there enough horses to buy locally?"

"Yes, if I don't plan to expand. I've looked into offering more services such as riding lessons. The horses I use for therapy wouldn't be the same as the ones I'd use to teach cowboys how to ride and rope."

Her eyes flitted up to meet his. "Oh."

"And I worry if I expand too quickly, I'd be taking horses from the locals who need them for their work."

"That makes sense." She glanced at the paperwork again. "May I?"

Shane shrugged. "Be my guest."

She read through the first few lines, then let out a laugh. "This is a joke, right?"

He frowned. "I'm sorry?"

Eloise shook her head and handed him the paperwork again. "For what you're describing, that proposal is a rip-off. They're not cutting you a deal at all. My father gets livestock for at least ten percent less and he doesn't have a contract with anyone. I'd suggest getting a few other bids."

"Their offer includes training."

"That's great and all, but you have trainers who probably do a better job because they know what you need."

He stared at her. In under five minutes she'd made it perfectly clear what he needed to say to this company. He'd nearly been prepared to sign on the dotted line simply because he couldn't see anything wrong with what they were offering.

"Seriously, if you get an exclusive deal, it's not supposed to benefit them more than you. You've created a brand for your therapy services. If you were to expand to other states, then they would be able to wear that badge of honor and advertise it. They should be giving you a steeper discount if they want to win you over." Eloise snuggled back into her seat.

A smile stretched across his face unbidden. "Point taken." He placed the paperwork on the table in front of him. "I take it that your father was the one to teach you this sort of thing?"

"A little here and there, maybe. But most of it is common sense. When you grow up around this sort of thing, you pick up on stuff that you might not have otherwise. I'd imagine you picked up a lot on running businesses when you were younger from your parents."

He shook his head. "Actually, it was my grandfather."

Eloise frowned. "Your grandfather raised you?"

"Well, he wasn't technically my grandfather either." He let out a strained chuckle. It was time to lean into this plan with all he had. He didn't want to share any of this. But it was what Brielle had insisted he do, and so far she hadn't been wrong. Shane took in a deep breath, then let it out. "I was adopted by my folks when I was four. But then a few years later, they passed away in a car crash."

She sucked in sharply. "I'm so sorry."

"It's fine, really." His chest was closing in. He could feel it, and at the same time, he pushed against it. Wasn't this sort of thing supposed to feel normal? "My mother's father took me in. He raised me like I was his blood. And yes, he was the one who taught me how to be a good businessman."

"Wow. That's amazing." Her brows creased. "Marc said his grandfather passed away a few years ago. Was that—"

"Yes. That was the man who raised me. He gave me everything I have and more." He turned toward the window wistfully. No one in his family had appreciated what his grandfather had done for any of them, but he'd seen it first-hand. Marc and Madeline had soured everything with their greed.

Eloise's hand landed on his, and he turned his attention back to her. "I'm so sorry," she whispered.

"It was a few years ago."

"Doesn't mean it can't still hurt."

She was right about that one, too. He would have given anything to have his grandfather back. He would have sacrificed everything he owned to see him again. "Thank you." Those were the only words he could say in that moment.

He'd underestimated how hard sharing that part of his past would be. He'd never felt this vulnerable in his life. Brielle knew he'd been raised by his grandfather, but that was about it. She hadn't even known he was adopted.

It wasn't fair how easy it was for some people to share their histories. But he wasn't going to tell her everything. There was no need for that.

"I'm guessing that's where your fortune came from."

He stiffened. "What?"

This time she blushed and looked away. She tucked a strand of hair behind her ear and let out a soft laugh. "You must have realized that everyone in town likes to gossip, and when someone new arrives here, people are bound to talk."

But there was nothing to talk about. He had been very careful what he shared with everyone he'd met.

She laughed again. "You bought a property from one of the most talkative realtors of Copper Creek. She didn't know much, but she knew you came from money."

Shane rubbed the back of his neck. "Oh, is that all?"

Eloise glanced at him. "Well, that and you weren't married." Her blush deepened. "But that was back when you arrived. A lot has come out since then."

He'd lost track of how many times he'd felt put on the spot. What else had people figured out about him? Did they know about his terrible family? Had he been going along this whole time worried they'd find out for nothing? He met her gaze, curiosity burning a hole in his chest. "And what is that?"

"Well, we know you're generous. You care about veterans and children. You want to help the community." She looked away again. "And you're still a complete mystery. Even Brielle said she couldn't believe you didn't tell her about your cousins."

"Right. Well, we've been estranged for quite some time. They have different... values than I do."

Her brows creased as she studied him. "How so?"

He shook his head. "Can we not talk about Marc? I'd rather focus on you and me."

A small smile touched her lips. "Sure."

"What do you like to do in your spare time? Other than riding and cooking?" This was his chance, and he was bound and determined to take it. He'd get the attention off him and onto her. Women loved talking about themselves. He just needed to get her started.

She tilted her head, her eyes bright. "I like dancing. Right after you opened, I went to the country club almost every night. The problem is, most of the guys around here don't know the kind of dancing I'm into."

"Oh? What kind of dance is that?"

"I'm a sucker for ballroom dancing." She peered at him again. "Do you know that style?'

He chuckled. "Unfortunately, no. I'm afraid I have two left feet."

"So what is it you like to do? Besides working 24/7, I mean?"

Shane tossed back his head and let out a laugh. "I see you know me far better than you let on."

12

Eloise

hat had started out as a strange and awkward beginning had soon shifted into something more comfortable. Eloise looked at Shane a little differently. It was funny how his disheveled appearance had been enough to humanize him, and hearing about his upbringing had solidified it.

Shane wasn't some untouchable billionaire or whatever. He could bleed and lose just like the rest of them.

She found herself drawn to his features more so than before. When he was uncomfortable, he had a tell. That endearing twitch in his cheek could alert her to when they were nearing a topic he wasn't willing to discuss.

Then there was the dimple in his chin that deepened when he had completely let down his walls. Usually that only happened when she caught him off guard or made him laugh. She no longer wondered what Brielle had seen in him.

Something tugged on her heart, demanding that she continue to peel away the layers he had wrapped around him. There was someone softer beneath his closed-off exterior.

After their plane ride, they were taken to a ranch that was about thirty minutes from the airport. Before they got out of the car, Shane turned to her. "You can stay here, or you can take a look around. These folks are great. Just don't get into trouble."

"Me?" She snickered. "Since when have I ever gotten into trouble? That's Brielle's doing." Almost immediately, she regretted saying her sister's name. Eloise wasn't certain how much of Shane's heart her sister still held. But from the looks of it, enough.

Shane's expression faltered. It was so quick she almost thought she'd imagined it.

Almost.

He nodded toward several structures. "Those barns are filled to the brim with horses you're gonna love meeting. I'll be at the main building. If you need me, just text my cell phone."

Eloise nodded. She watched him leave, feeling terrible over what she'd said even though it really wasn't all that *bad*. She'd simply reminded him of someone he had lost. She couldn't help but feel like she was competing with a ghost. Deep down she knew they were over; that wasn't the problem. She just didn't want to be compared to her sister.

Heaving a sigh, she wandered toward the barn. She needed to be more careful about what she said around him—especially since she was beginning to like him.

A small smile graced her lips. She was looking forward to their date more than she cared to admit. Shane wasn't her usual type, but maybe she could get used to someone who spent his money a little more frivolously than the average joe.

The barn she stepped into was painted red with white trim. It looked just like a barn right out of the movies. The paint was kept up well, indicating this ranch had the money and means to take care of it.

Eloise shook her head, a chuckle escaping her. Why was it wealthy people had a tendency to attract other wealthy people? If she had been completely honest with Shane, she would have told him to hunt for a supplier closer to home. There were several ranches that could accommodate Shane's endeavors. They could work together and help his expansion over a few years rather than all at once. She wasn't a businesswoman by any means, but she knew horses.

Her fingers trailed along the smooth wood on the side of the barn as she wandered alongside it until she reached the door. Her heart stuttered when she turned the corner and entered the building.

The Callahan ranch was one of the largest and most profitable places in Copper Creek. But it was nothing compared to what she was staring at in this moment. There had to be at least two hundred stalls. From the front of the building, it had been rather deceiving. The barn stretched far longer than she'd been able to see from her vantage point.

No wonder Shane had gravitated toward this company. They had the ability to give him everything he wanted. Their price point was also more understandable, though it didn't change her mind on what route he ought to take.

One step in front of another, Eloise wandered along one side of the barn and then up the other. Time seemed to pass slowly as she admired each animal one by one. Finally, she stopped in front of a stall with a starkly white horse.

This wasn't just any horse. Its beauty was clearly showcased from the way its mane was styled to the way its hair was maintained. This steed had to have won several awards.

Eloise crossed her arms over the top of the stall door and

gazed at the animal. It caught sight of her and shifted until it wandered close enough to nudge her.

She let out a laugh, rubbing the horse's nose. "What's your name, beautiful?"

"That would be Snow White."

Eloise let out a yelp, spinning around so she could stare down the intruder. The cowboy before her wore a black shirt and jacket with a matching hat. He sported a beard and dark blue eyes. There was a bag of something over his shoulder and he grunted as he placed it on the ground. His lips quirked upward. "You don't belong here."

Her heart was still reeling from the surprise of his arrival. She nibbled her lower lip and glanced toward the door. Perhaps she should have insisted she tag along with Shane. "I'm just waiting for my—" Date? Friend? What would she call Shane? "Mr. Owens is in a meeting with the owners of this place."

The cowboy chuckled. "That would be my father."

She lifted her brows. "Oh." Shifting a little, edging closer toward the door, she mumbled, "Why aren't you in that meeting?"

He wandered toward her, then stopped and leaned against a post a few feet away. "I prefer more hands-on work." His eyes swept over her. "Mr. Owens... I take it he isn't your husband."

Eloise shook her head. "No. He's not."

"Boyfriend?"

She tilted her head, her eyes dancing with amusement. "Why do you ask?" She'd interacted with men like this back home. They all flirted until they found something or someone they found more interesting. They weren't *bad*. In fact, she'd had several enjoyable dates with such men. Between Marc and Shane, she didn't need another guy showing her interest.

He shrugged, his smile widening. "Depending on how long you'll be in town, perhaps I could take you out for a drink."

Funny how his request was the furthest thing from being appealing. "Thanks, but—"

Someone cleared his throat, and she turned to find Shane moving toward them. His soft, kind expression had been replaced by a hardened one and he had it locked on the cowboy. "Eloise, are you ready to go? I'm done here."

The cowboy stepped forward, holding out his hand. "Mr. Owens, nice to see you again."

Shane glanced at his offering, then back to the man's face. "Chase." He stopped when he reached Eloise's side. Without preamble, he grabbed Eloise's hand. His fingers laced between hers. A spark of something strange electrified her, traveling up her arm, but Shane's grip made it difficult to pull away.

Chase dropped his hand to his side, but his easy smile remained. "I trust you had a good meeting? Was our proposal to your liking?"

"Unfortunately, I've decided to take my business elsewhere."

Eloise's eyes shot up to stare at Shane. *What*? Why would he do such a thing?

Chase seemed equally shocked. "My apologies. Was there something wrong with it?"

Shane glanced down at Eloise and his expression softened ever so slightly. "I've just decided to keep my business local."

Her stomach knotted and twisted. Though not entirely unpleasant, it still threw her off. She couldn't tear her gaze from him. There was no way he'd made this decision just because of her. That was a silly notion. But she liked to think that she was able to influence him a little.

She brought her free hand around and clasped it to the hand he held.

It was Chase's turn to clear his throat. "Well, it's obvious that the two of you have somewhere better to be. If you change your mind—"

"I won't," Shane murmured, not pulling his eyes away from her.

"I was talking to Eloise."

This time Shane shot a dark look in Chase's direction. The cowboy held up both hands and laughed. "It was nice seeing you again, Mr. Owens." He retreated toward the barn entrance until he disappeared outside.

Eloise shook her head, biting back a laugh. "You have a lot of explaining to do."

He shrugged. "You made a good point. And I started to wonder if I hadn't considered all my options before settling, how things might differ."

Her smile widened. "How very intelligent of you. But that's not the only thing I was referring to."

"Oh?" His cheek twitched. Oh, how she wanted to reach up and place her palm against that spot to soothe it.

She ignored the way that thought had come out of nowhere and instead lifted their hands. "This."

His eyes darted to glance at their intertwined fingers, and his smile returned. "What about it?"

"Not exactly what I was expecting."

"But not bad." It was a statement, though the way he'd said it made her think he still wanted confirmation.

"Not... *bad*." The flutters in her chest returned. "Like I said. Unexpected."

Shane turned to face her. His body blocked her in. With the stalls at her back, Shane blocking her front, and their clasped hands preventing her from edging to the side, there was no escape. While her mind sought one, her heart insisted she didn't need it. His voice had lowered, but it wasn't menacing. "Admittedly, I wasn't thrilled, hearing him hit on you like that."

Her lashes fluttered. "You weren't?"

Slowly, he shook his head. It was as if he wanted his words to sink in.

"Are you suggesting you were… jealous?"

He grimaced. "That sounds harsh."

"But you were."

"Would it upset you if I were?"

She lifted a shoulder. "I think healthy jealously has a time and a place." She cocked her head to one side. "Though historically, a first date isn't typically when that happens."

"I suppose I'm not a typical guy." He was so close.

Eloise didn't know when it happened exactly, but he'd continued closing in and now his face was inches from hers. She could feel his warm breath against her cheek, and it forced chills to course through her whole body. She tilted her face upward, inching ever so closer to him.

Two inches was all that stood between her lips and his. He could kiss her right now and there would be nothing she could do about it—not that she would want to. Her hand had tightened around his. Time froze in that moment. What would it feel like to be held by him, kissed by him?

Voices drew near, and she blinked. Shane released her hand, leaving her feeling chilled. He took a few steps back. Disappointment swirled within her. What a ridiculous emotion to feel in this moment. She should be more focused on getting to know him better.

Forcing a smile, she moved toward him and took his hand in hers once again. "Where are we going next?"

He stared at where they were connected, then brought her hand upward. His lips barely grazed her hand but nevertheless caused a fresh wave of shivers. "I have the perfect place."

~

Eloise had thought Shane was going to take her to some fancy restaurant. She'd expected him to spend excessive amounts of money to impress her. But she'd been wrong.

She stared out at the lake before her as the red sun set on the horizon. White Rock Lake was the most beautiful place she had ever seen. It had an old-time sort of feel from the wooden dock to the way the water crept up right to the edge of the grass growing along its perimeter.

Her eyes locked with Shane's for a moment, and she let out an appreciative sigh. "How did you know about this place?"

His focus swept through the area, and his serene smile was hard to miss. "Not many people know this about me, but I'm a sucker for places like this—the simple pleasures in life." He glanced toward her again. "I think I have my parents to thank for that. My mother was raised with money, but my father wasn't. We spent every Sunday finding new places to watch the sun set."

There went one more layer, and she could see him a little more clearly. Eloise studied his profile. A billionaire who could appreciate the simple things. Now she'd seen it all. "You're not normal, are you?"

He gave her a funny look, and her eyes widened.

"Please tell me I didn't just say that out loud."

Shane chuckled. "I suppose you're right. I'm not very normal."

"I didn't mean it in a bad way, I swear." She blushed hotter with each passing second. "I only meant..." What did she mean? Even in her head, it sounded stupid to tell him she was impressed that he liked sunsets. She cleared her throat and looked away. "I only meant that you're not what I expected."

He turned toward her, then tucked a stray wisp of hair behind her ear as she met his gaze. "I assume that's a good thing?"

"I wouldn't be here if it wasn't," she said.

His eyes searched hers, darting from one to the other. He was going to kiss her. She just knew it. This was that moment when he would try to *show* her that he found her attractive. Eloise leaned into him, and her eyes closed. But the kiss never came.

"You aren't quite what I expected either," he whispered.

Her eyes flew open and she stared at him. When he took a step back, she allowed herself to breathe again. Shane nodded toward a little ice cream stand. "What do you say to some dessert before dinner?"

Eloise gnawed on her lower lip, but it didn't stop her from grinning. "I say that sounds like heaven."

Shane's smile matched her own except for that cute little dimple. He tugged on her hand, and she finally allowed herself to relax and enjoy the moment.

13

Shane

Shane was finding it harder and harder to differentiate between pretending and actually wanting to be with Eloise. He never thought he'd be able to look at her and not think of Brielle, but somehow that wasn't an issue.

The jealousy he'd experienced when they'd been in the barn had thrown him off guard. Now he didn't know what to do with the information he'd learned from that situation. Preventing Eloise from dating Marc was one thing; allowing himself to fall for her was completely different.

There was one glaring problem.

They stood at the edge of the lake, pants rolled up to their calves. Water lapped against their ankles. What should have been a perfect moment as he watched her enjoying the sunset, her face glowing from the golden hues, simply wasn't. Right now, his gut reminded him this wasn't a matter of *if* he was falling for her.

He already was.

Shane bit back a curse. Brielle was going to be outraged. She'd made him promise this wasn't going to be serious. And all it had taken was one date with Eloise to have him going against his word.

What was he going to do?

Eloise glanced toward him and let out a laugh. "What? Do I have something on my face?" She rubbed at her cheeks with the heel of her hand, then faced him. "Better?"

His eyes locked on her face. There was no denying her beauty. All of the Callahans boasted good looks. It wasn't what she had on the surface that intrigued him. It was her heart—the way she lit up over the small things.

And yet, he wanted nothing more than to reach out and caress her, to trace his thumb over her lower lip, to tease her with his touch.

Shane jerked his head around and stared at the sunset. "Nope."

"It's not better?"

He glanced at her out of the corner of his eye. "I mean, yep. It's better. Great. You're great." He grimaced. Geez, where was the charm? Where was his ability to win her over like he had with Brielle? He'd lost his mojo.

Eloise laughed, drawing his attention. "This isn't exactly what either of us was expecting for a first date, was it?"

Shane arched a brow. "To be fair, you didn't exactly make it easy to ask you out."

She tilted her head, her smile not wavering. "I suppose you're right."

"What were you expecting?" He knew he probably shouldn't ask. Anything she might say could be the thing to knock him down a few pegs, and he was already beating himself up over how it was going.

Eloise shrugged, then leaned back on the bench, one arm crossed over her stomach. She took another lick of her ice cream. "I guess I had expected you to show off your money."

"Show off my money?"

She shot him an embarrassed look. "Well, yeah. Isn't that what you guys do? Fancy restaurants. Expensive gifts. You know, the works."

He shifted his weight from one foot to the other, hating the way her words made him slightly uncomfortable. Yes, he had money. But he didn't just throw it around. His grandfather had taught him well how to manage it. "Actually, I think that's a common misconception. The people who have a lot of money only do because they are careful with it."

Eloise peeked at him, giving him a sideways smile. "I guess that makes sense."

"Are you... disappointed?"

Her eyes widened, and she faced him suddenly. "Oh, on the contrary. I was ready to accept that you were a pompous jerk who valued the money you owned above all else. One date was all I agreed to, remember?"

"So you aren't impressed by it." From what he recalled, Brielle hadn't mentioned a single thing regarding his wealth. She'd only given him ideas on how to win Eloise over, which mostly consisted of getting to know her on a deeper level. The date ideas were all on him.

Eloise shook her head vehemently. "Think about it. I grew up with money, but my father taught us to appreciate what we have. Nothing is for free and all that." Her cheeks flushed and she let out a soft laugh. "I can't believe I'm talking to you about money right now. I'm so sorry."

Her words resonated with him in a way he hadn't expected. She didn't care about his money. And it almost sounded like the thought of it turned her off. Her view of wealth was like a breath of fresh air after his dealings with his cousins. "You don't have to be sorry."

Once again, she glanced at him.

"It's refreshing to meet someone who isn't constantly thinking about how much I might be worth." He moved a fraction of an inch closer to her. "Does this mean I passed the test?"

Her features scrunched into an adorable frown. "What test?"

"Do I get a second date?"

Immediately a smile replaced her confused expression. "I'd say I might be convinced to go on another date." She finished off the last of her ice cream cone and brushed her hands together to rid herself of the crumbs.

"*Might* be?"

She nodded. "On one condition."

"And what is that?"

In one swift motion, she dropped lower and scooped a wave of water toward him.

He only had a moment to realize what had just happened when she threw her head back and laughed. Shane stared down at his expensive suit. He *should* be irritated. Any man in his position would be.

But he wasn't. He stared at her, completely in shock.

Eloise's giggles dissipated, and her eyes widened. "Oh. I totally read that wrong. I shouldn't have—"

Shane tossed the last of his ice cream aside. Then without warning, he scooped her up into his arms like a baby and sloshed out into the deeper area of the lake.

Eloise clawed at him, screeching loud enough to draw the attention of the few bystanders who were taking in the view. "Shane! Shane, you can't. I don't have a change of clothes." Her arms wrapped around his neck tight as she clung to him. "I'm sorry. I shouldn't have done that."

"No, you shouldn't have," he murmured, his voice huskier than before.

She laughed again. "Seriously, Shane. I don't want to get wet."

His lips quirked upward. "You should have thought about that before you created a tidal wave back there." He lifted a brow, waiting for her to meet his gaze. When she did, he chuckled.

"Don't. You. Da—"

Her final word ended in a scream followed by a splash.

This time Shane was the one who couldn't contain his laughter. Her mouth hung open and water dripped from her hair, trailing down her face in rivulets.

"I can't believe you just did that."

"You started it."

He put her down and the battle that ensued was wrought with splashing and dunking.

But best of all, laughter.

He couldn't remember the last time he'd just let go like this. It actually made him feel human again.

Eloise splashed at him, then attempted to dart away, but the water slowed down her efforts. His arm snaked around her waist, pulling her tight against him. Their bodies collided. He wasn't sure what he'd planned on doing, but whatever ghost of an idea had started, it evaporated faster than water on a hot summer sidewalk.

Droplets of water clung to her lashes. Her cheeks were flushed from their battle. She was breathing heavily, and her eyes remained locked with his. As time slowed, he could feel every single beat of his heart. Each pounding thump hit him with a force that could have easily knocked him to his feet.

Shane's gaze dipped lower to her parted lips. He'd nearly kissed her in the barn earlier. It would have been so easy to steal that part of her that he so desperately craved had they not been interrupted.

Perhaps the universe wanted this to happen. They continued to be thrown together like this; he should just take what it was offering.

"Excuse me! Ma'am, sir, you're not supposed to be swimming in the lake."

Just like that, the spell was broken.

Eloise smiled as she extricated herself from his arms. She tucked a strand of wet hair behind her ear and brushed past him.

Shane released a pent-up breath before facing the reason for the intrusion. The woman who stood on the edge of the bank had her hands on her hips and the most judgmental pair of eyes he'd ever seen. That wasn't the strangest part. She seemed to want to watch him until he was completely out of the lake.

Once he was on the bank, she huffed and then strode away.

"Do you think she works for the parks and recreation department?" Eloise snickered under her breath. "Or do you think she's just a concerned citizen?"

"Neither," he muttered, though he couldn't hide his own smile. "She's just someone who doesn't like to see people breaking the rules and having fun."

Eloise pressed her lips together in a thin line, but it didn't hide her grin. Her gaze trailed over him, and her laughter returned. "You look terrible."

He threw a hand to his chest, covering the spot where his heart lay beneath. "You wound me."

"What are we going to do? I don't think the pilot is going to be all that thrilled about us showing up dripping wet."

"Technically, it's my plane." He winked at her. "My rules."

She rolled her eyes. "I guess you're not wrong."

"Though I don't think there is a restaurant on this planet that would seat us the way we are. So let's get ourselves a change of clothes. My treat."

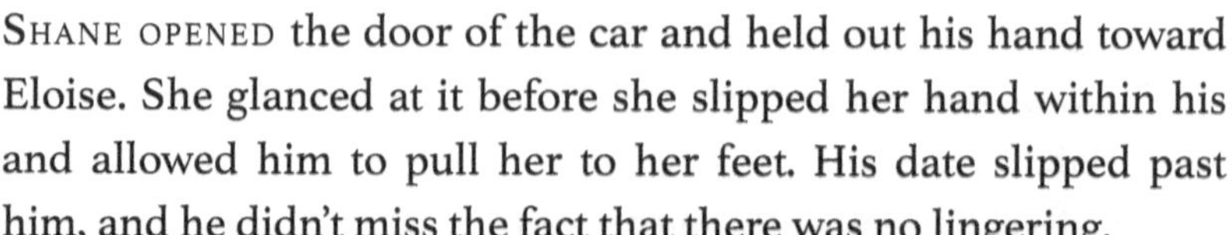

SHANE OPENED the door of the car and held out his hand toward Eloise. She glanced at it before she slipped her hand within his and allowed him to pull her to her feet. His date slipped past him, and he didn't miss the fact that there was no lingering.

She hadn't lifted her face to his, offering her lips for the taking.

He shouldn't have been disappointed. This was a first date, after all.

But something inside him thought that was where this was going. She'd thank him for a wonderful day, agree to call him, then kiss him goodnight.

His emotions were going haywire. The conflicting thoughts he had were going to be the end of him if he didn't get them in check. This date wasn't supposed to be real. He wasn't supposed to fall for her.

This whole outing was a means to an end.

Shane shut the door and followed in her wake. The sundress she'd picked out swirled around her knees, drawing his attention and causing those betraying reactions to worsen. His heart thundered, and his stomach tightened so much that he thought he might lose the dinner they'd shared.

Eloise stopped in front of her door and offered him a smile. "Today was fun. Thanks for inviting me."

"I had a good time, too."

The pregnant pause was torture. Was he supposed to go in for the kill? Or was he supposed to leave her wanting? She answered the questions banging around his head when she placed her hand on the doorknob.

"Wait," he barked.

She stilled, her large, clear eyes meeting his.

"What about that second date?"

The smile he'd grown to love filled her face, and she tilted her head slightly. "I'll call you."

His triumph was short-lived as she pushed the door open and headed inside.

"Goodnight, Shane."

Letting out a pent-up breath, Shane shuffled to the top porch step and collapsed.

"That bad, huh?" a voice said, one he recognized.

His head snapped up and he spun around to find Brielle standing where Eloise had been. She wore a smirk on her face and her arms were crossed. He had never seen her looking so smug.

Shane dragged his hand down his face.

Wonderful. It would take all of three seconds before she noticed that he had a thing for Eloise. Could this get any worse?

She moved from behind him and settled on the step beside him. "How did it go?"

"Great," he muttered.

"Really? Because you look miserable."

"I'm miserable because I'm stuck, Brielle. I've been pinned with my arms behind my back, and I can't figure out how to fix it."

Her expression softened, and she stared out at the property. "Is this about your cousins? Because I haven't heard a peep about them. Maybe they're just blowing hot air."

"That's only part of it."

Brielle peered at him, her eyes narrowing. "You're upset about our arrangement."

He stiffened. This was when everything came crashing down and she told him to walk away. The sad part was that he couldn't blame her. Shane leaned over, resting his forearms on his knees. "I can't pretend anymore, Brielle."

"Why? Eloise will be fine. It's more important for her to stay away from Marc—you said so yourself."

"That's not what I mean." He glanced at her out of the corner of his eye. "I can't explain it, but... I think I might be developing feelings for her."

Brielle didn't move. Her features tightened as she drilled her angry gaze into him. "Tell me you're joking."

Slowly, he shook his head from side to side.

"You promised, Shane."

"I know. And I'm sorry."

She shot up and strode toward the door. He could practically see the steam rising off her shoulders.

Standing up and spinning around, he stared after her. "What are you going to do?"

Brielle stopped, her hand on the doorknob. "What am I going to do?" She let out a dry chuckle before she faced him. "You think I have *any* control over what my sister does or doesn't do?" Shaking her head, she let out a sigh. "Eloise is her own person. If you've managed to win her over, then there's nothing I *can* do."

"So you're not going to poison her against me?"

Her expression softened momentarily. "Shane, I cared about you more deeply than even I like to admit. I could tell we weren't going to work out. Do I want you dating my sister? That's a huge no. But could she do better?" Brielle lifted a shoulder. "Maybe not."

That was probably the closest he would ever get to receiving a compliment from her.

"Shane?"

He glanced up at her again.

"If you hurt her..." Brielle's threat hung in the air, sending chills down his spine.

"I won't."

"You better not." She yanked open the door and disappeared.

Shane let out a heavy breath. There was one problem solved. Now he just had to deal with the two bigger issues that had gone suspiciously radio silent. One thing was for certain. Dating Eloise would come with its own set of problems. She'd become a bigger target for Madeline to manipulate. He'd have to figure out a way to keep his cousin from discovering exactly what was going on.

14

Eloise

loise hurried up the steps and out of the rain into the country club. She stopped just inside before she shook her head to allow the droplets to cascade to the floor. An umbrella would have been a smart decision had she thought to grab one on her way out of the house.

Brielle had been distant since she'd gotten back from her date with Shane. She wasn't exactly angry, but she didn't seem at all thrilled either. Eloise had to come to the realization that Brielle would never truly be on board with her interest in Shane.

Unfortunately, her sister's behavior was the one reason Eloise hadn't done anything to pursue Shane since their date.

One week.

Eloise had been stealing glances and flirting horrendously with Shane for an entire week, and it still hadn't gotten old. There was something to be said about the taboo nature of their budding relationship. She almost didn't want it to shift into anything else—except if she never allowed it to go further, she'd never be able to satisfy the dreams she'd been having.

On more than one occasion, she'd dreamt Shane was about to kiss her, but then she'd be dragged from her slumber by her alarm or the crow of the rooster. Even in her dreams, his kisses eluded her.

Maybe she should just bite the bullet and ask him out. Would that be so bad?

Probably.

So many reasons why she shouldn't be dating him.

Brielle.

Marc.

And the big one... he was her boss.

But none of them affected her as much as the simple fact she couldn't get him out of her head. Shane Owens had taken up permanent residence in her thoughts.

"I love the way your hair looks when it's wet."

Chills rocketed through her body at the soft sound of Shane's voice. She spun around to face him, offering him a smile. They were out in public where anyone could see them. Somehow, she knew that they couldn't showcase their interest.

Then again, her interest might not even match his. There was a very real possibility he was toying with her, and she'd tried very hard to keep those thoughts buried.

She slipped a strand of hair behind her ear with her fingertips. "How are you doing today, Mr. Owens?" There was something to be said about the way he kept his emotions in check when he didn't want anyone else to take note. This past week, she'd grown used to the way his eyes could cloud over. It was aways brief, but she'd gotten pretty good at catching it.

Shane didn't disappoint. His eyes darkened briefly, and he glanced up at the clock on the wall. "You'd better get in the kitchen before your shift starts."

He was so quick to send her off, to make sure nothing inappropriate occurred between them. She couldn't decide if this was part of what made their interactions so exciting or if it was the thing that reined her in.

Eloise worried her lower lip. "I won't be late. I just have to fix my hair before I head in. This rain did nothing but turn it into a mass of messy waves."

His gaze darted to her hair, then swung back to her face. She almost thought he might say something to her, to compliment her or to flirt like he had all week, but he said nothing. She brushed past him, taking care not to let her arm touch his. The last thing she needed was to be caught by someone who spent the majority of their days gossiping about anything and anyone.

She made her way into the restroom to do something with her wet hair. She couldn't help but feel that her reflection was staring back at her, judging her.

While she'd spent the week obsessing over her date with Shane, Marc had left several messages. She'd returned one of them but brushed off his request for another outing. One date with Shane had been all it took to win her over. She simply didn't know what she should do about Marc.

Well, that wasn't true.

She knew exactly what she had to do about Marc. She needed to make sure he knew her intentions so he didn't think she was leading him on.

That was a lot easier said than done.

Eloise sighed, gripping the edge of the sink as she stared at her reflection again. She knew what she was doing. She was waiting until she knew how Shane felt before she made her decision about Marc. That's why she felt like a terrible person.

If Shane wasn't in fact interested, then she would have a backup.

Yup.

She was a terrible person.

What was she thinking? Before Shane came into the picture, she wasn't even sure she wanted a relationship. She'd been content to follow in Brielle's footsteps, however misguided they might have been.

Eloise couldn't do that anymore.

She took a deep breath and nodded to her reflection. Regardless of whether or not Shane was interested, she needed to tell Marc where she stood. She headed out of the bathroom, and the second she let the door shut behind her, a hand wrapped around her forearm and pulled her down the hall. Shane turned a corner and pushed her gently against the wall, his finger held up to stop her exclamation.

Eloise snapped her mouth shut as she stared at the man before her. He was currently peering around the corner, and when he pulled back to meet her gaze, she saw that same familiar steaminess in his gaze. Her stomach knotted pleasantly, and there was no use quelling the flutters that erupted within her. It was a miracle she found her voice at all. "Shane!" she hissed. "What are you doing?"

"I thought I could take my time. I figured that would be what you wanted, but I can't." She let out a laugh and he pressed his finger to her lips, a warning look on his face. "Shhh. I don't want anyone to hear us."

She blinked, her voice dying in her throat. This whole situation was ridiculous. "If you wanted to talk in private so bad, then why not meet in your office? Or stop by my place?"

He cocked his head, and at that moment, he appeared almost like a predator. Eloise shrank back even though she had no cause to be concerned. Shane edged closer, his lips quirking upward at the corners. "I haven't been able to get you out of my mind."

Her mouth went dry. Wasn't this exactly what she'd wanted to hear him confess? She *had* to be dreaming. There was no other reasonable explanation.

"On our last date, you agreed to see me again." He chuckled. "Though your terms were quite ridiculous."

She bit back a smile. "But totally worth it."

His gaze swept over her face, the adoration in his eyes hard to miss. The way he was looking at her was the way she'd always wanted a man to.

Was there such a thing as too much perfection? Because she might have found it. "So what is this little rendezvous for? Are you here to steal me away so we can run off into the sunset?"

"Perhaps."

"Are you always this forward?" This time she couldn't speak over a whisper. Never had a guy shown this much interest in her.

Shane reached for her hand, placing all of her fingers in his before running his thumb over the ridges of her knuckles. "Never," he murmured before lifting his eyes to lock with hers. "I am so out of my depth right now. I wasn't expecting any of this to happen. I suppose I have my cousins to thank for this one thing."

She grinned at him. "I tend to find that family can either be the best advocate or the worst enemy when it comes to relationships. I'm happy to hear it's the former with yours."

His expression faltered so briefly that she wasn't sure what she actually saw. He quickly covered by lifting her hand to his lips.

If her involuntary shiver was any indication of how that made her feel, she was a goner. "So... what now?"

"What now?"

Eloise nodded. "I assume this is your way of proclaiming your undying love for me." She snickered at the shock on his face. "I'm kidding. But seriously, where does this put us? I *work* for you. Will that present a problem? What about Marc? And Brielle?" These issues needed to be addressed—probably not right now in the hallway down from the bathrooms. But soon. "Are you sure that getting serious right now won't create more problems than it's worth?"

He shook his head. "I know it will." Shane glanced down the hallway once more. "Meet me in my office when you take your break."

She arched a brow. "I get the feeling you're trying to keep this under wraps." If it weren't for his crooked smile, she might have been a little annoyed. Sneaking around might be appealing in the beginning, but what would come next?

Did it matter?

This was the start of something new. Maybe she just needed to allow herself to let go and have some fun.

Shane dropped her hand and placed his palm against the wall just above her shoulder as he leaned in closer to her. "How do you feel about that?"

"About sneaking around?"

He nodded.

"I don't know. I guess we'll have to see." Her voice was a breath above a whisper. The tension between them had been mounting since that moment in the barn, then again at the lake. It felt like a big game of cat and mouse at this point. She couldn't tell if he was toying with her, and at this point she wasn't sure she minded all that much.

He moved closer, his eyes glancing toward her mouth. "Yeah?"

In a moment of clarity and perhaps flirtatiousness, Eloise ducked under his arm and scooted along the wall before turning to face him. "My break is at nine." With that statement, she turned on her heel and headed back the way they'd come.

Her heart was beating too fast, and her face was flushed. Hannah was bound to notice that something was up. Her only chance was to blame it on something else... or perhaps someone else.

As she walked back into the kitchen, Hannah gave her a suspicious side-glance. "I know that look. You're seeing someone." Hannah placed a few dishes in front of them with a flourish. "So who's the guy?"

Eloise avoided looking directly at her friend. Instead she focused on grabbing the materials they needed for the chef salads. "I don't think you know him. We've spent some time together recently, though. It might turn into more." A smile tugged at her lips.

Hannah gasped, snapping her fingers. Even though the kitchen was full of busy workers, it felt like they were alone. "It's that guy. Shane's cousin. Matt? Michael?" Her smile widened. "Marc. That's who it is, isn't it?"

Eloise pressed her lips together, still avoiding her friend's gaze.

"That's totally who it is. *Girl*, that's so exciting. He was cute."

"You met him?"

She shook her head. "No, but I noticed him once when I got here for work." Hannah nudged Eloise with her elbow. "Good for you. So, how serious is it?"

"Not very serious. It's just starting out." At least that was the truth. Eloise didn't even know what would come of her meeting with Shane when she slipped away to see him during her break.

"*Okay*," Hannah drawled, "then how serious do you *want* it to be?"

Eloise's thoughts shifted to Shane. Their little date had shown a side of him she wouldn't soon forget. He had the potential to be the kind of guy she could see herself with for the long haul. "I don't know."

"You don't *know*? Sweetie." Hannah gave her a pointed look.

"Deep down you do. I don't care what anyone says. The moment we meet a person, we *know*."

"It's... complicated."

Hannah shot a confused look in her direction. "Nothing is worth *complicated*. It either works or it doesn't."

"I don't believe that for a second. Things can be complicated until they're not." Eloise wasn't sure she believed her own words. Was she just making excuses? Maybe. Then again, maybe not.

HANNAH'S WORDS ran laps in Eloise's head throughout their shift—which unfortunately felt shorter than usual. When the time for her break arrived, she almost didn't know if she had the guts to follow through with meeting Shane—not until she was standing in front of his office, her hand poised to knock.

She was doing this. She was *actually* doing this.

Eloise took a deep breath, then just as she was about to make contact with the door, it swung inward. Shane's cousin—Madeline—nearly ran into Eloise. Her eyes widened, and she glanced over her shoulder toward her cousin.

Shane looked worse for wear. His hair was mussed, and his face was drawn. There was a look about him that suggested he'd been in a fight.

Strange. Eloise had thought that Shane got along alright with her.

Madeline smiled widely at her. "Well, hello there. Lovely to see you again. Eloise, wasn't it?"

Nodding, Eloise matched Madeline's smile. "How are you settling in? Marc mentioned that you two were going to buy a ranch."

"Oh, we've just closed on it."

Eloise blinked rapidly. "Wow. That was fast. I thought there was a waiting period for something like that?"

"Oh, there was. But the owners opted to bypass on a few things, as did we. Who needs an inspection, am I right?" Madeline winked twice, then brushed past her.

"Actually," Eloise held up a finger, "it's a good—"

"Save your breath, Miss Callahan. My cousin has a habit of making very poor decisions, and this is just one of many."

Eloise spun around to face him, confusion written on her face. He'd called her by her last name rather than her first. Perhaps this was just his way of maintaining his distance before they discussed the steps they wanted to take next.

"You can shut the door," he motioned toward it while he remained perched on the edge of his desk.

Her fingers fumbled with the edge of the door before she eased it closed. The metal knob clicked, and they were alone. Eloise pressed her back against the wood, her eyes locking with Shane's. "I have fifteen minutes. What did you want to talk about?"

Shane pushed himself into a standing position. "I've thought a lot about what you said earlier—about Marc and your job."

"And Brielle."

He nodded. "And I think I have a solution."

15

Shane

After Madeline's visit, there was no other option. Shane needed to keep his interest in Eloise a secret—well, as much of a secret as he could keep from this point forward.

Eloise continued to hover by the door as if she wanted a quick escape. If she was nervous, it was best to keep at least a small distance between them. At least she was still here.

"After our date, I haven't been able to stop thinking about you."

"I feel the same." She said it without hesitation, throwing him off so much he'd lost track of what he had planned on saying. Eloise smiled. "I take it that surprises you."

"Yeah, you could say that."

"So what now? You're thinking of me. I'm thinking of you. Seems to me we have only one path ahead of us."

Shane chuckled. "But like you said, there are a few obstacles. My cousin, for one."

"Do you think there might be a problem? Would he do something?"

"My cousin's morals don't exactly point true north."

She frowned, her eyes shifting away from his as she seemed to consider his words. "Why do you say that? He seems nice enough."

"Oh, he's nice. He's just not genuine." Shane took a few more steps toward her, closing the distance between them. "You deserve someone better."

Eloise tilted her head, her eyes dancing with amusement. "Oh? And you think you would fit the bill?"

He studied her flawless face, the way her smile could make him melt, and how her voice sent shivers through his body. Without a doubt, he knew he would be better for her than Marc. "I'm not saying I'm perfect. I'm only suggesting I would be a step up."

"I wonder what he'd say if he heard you say that."

Shane shrugged. "I'd rather Marc *not* find out about any of this until we really know where we want this to go."

She went quiet, and for a moment he didn't know whether he'd said something wrong. Then she lifted her chin. "And where do you want this to go?"

During this whole meeting, he'd wanted so much to touch her. What he wouldn't give to hold her hand and feel the softness of her skin. She would probably think he was a little crazy if she could hear his thoughts in this moment.

It was definitely a little late to take this slow. He'd built up to this meeting all week long—at least he had in his head. "I want to see how far this attraction we clearly feel for one another can go. I want to take you on more dates and spend as much time as I can with you."

Her brows furrowed. "I guess we've come full circle then. You still haven't told me what you want to do about my sister and your cousin."

And that was the problem. This was where he didn't know if his idea would even appeal to her. But he had to try.

"For the first little while, I think we need to keep our relationship a secret."

It was written all over her face. He could practically hear her telling him that was a terrible idea. "You want to date... in secret?"

Shane rubbed the back of his neck. "Yeah. I think that would be easiest. We wouldn't have to worry about hurting feelings. No one would be making comments about whether I'm giving you preferential treatment."

"But you're not."

"I know that, and you know that. But who's to say anyone else might not see it the same way?" This was the perfect solution; he just couldn't tell her why. Madeline's visit had done one thing. It had solidified the threat she presented. She still wouldn't tell him the plan she was cooking up. But he could tell she was searching for anything he might find of value.

So far, he'd been lucky that she hadn't heard about his date with Eloise. That would have tipped her off immediately. For all his cousin knew, he was only trying to step in the way of Marc dating Eloise.

Shane cleared his throat. "Brielle wouldn't have to witness anything that would make her uncomfortable, and neither would Marc. You could just tell him that you're seeing someone and you'd like to keep your personal life private." Eloise didn't need to know that Brielle had basically given her blessing on this budding relationship. She only needed to know that he'd prefer it to stay under wraps for the time being.

His face scrunched up and he tilted his head as he reached for her hand. The gesture was entirely instinctual, but the moment he made contact with her, it was as if a wave of peace settled over him. His idea was the right thing to do. It would help him keep her safe, which was the most important part. "I know it's a little soon to ask you to trust me, but that's what I'm doing. I'm standing here, asking you to take a leap of faith."

The seconds ticked by with such a finality to them that he wasn't sure how long he'd be able to handle standing there without her answer. He'd asked her for one date, and he'd gotten that. To beg her for more seemed like too much. He needed to have a little faith of his own.

"Okay."

Shane stilled. Every fiber of his being didn't trust the words that had come from her lips.

Dreaming.

That's what he must be doing at this very moment.

Eloise nodded. "Sure, okay. I can keep a secret, and if it would help Bri and Marc in the long run, then I don't see why we shouldn't." She smiled at him. "There's only one problem I can foresee."

"What's that?"

"This town is *way* too small. I doubt there would be anywhere we could go to spend time together where we wouldn't be noticed. We can't use the trails on my property because of Brielle. We can't use the facilities here because of Marc."

"Marc wouldn't come..." It was true that Marc might not come to the country club often, but that wasn't the biggest problem. The gossiping women in town would blow his cover if any of them got wind of who he had decided to spend his time with. "Never mind. I suppose you're right."

Eloise bit down on her lower lip, nibbling the pretty pink flesh until it turned a deeper shade of rose. "I suppose we *could* have our dates outside of Copper Creek. Unless you know anyone locally who could keep a secret."

His smile returned. "I think I have just the place in mind."

"THIS PLACE IS NICER than Brielle made it out to be."

Eloise was perched in her saddle as they rode a pair of horses along the trails in the far reaches of the Keagan property. She was the epitome of a cowgirl, through and through, which begged the question of why she wanted to be stuck in a kitchen. That was a question he wasn't willing to ask at the moment. Doing so might risk losing out on seeing her every day as she worked in his restaurant kitchen.

Shane still couldn't believe that Eloise had agreed to keep their relationship secret. But then she *was* a Callahan. Brielle had wanted something similar. Granted, Brielle was okay being seen with him at the country club; she just didn't want their relationship to be that serious.

"What?" Eloise asked.

His eyes focused, only to find Eloise staring at him with a small grin on her face. "Huh?"

"You're staring again."

Shane ran a nervous hand through his hair. "A lot has happened in the past month. I'm just grateful that this is where we ended up." Boy, how he loved the way she looked at him. She could start wars with that smile. Eloise stirred something within him that not even Brielle had been able to do, and he wouldn't soon take it for granted.

She glanced away and let out a sigh.

"Something the matter?" he asked.

Her gaze sought his and she shook her head. "I can't believe Wade was willing to let us use his property. What did you say to him?"

It wasn't a secret that he'd given the eldest Keagan brother the money to get this place on its feet. And Wade wasn't about to take any amount of charity. But there were certain necessities the man needed to keep his family's finances from going under.

Shane wasn't proud of it, but he'd managed to convince Wade that they needed each other. The youngest Keagan kid had just turned twelve. They all needed clothing and some of them needed jobs. It was a no-brainer—a quid pro quo. Which was why Shane felt so manipulative about the whole thing.

"We have a mutual understanding on a few things." That was all he could say on the matter. Somehow, he didn't think Eloise would approve of an arrangement where one party benefited at a different rate than the other.

"A mutual understanding, huh?"

He nodded.

"Like the mutual understanding that led him to scare the pants off your cousin?"

Shane stiffened. Right. He'd nearly forgotten about that. "Something like that."

"I suppose letting us use his property isn't gonna get him arrested or anything."

"Of course not."

They continued to follow the trail they were on in silence. His thoughts shifted to Madeline and the threats she'd made during her last visit. She'd complained about Marc not getting through to Eloise, then blamed Shane for that happening. The truth was right under her nose. It wouldn't be long before she found out he was dating Eloise, and when that happened, he didn't know what he would do.

A quick glance in Eloise's direction and his heart constricted. He would never let any harm come to her or her family. No matter what it took, he'd do it to keep them safe. But he couldn't do that if he didn't know what Madeline was planning.

Eloise caught his gaze again and let out a soft laugh. "Seriously, why are you looking at me like that?"

In a swift motion, he pulled on his reins to turn his horse in the path of hers. He climbed down from his saddle and then walked right up to her, holding out his hand.

She glanced down at his hand and shook her head. "You wanna tell me what you're planning? Because a normal person wouldn't just trust a guy who does what you do."

He lifted a brow and chuckled. "A guy who does what I do? What exactly are you referring to?"

"Oh, you know. Stealing me away for a date several hundred miles away from home to show off how powerful he is. Hiring thugs to rough up other men who are interested in me. Dunking me in a river."

He pointed a finger at her. "That was a lake, not a river."

Eloise rolled her eyes, but a laugh still escaped her lips. She rose out of the saddle and jumped down in front of him. "But then you surprised me." She stepped toward him, closing the small amount of distance that kept them apart. Her fingers trailed along his chest, eliciting sparks of energy. Her voice softened further. "You showed me you care about other people—your friends... your *family*."

She couldn't be more wrong on that last one.

"You showed me you could be impulsive, reckless, and fun without caring about maintaining a certain reputation. Brielle talked about that, you know—she thought you were a little stuffy, and she didn't want to be arm candy for a guy who couldn't understand her roots."

He was thrown off momentarily by this confession. Brielle had never mentioned anything like that before. But he couldn't deny that it wasn't surprising she had realized that was part of his personality. Everything Eloise had mentioned—right up to the being more carefree part—had been recommended by Brielle.

Eloise tilted her face upward. "My life needs balance. I want to be with someone who can enjoy the little moments but who also understands the importance of family." She gave him a pointed look. "I need someone who can be honest with me."

A lump large enough to cut off his breathing formed in his throat. His chest constricted and he felt frozen to his spot. Did she know what was going on? Had she figured out he was hiding what was happening with his cousins?

She lifted a shoulder. "Brielle mentioned that you didn't tell her about your family. She wasn't thrilled to find out you'd been hiding them from her."

"That's because—"

Eloise pressed a finger to his lips. "I rationalized that there were certain things that needed to remain private until a relationship deepens." She dragged her gaze from his. "If there are things that I keep from you, it's for a good reason. And if you decide to keep something from me, I'll understand. I'm not going to babysit you. I want to make that clear." Her eyes flitted back to meet his. "I trust you, Shane. Implicitly."

There was something strange about her words—something off. It was as if she made this speech to protect herself in the future. Was she already keeping secrets?

He could have dumped a bucket of cold water over himself.

What right did he have to worry about something like that? He was keeping so much more from her—and her family. Fair was fair.

Shane cupped her cheek gently with his hand. "We're in agreement then—dating without telling the world about us." A thrill shot through him at the thought. They could be together in secret until Madeline lost. Then he'd show her to the world. "For now," he amended.

Eloise's brows creased. "For now?"

"This is our little secret for the time being."

Still, confusion seemed to linger on her face.

"Oh, you must know by now, Eloise. I fully intend on figuring out the best time and place to make this public. It just makes sense to enjoy our newfound..." What? Love? Attraction? What should they be calling it?

"Relationship," she offered.

"Exactly."

His whole life had been building up to this moment—like a contract he had organized for a potential client.

No, it was definitely better than that because he wasn't allowed to kiss his clients.

Shane dipped his face closer to hers and brushed his lips against her soft, supple lips. Her eyes fluttered closed, and she leaned into him. His arm wrapped around her waist, securing them together. Her body melted into his, easily fitting with him like they were two parts of a puzzle that had finally found one another.

Electrifying sparks exploded behind his eyes, filling his whole body with warmth right down to his toes. His kiss grew more passionate as he allowed himself to let go of his inhibitions. He couldn't fathom a scenario where anything could go wrong, not when he had Eloise in his arms.

She was perfection.

And she was all his.

16

*E*loise did her best not to feel the guilt that continued to grow over the next two weeks. Marc still called her, though she hadn't accepted any of his invitations to see him in person. His persistence wore on her.

It was getting to the point where she thought it might not be such a bad idea to just tell him that she was dating Shane now. The problem with that idea was Shane.

He still insisted that they shouldn't tell anyone. If even one person were to find out, he said that others would too and that could spell disaster.

She continued to tell herself it was fine. She was happy with Shane. They had found something that worked. They'd seen each other every single day since they'd stolen that kiss. He'd shared a lot about himself that only made him more endearing to her.

Shane was a good man through and through. Even if Eloise

had tried, she wouldn't have been able to find something wrong with him.

Well, except for his strange insistence that people couldn't handle seeing them together. He'd made such a compelling argument that she couldn't deny that it made sense.

If only Marc would get the hint and stop calling her.

Eloise glanced at the clock on the wall of the kitchen. Her break would start in just a minute or so, then she could sneak away and steal some time with Shane. Admittedly, sneaking around wasn't *all* bad. There was a sort of danger and excitement about being caught.

A smile touched her lips as she headed toward the kitchen sink to wash her hands. Already her legs felt weak, and her heart fluttered wildly. Just the thought of seeing him and being held by him was enough to stir those feelings. Then they grew more pronounced when she was actually in his presence.

"Hey, Eloise."

She glanced up to see Hannah heading toward her.

"Did you hear about Shane?" Hannah's wide eyes and broad grin were all it took for Eloise to know Hannah had some gossip. Usually, it was about one of the staff at the country club. Never had it been about their boss.

Eloise's heart shifted from a happy flutter to an anxious pounding. "What about him?"

"Sounds like he's dating someone."

She fought the blush that threatened to give herself away. Rumors. That's all they were. If people actually knew she was dating their boss, she would have already gotten more than one stink-eye. At least, that's what Shane had said would happen. Eloise grabbed a hand towel to dry her hands, then tossed it back in its place. "You know better than to give power to useless gossip."

Hannah reached out and placed her hand on Eloise's arm.

"It's not just gossip. Someone said that there's been a woman who has repeatedly visited his office over the last few weeks. The *same* one."

"Shane has a lot of people who work for him. I don't—"

She shook her head. "No. This isn't someone who works here. And it's not a client either."

Eloise's heart dropped. He wouldn't do something like that. Right?

Then again, what did she know about him besides his affinity for helping everyone he met and trying to keep their relationship a secret? As much as she tried to make sense of these strange thoughts, Eloise couldn't shake the feeling that something was off.

"I know, right?" Hannah let out a little laugh. "I just hope the woman he picks is someone who understands how this place runs. The last thing we need is for Shane to date someone who will try to change it."

"I don't think he'd let anyone do that," Eloise said.

"Callahan. Time for your break!"

She glanced over to the chef, then nodded. "I'll be back." Her steps were slower than usual. It was just like her to overthink this. But she'd never given in and believed everything she heard without investigating for herself. Not only that, but a lot of the gossip in town wasn't any of her business.

It just so happened that this tidbit was.

Eloise made it to Shane's office, but rather than knock, she just let herself in. "Shane, I need to ask—" She stopped in her tracks, finding Madeline sitting on the edge of Shane's desk while he was settled into his chair on the other side. They both shifted their gazes toward her. Both looked surprised.

The first emotion Eloise registered was relief. Madeline must have been the woman everyone had been talking about. Nobody knew she was his cousin, so maybe that was the reason the gossip was so chatty about what they'd seen.

But that relief quickly dissipated. Shoot. She'd called him by his first name in front of Madeline. Eloise didn't know how close Marc was with his sister, but if she even glimpsed a hint that Shane and Eloise were involved, Madeline would likely say something.

Eloise placed her hands behind her back and ducked her head. "I'm sorry, Mr. Owens. I was just coming to ask you a question." When she lifted her gaze, she found Madeline appraising her with a shrewd expression.

Shane got to his feet. "My apologies for the intrusion, Madeline. Before I see to what Miss Callahan needs, is our meeting over?"

Madeline's eyes remained locked on Eloise for what felt like an eternity. Then it was as if someone had pressed the play button. She sucked in a breath and faced Shane. "Not quite." She swung her focus back to Eloise. "Miss Callahan, perhaps you can help me with something. I was telling Shane here that he needed to get out into the world and stop working so much. He needs a girlfriend, don't you think?"

Eloise snapped her eyes to Shane's. She couldn't read his expression, only that he wasn't comfortable with this conversation. "I don't think Shane—I'm sorry—Mr. Owens needs to do anything he's not ready for. He used to date my sister, and she's been known to do a number on every guy she's dated."

"Oh, *really*. Now *that's* interesting."

"Is it?"

"Of course, dear. Now I can figure out if my sweet cousin has a type."

Eloise let out a strained laugh. "I doubt that. There's no one like Brielle. She's one of a kind."

Madeline's laugh raked against Eloise's nerves. It sounded

incredibly fake and almost menacing. But that was probably because Eloise was so on edge at the moment. She needed to get her head on straight and maybe get some air. There was something about Madeline that set her teeth on edge.

Whatever the reason, Eloise couldn't wait for Shane's cousin to leave the room.

Madeline's movements were more catlike than anything else. She brushed past Eloise near the door, then paused. "I'll see you tomorrow, Shane. I'm sure we'll have a lot to talk about."

When Eloise turned back to Shane, she nearly gasped. This wasn't the man who could make her laugh or who wanted to have a water fight with her. This was a man who was stressed beyond a shadow of a doubt.

Eloise closed the door behind Madeline, then hurried through the room toward him. "What's the matter?"

"Why did you do that?"

She glanced over her shoulder toward the door, almost expecting Madeline to have opened it. The dark sound of Shane's voice sent a shiver through her, turning her blood to ice. She looked up at him again. "Do what?"

"Why did you tell her that I dated your sister?"

Her brows creased with confusion. "Was I not supposed to?"

Shane pulled away from her and paced from one side of the room to the other. He raked his hands through his hair until it was a complete mess. "No, you weren't supposed to. Madeline is manipulative. She wants something from me, but I can't tell what." He glanced at her, and his mouth snapped shut like he'd said too much himself.

This was all news to her. From the brief conversations she'd had with Marc and Madeline, she had assumed that while they weren't *close,* they still got along. Why else would Shane's cousins come out all this way to be closer to him?

He resumed his pacing. "You don't get it."

"Then help me understand. What is it about Madeline that makes you so upset?"

"I'm not upset," he muttered.

"Sure sounds like it."

Shane snapped his head around to stare at her. "Just forget it. I'm under a lot of stress over a few things right now, and I don't mean to take it out on you."

She moved toward him, wishing she could do something to help alleviate the pressure he was under. "Is it the restaurant?"

He stopped his pacing, looking at her once more. "Why are you so good to me?"

Eloise laughed. "That's an odd question."

Shane closed the distance between them and took her hands into his. "No, it's not. You're the one thing in my life I still can't believe I have."

Her brows pulled together. The way he was talking, it sounded like he had quite a bit more he was dealing with that he wasn't letting on to. She burned to demand an explanation just so she could help him. Heaven knew that venting was one of the best ways to get out of a slump like this.

He lifted his curled hand to brush his knuckles along her jawline. "You are... too perfect."

Stomach knotting, she looked away. "I'm not perfect."

Shane continued to hold her hands. "You're perfect for me."

That poisonous guilt she felt over Marc's incessant calls eased somewhat.

"And you're perfect for me." She looked into his eyes, placed her palm against his cheek and rose on her toes to kiss him. When she pulled back, she let out a little laugh. "You should hear what the gossip is in the kitchen."

"Oh?"

"Yeah. Everyone thinks you're dating someone."

Almost immediately that troubled expression returned.

"Don't worry. It's not me. They think you're dating Madeline." She laughed again. "Can you believe it? Your cousin."

"Well, she's not related by blood. I suppose I could…"

Her eyes grew wide and she smirked. "Don't even joke about that."

He chuckled. "Okay, okay. How much time do we have left?"

Eloise glanced at the clock on the wall and grimaced. "Only like five minutes if I want to get back in time."

Shane wagged his brows up and down. "I think I know just what we could do in that amount of time."

She laughed, pushing away from him. "I know what you're thinking. And you don't want to do that." Eloise took a step backward as if to emphasize what she was saying.

He snaked his arms around her waist, capturing her from her retreat. "Oh? And why is that?"

Once again, she pressed her fingertips to his chest. "Because once you get started, it's that much harder to stop."

A smile played at his lips. "Maybe this time would be different."

"Or maybe—" Before she could complete her statement, Shane crushed his lips over hers, claiming his prize.

Euphoria.

There was no other way to describe the way Shane made her feel when she was with him. The world managed to fall away and with it all her cares and concerns. It was just the two of them, forever being entangled with the other.

To anyone else, her thoughts might have sounded a little crazy. But in her heart, she couldn't deny that they had a shot at being with each other for the rest of their lives.

She shoved her hands into his hair, pulling him closer and kissing him more fervently than before. Theirs was a kiss full of promises.

While the future didn't have any guarantees, at this moment

it didn't matter. They could work out anything if they did so together.

Shane was the first to pull away. His face was flushed, and the haze in his eyes gave her all the evidence she needed to know how he felt about her. She threaded her fingers through his hair in an attempt to get it under control just a little bit before she left him. When it refused to cooperate, she let out a laugh.

"I think you're out of luck. People are definitely going to talk."

"Let them. They can assume away." He leaned down and kissed her forehead. "I've got what truly matters right here and no one can take that away from me."

She rested her head against his shoulder, reveling in everything that had happened over the last several weeks.

Crazy didn't begin to cover it.

And now, she knew without a doubt that she had something she had to take care of before this relationship continued on its projected path.

"I'M surprised you finally agreed to meet with me." Marc gestured toward her house from where they sat on the porch steps. "And at your home, no less. I get the feeling you have something important to tell me."

Eloise wrung her hands in her lap. Why did this seem so difficult? She was happy with Shane. She didn't need anyone else in her life. And yet she couldn't shake the feeling that she was doing the wrong thing. She glanced up at Marc and forced a smile. "I need you to stop calling me—stop flirting with me."

His eyes narrowed, and he turned away from her slightly.

"I know it doesn't make sense. We started off seeing each other quite a few times in a short amount of time and then I ghosted you."

"Yeah, you did. I guess I should have gotten the hint. Is it something I did?"

She stiffened, her hand landing on his knee as if the gesture would offer him some comfort. "No, of course not. It's just that... I'm seeing someone."

He shot a look at her, full of pain she hadn't expected.

"This has nothing to do with you and everything to do with me."

"Does he treat you right?"

"I—what? Of course he does. He makes me very happy."

Marc studied her, and she squirmed beneath his gaze. Finally, he let out a sigh, shaking his head. "Does Shane know who this is? Would he be able to vouch for the guy?"

Eloise gnawed on her lower lip. "Actually, yes." She should just tell him. What harm could it do? "Because it sorta... is... Shane."

Marc gave her a sharp look but then just as quickly schooled his features. "You're dating Shane."

She nodded. "I'm so sorry. I didn't mean to lead you on. It just sorta happened." She reached out and squeezed his forearm. "But you can't tell him I told you. He doesn't want anyone to know yet and it's just better this way. Please don't say anything."

Marc's brows creased. "I guess I can't say I'm surprised. Shane is a catch."

Her small smile returned. "Yeah, he is."

"Does that mean we can still be friends?"

She stiffened. "Really? You want to be friends?"

He shrugged. "I like you. Is that so surprising?" Marc bumped his shoulder into hers. "And we can keep *that* our little secret— mostly because Shane wouldn't like it if he knew I was hanging around."

"Yeah, I could see that." She gave him a smile. "I can always use a friend."

17

Shane

Shane felt like his neck was in a noose twenty-four-seven these days. He kept expecting Madeline to show up and do something terrible. She never did stop by after her conversation with Eloise.

And that utterly terrified him.

She was cooking up something, and he had a feeling it was going to be catastrophic. The longer she remained quiet, the more anxious he became. All this stress was messing with him, and now he'd just found his first gray hair.

Madeline and Marc needed to leave town, and soon. Otherwise he might start losing his hair. At this point he didn't know if he'd prefer that over the grays. There were some pretty powerful men who were completely bald.

His hand reached up and he ran his fingers through his thick locks. No, he'd rather go gray than lose any of this.

Shane started pacing his office once more as he tried to figure out Madeline's endgame. She wanted money. She wanted power. But coming out to this area would only give her one of those things. It was probably obvious. The problem was he'd never been very good at predicting what Madeline was capable of.

On the surface, it appeared everything had settled down. His relationship with Eloise continued to grow. Marc had stopped sniffing around.

But Shane knew better. The other shoe would drop. He just didn't know when.

His office door opened, then shut just as swiftly. Shane glanced up and smiled.

Eloise was the breath of fresh air he never knew he needed. She leaned against the door, her eyes locking with his. If time were to be frozen in this very moment, he would happily accept it. She tilted her head in that way that drove him crazy and that soft smile she wore widened. "Hey," she said.

"Hey."

Pushing away from the door, she headed toward him. "I was wondering if you were free tomorrow morning." Her hand trailed over the back of the chair she passed by. "Because if you were... I wanted to take you riding."

He met her halfway. "Oh? You want to head out to the Keagan's ranch again?"

She shook her head. "No, I wanted to show you my favorite places at my family's property. And maybe we could do a picnic breakfast."

The mention of her family's ranch put him on edge. If *anyone* saw them together, there would be no telling how quickly Madeline would find out. She was bound to use Eloise to her benefit. He wasn't sure how, but he had a feeling she wouldn't hold anything back.

Shane swallowed hard, reaching out to graze Eloise's cheek with his thumb. "I don't know if that's such a good idea."

She stiffened beneath his touch and grasped his hand to pull it away from her face. "You're still on that? We've been seeing each other for a couple weeks and—"

"And I still haven't figured out every possible outcome that could happen if my employees found out. Technically, you're a subordinate—"

"*Subordinate*?" Her tone was sharper than he'd anticipated. "You realize I don't need this job, right? I could just as easily quit. That seems to be the one thing that you need me to do in order to be comfortable with dating me in public."

He shook his head. "No, that's not it."

"Really? Because you continue to insist on keeping this relationship a secret, and your only excuse is that you worry about what your staff would think. I feel like there are ulterior motives or something going on—like you're keeping something from me."

She didn't sound angry anymore. The tone of her voice sounded more like someone who was unsure. *He'd* done that to her. He'd made her worry about where they stood. If only he could tell her that this was all for her own good.

Maybe he needed to tell her everything—about Madeline and Marc, about what they were capable of and why he'd kept it from her in the first place.

That was a very bad idea. If she found out what he was up against, would she leave him? Would she decide to tell everyone he knew and, in the end, hurt his business?

He was stuck. Neither option appealed to him. Both would hurt her and himself.

"I have a different idea."

Her brows pulled together, forming a crease between them. "You do?"

"Come to my house—for dinner. I'll make you something delicious and we can spend some quality time together."

Eloise pressed her lips into a thin line and tilted her head as she studied him. He shifted beneath her penetrating gaze. He wouldn't be the least bit surprised if she could see right through him. Shane only hoped that she would look past the totally obvious fact that he was changing the subject. If she took the bait, maybe he'd have a shot at keeping this relationship under wraps a little while longer.

The ironic thing was that he'd never brought a woman to his place before. Brielle was the closest he thought he'd ever get to a woman, and she hadn't been interested. Her strict policy of keeping everything casual kept them from taking that step.

Now his stomach hurt just thinking about the reason for extending this offer. Was he ready to bring Eloise to his place?

Immediately he knew the answer.

Yes.

Shane wanted more with Eloise. He just wished the circumstances were different. If only he'd met and started dating Eloise before his cousins had arrived. Then everything would have been different. Madeline wouldn't be this sliver of glass in his finger that had been embedded beneath the surface.

He blinked when Eloise waved her hand in front of his face. She wore a worried smile. "Is everything okay?"

Nodding, he shifted again and looked away. "I was just thinking."

"Yeah, I could tell." She nibbled on her cheek, pursing her lips to the side. "You don't really want me to come to your place, do you?"

His whole body went stiff and that swirling sensation in his stomach cramped up. "What? Of course I want you to come to my place. I wouldn't have offered if I wasn't sure."

Eloise shook her head. "No, you don't. I can tell. The thought of it makes you nervous or something."

Shane reached forward and took both her hands into his. He

fought to keep his voice steady as his gaze locked on her. "I could not be more certain of anything. I'm ready to share my life with you in whatever way I can."

She gave him a flat look. "Anything except announcing to everyone that we're an item."

As much as he didn't want to, he grimaced. She'd caught him again. Yes, he wanted to shout about their relationship from the rooftops. But he *couldn't*. If they both survived this situation, he made a mental note that he would be upfront about *everything* regarding his past and his family. He just needed to get through this thing with Madeline and then he could move forward.

Eloise squeezed his hand. "There you go again."

"Hmm?"

"You get all distant and zone out like you're floating in some interdimensional timeline or something."

His lips quirked upward at the corners. "I wasn't aware that a cowgirl such as yourself would even know those vocabulary words."

She snorted, rolling her eyes at him. "I read *and* I watch the occasional sci-fi movie."

Shane took this opportunity to slip his hands around her waist and pull her into him. He stared at her, memorizing every plane and dimple her face had to offer. She was something special, and already he could feel her slipping through his fingertips even though their relationship had only recently started.

Was this what it felt to be in love—to feel so much anguish over the possibility of losing her?

It wasn't just that. Whenever he saw her—caught a glimpse of her in the hallway—the tightness in his chest was almost unbearable. He found himself longing to spend every waking moment with her. He *needed* her.

"Come to my place. Let me cook for you and we can talk about our plans for the future," he said.

"You cook?"

"I cook," he said, then added, "not as good as the chef and probably not as good as you, but I can put together a mean plate of spaghetti."

For the first time since she arrived, he noticed her expression relax. Her walls had come down. He'd made progress.

Eloise placed her hands on either side of his face. "It's a date. But the next one is riding and it's gonna be at my place."

His stomach knotted, but he agreed with a short nod. "Deal." There were several reasons he could give if people caught him going to the Callahan property. He didn't have to admit to anything, right? Shane pushed the doubt and worry down as far as he could muster before brushing a kiss to her lips. He pulled away, immediately noticing the cool air that slipped into the space between them.

Grabbing a sheet of paper, he scribbled his address on it and then held it out to her. He couldn't remember the last person he'd given that to. In fact, he wasn't sure he'd given it to anyone since he'd bought the place. It was completely separate from the country club property, and for good reason. Even his cousins didn't know where he lived—for security purposes.

Eloise peered at the paper, then her eyes bounced up to meet his. "I don't think I've ever been here. Is this out past the Keagan's property?"

Shane nodded. "There's a security gate that prevents anyone from coming up the private drive that leads to the property, but it isn't too hard to find if you put that address into the GPS." He placed his hand over the paper, causing her to meet his gaze again. "I've not given this to anyone local. Please help me retain my anonymity. I'd prefer if no one—not even my cousins—know where I live."

Confusion flitted behind her eyes, but she nodded anyway,

without questioning his motives. "What time will dinner be served?"

He chuckled, if only to quash the nerves that still lingered. "You make it sound like I'm going to be giving you this Michelin treatment. I assure you, while my spaghetti is good, it's only just."

"I'm sure the food will be fantastic." Her eyes seemed to tease him. "Though, I must admit I was sorta expecting you to admit you had a personal chef."

Shane didn't know how to react to that statement. Did he have the money to hire such a person? Yes. But his grandfather had never had anyone other than a housekeeper. She'd helped prepare meals every so often, but he'd learned a few things from his grandparents about running a household. He cleared his throat. "Really?"

She nodded. "Why not? Don't people in your position do that sort of thing? Have a staff or something?"

The look on his face must have been enough to set her back because her face flushed and she dropped her hands from his face before glancing away. "I'm sorry. That was a little judgmental, wasn't it?" She covered her face with her hands and let out a little laugh. "I can't believe I said that."

He stepped toward her, hooked his finger beneath her chin and offered her a small smile. When she lifted her gaze to meet his, he shook his head. "While your statement was a surprise, it wasn't entirely misguided. There are a lot of people with my financial background who do exactly what you suggested—not because they need it but because they have the money to do so. I just don't."

"You don't?"

Once again, he shook his head, letting that answer sink in. "I have three people on *staff*—as you put it."

"Oh?"

He could hear the notes of disappointment in her voice, and for a moment he wondered for the first time in his life if the people he had working for him was a bit much. His brows pulled together as he let himself hope that she would understand. Brielle was the one who mentioned that Eloise wasn't impressed by money or status. "I do. I pay a housekeeper to keep my home tidy and help prepare the occasional meal. Then there's the landscaper who tends to everything outdoors. And finally, I have a security guy."

Her brows lifted. "*Security*? I haven't seen any bodyguards or anything."

This time Shane laughed. He couldn't help it. "Not that kind of security. I don't fear for my life by any means. But I do have a nice home on a big property, and I do have valuables. My guy monitors the gate and the people who come and go—or rather, the ones who would if I invited more of them to stop by." Shane dropped his hand to grasp hers. He rubbed his thumb over the back of her hand and let out a sigh. "Like I said, I don't usually invite people over. But you're important to me. I want you to know that more than anything."

She squeezed his hand, and he lifted his eyes to meet hers. "I know," she whispered.

"Then I'll see you tonight at seven?"

Eloise nodded. "I'll see you tonight."

18

*E*loise drove her car up the winding road toward what could only be Shane's house. The code he'd given her did open the gate she passed a little while ago, but the property was shrouded in trees. If she hadn't gotten his address, she wouldn't have even seen the gate.

No wonder he could remain such a private man. He only gave people access to what he wanted them to know.

Brielle's concerns over his secrecy about a month ago came rushing back to her mind. On the one hand, her sister had made several good points. Shane should have told her more about his family. But on the other hand, someone like Shane was allowed his privacy to a certain degree.

Eloise let out an audible groan. Why couldn't she let go of this nagging feeling of doubt? Shane had been nothing but sweet to her, and now he was fixing her dinner. She should just enjoy herself.

The house came into view, and she slowed the car to a stop as she peered through the window. It wasn't as large as she'd expected based on what he'd said about his home life. The size didn't really warrant a *staff*. Suddenly the few people he had working for him seemed to make sense.

Just seeing the house made her like Shane even more. Clearly, he had the money to build a mansion. And yet his home might be smaller than the one she grew up in.

Eloise couldn't fight the grin that crossed her face. How was it that without even trying, Shane was able to win her over time and time again? She was finding it harder to come up with reasons she should keep her walls up. The only thing that held her back was her gut feeling that he was hiding something.

She pulled up to the front of the house, leaving her doubts behind. Tonight, she was going to forget all about what Brielle had said.

That was the smart move.

When Shane opened the door, he looked more haggard than she expected. His hair was mussed, there was sauce on his cheek, and he wore a pink plaid apron that seemed to pull the whole look together.

Eloise clapped a hand over her mouth to muffle the laugh that erupted from her lips. "You look like..."

"What?" He glanced down at the apron.

She shook her head, laughing again. "Like you've had a rough evening. Do you need any *help*?"

Shane huffed. "What makes you say that?" He gestured toward the apron. "I'll have you know this apron is very fashionable... in certain places."

Shaking her head, she stepped through the doorway and then wiped her finger against his cheek. Eloise showed him the sauce and then let out a chuckle. "Isn't this supposed to stay in the pot or something?"

His gaze dipped to her finger then he snatched her wrist. His brow lifted and his lips quirked upward at the corners.

Eloise gasped. "Don't you dare."

"I don't know what you're talking about."

She tugged on her hand, expecting him to lick off the little bit of sauce from her finger. But instead, he pulled her toward him.

Shane held her hand out to the side and pressed a kiss to her lips. "Come on. You got here just in time. Dinner's almost ready." He guided her away from the entrance and shut the door behind her. Then he nodded toward her finger. "You know, even though I'm well off, I hate when people let things go to waste."

Her eyes widened, and without thinking about it, she popped her finger into her mouth.

Shane laughed, and she would have joined in, but the taste of the sauce distracted her. It had a little more kick than she had anticipated. There were notes of Italian seasoning and basil, along with something more savory.

Eloise's focus darted up to meet his. "This is *really* good." Her stomach growled, echoing the way she felt.

"Better be careful. You don't want to give me a big head."

Eloise shook her head. "I will never lie to you."

There was a moment when she thought she saw something change in his countenance. She couldn't be certain, but she thought he looked uncomfortable. That was silly. She was just getting into her own head again.

She slipped her hand into his and leaned into him. "Do you have time to give me a tour?"

Shane gestured before them. "Of course. This is the foyer, obviously."

Eloise glanced around at the fifteen-foot ceilings and the ornate chandelier. Okay, so he did splurge a little on his home. It might not be huge, but it was decorated by someone who had good taste. Beyond the foyer appeared to be a great room for entertaining.

He tugged her to their left toward an open archway that led to the dining room. A distressed table that could seat at least eight guests was situated beneath a more modern lighting fixture. He continued to lead her through another doorway into the kitchen.

Her eyes rounded as she took in the white cabinets and marbled countertops. Five pendant lights hung over the island. A pot of something simmering sat on the stove, adding to the wonderful smell. "Your place is really nice." She moved ahead of him, tracing her fingertip across the edge of the countertop.

Shane shrugged. "It's alright, I suppose."

She snorted. "I don't know why you don't invite more people over. This is the kind of place I would use to entertain people all the time." Eloise turned toward him, her eyes meeting his.

"Maybe one day you could." He'd said it so quietly that she wasn't sure she heard him correctly or if she'd imagined it. Either way, her heart beat just a little faster. It was crazy how much she wanted this.

He removed his apron and raked a hand through his hair, not looking at her anymore. "I'm glad you came tonight."

"Me too."

Brushing past her, he set to work putting the meal in its serving dishes. He'd grown quiet as she watched him.

"Is there anything I can do to help?"

"I don't want you to lift a finger." Shane picked up a salad bowl and guided her back to the dining room. He placed the bowl on the table before pulling out her chair. "I'll get the rest of the food."

They didn't speak much while they ate. Shane's spaghetti was to die for. "Where did you learn to cook?"

Shane smiled. "I didn't really learn to cook anywhere. I

picked up a few things here and there from my grandparents and then from Ingrid."

"Ingrid? Is that your housekeeper?"

He nodded. "She was the last person my grandfather hired before he passed. I took her on after that."

Eloise's brows shot up. "She still works for you?"

"Yes. Is that so strange?"

"She moved here. To work for you?"

He laughed. "I think I answered that question already."

"I just can't believe it. Why would someone—" She snapped her mouth shut and shook her head. "Never mind. It's none of my business."

"I find it... hard to trust people."

Eloise stilled. She hadn't gotten that from the way he was around other people, but the more she thought about it, the more she had to accept that his words made sense. He'd hired someone from his previous life to be the chef. His housekeeper and probably his security guy were people he knew before he moved out to Copper Creek.

According to Dianna and Grace, there wasn't much in the way of turnover in his staff. Even the woman Eloise was covering for hadn't quit. She was on maternity leave for the next couple of weeks.

A twinge shot through her heart. She thought she'd gotten to know Shane at least a decent amount, but she was still learning things about him that surprised her—like the modest way he lived his life. This home didn't look like the home of a billionaire.

She twisted her fork into her pasta and then lifted it to her mouth. "Well, I think people following you out here to work for you says a lot more about you than it does about them."

"How do you figure?" Shane bit off a piece of his garlic bread, but his gaze didn't leave her face.

"Well, it shows that you're the kind of guy that people

would follow anywhere. You must resonate with people in a way you don't even realize." She placed her fork beside her plate, then clasped her hands in her lap. "I know you did with me." Already she could feel the warmth seep into her face. She didn't even know why she felt embarrassed over telling him this. They were more intimate than anyone she had dated before.

Stuff like that should be shared, right?

When she looked up at him, she found him staring at her with that strange expression again—the one that almost appeared as though he felt guilty over something.

The second she frowned, he schooled his features and looked away.

So much for ignoring that gut instinct. She'd always been right on the money when it came to stuff like that. Maybe it was time to talk to Brielle about what she was feeling.

"I've been meaning to talk to you about something." Shane put his silverware down and leaned forward.

Maybe this was it. The reason he was acting so shady. Immediately, her heart went haywire. She held her breath, waiting for him to drop whatever bomb it was that he was hiding from her. Eloise's hands tightened around each other until her fingertips turned white. "Okay." She finally let out a breath. *Let's just get this over with.*

"You mentioned earlier that you didn't need the job at the restaurant."

Not where she thought this would go, but okay.

"My employee who was on maternity leave has asked to come back early, but I didn't want you to think that we didn't need *you.*"

She blinked a few times. Definitely not where she thought this was going to go.

Shane shifted in his seat. "I wanted to make it clear that you have a permanent position with me—at the restaurant—for however long you would like to. We were short-staffed when you started, and it would be nice if you... stayed."

Something strange and a little bit warm flooded her stomach. In a family with seven sisters, she always thought she was the one that was the most forgettable. She was born second to last, and as such, it was easy to overlook her accomplishments and even the things she did wrong.

For all intents and purposes, Shane had been the first one to see her for what she could offer.

And this was Shane Owens. The man who could have anything or hire anyone. He was the wealthiest person she knew, but he didn't live like it.

A faint smile crossed her features. Her thumbnail dug into the cuticle of her other thumb, and she lifted a shoulder. "Well, how could I turn down a request like that?"

When she peeked at him, she was surprised to find the relief so clearly written all over his face.

She had thought he was going to tell her something more. Tell her that *thing* that her intuition keeps nudging her about. She studied his face for a moment longer. "Okay, I can't take it anymore," she said.

Shane froze.

"I can tell something is up. I have no idea what you're hiding, but I can't shake the feeling that you're keeping something from me. I can't just sit back and let that happen. Something's not right."

Was she seeing things? Or did he pale visibly? She'd hit the nail on the head, then. He didn't want her to know something. Great, why did Brielle have to be right?"

She shoved away from her seat at the table and shot out of her chair. "Thanks for dinner. I'll see you tomorrow." Eloise turned toward the door as she snatched her purse from where it hung on the chair.

"Where are you going?"

"Home."

"Eloise—"

She spun around to face him. "I care about you. Can't you see that? I have gone along with this whole keeping our relationship a secret, but I haven't seen any benefit to it."

"I told you—"

"Yes, I'm fully aware of *why* you want to keep it secret. I just don't see the value in it anymore. People had to have noticed by now. It's not like I haven't been caught coming and going from your office—"

"I love you," he blurted.

She couldn't move. It was as if her limbs had been turned to stone. There was no way she'd heard him correctly.

Shane moved around the table swiftly until he reached her. He took her hands into his. "I love you, and I don't want to mess this up. I need to be sure I go about this right, and right now the safest way to do that is to keep things secret... for the time being." His voice pleaded with her, begging her to accept his explanation.

That swirling uncertainty she'd felt all night lessened but only somewhat. Was this what love felt like? What if her nerves were just her body's way of saying she felt the same way as Shane?

Her blood turned hot and cold all at once.

Shane stepped toward her and she held up a hand, but the look of pain on his face was almost too much for her to bear. "Just—give me a minute." Her eyes flitted from him to the floor and back. "This is... a lot. Can I think about it?"

He nodded as he stepped away from her. "Of course," he whispered. "Take as long as you need."

Eloise closed the distance between them, pecked him on the cheek, then left the house like her tail was on fire.

"How was dinner?" Brielle muttered as Eloise entered the kitchen. She probably shouldn't have told her sister about it, but keeping that secret from Brielle had been weighing on her more than she wanted to admit. Thankfully, Brielle didn't seem fazed by it. In fact, she seemed to have come to the conclusion that Eloise was dating Shane rather than Marc. And it appeared she found out on her own.

"Terrible." Eloise dropped her purse on the kitchen table, then pulled out a chair and collapsed into it.

Brielle gave Eloise a funny look as she pulled a cup out of the cupboard. "Really? Didn't he invite you over for dinner at his place?"

"Yeah."

Her sister laughed. "Sorry to break it to you, but if that makes your night terrible, maybe you should break up. That's what I did."

Eloise gave Brielle a dark look. She wasn't in the mood for any of Brielle's flippant comments regarding her relationship.

Brielle filled her glass with some water and then took a seat at the table. She heaved a sigh. "Fine, what was so terrible about tonight?"

"He said he loved me."

One brow lifted, but Brielle didn't say a word.

Eloise groaned. That probably didn't sound bad at all.

"Let me get this straight. He invited you to his home—a place I have *never* been, by the way—made you dinner and told you he loves you, and you think that equates to *terrible*? Seriously, I think you need to break up."

"None of that is the problem," Eloise moaned. "I have this feeling that something isn't right. He's hiding our relationship from everyone. That can't be normal. Guys aren't supposed to do that." She glanced up at her sister, finding Brielle's unnerving gaze locked on her. "What?"

Brielle twisted her glass between both of her hands thoughtfully. "You know me. Gut feelings are usually something you should listen to."

"I know! That's why I can't get over—"

"But coming from someone who dated Shane..." Her eyes flitted up to Eloise from her glass and stayed there. "I can tell you one thing. Shane is a good man."

"You said he lied to you."

Brielle shrugged. "Yeah, well, I didn't tell him everything about my past either. I didn't want him getting to know our family. I always kept him at arm's length. I only realize now that he had been doing the same with me. And maybe he wasn't lying so much as he was just trying to keep us safe while we were in a relationship. Maybe neither one of us was ready for anything that serious. But you are."

Eloise snorted. "You don't know that."

"Sure I do. This ache you feel in your stomach, that feeling that something bad is going to happen—it's because you're happy when you're with him. And maybe you're terrified that it's too good to be true." Brielle sighed, her expression tinted with sadness. "Don't let your fears hold you back from something great. I've been there. It doesn't ever end well."

Was she still harboring feelings for Shane? Eloise didn't think she was the jealous type, but knowing that someone might want to take Shane out from under her tore at her heart. The relationship she had with Shane felt all too flimsy to allow these thoughts of doubt to tear it to shreds. At a moment's notice, Shane could decide he didn't have the patience for any of this.

It was time to commit or walk away.

And deep down, she had already made her decision.

19

Shane

Shane had thought keeping the secret about his cousins was bad, but this was worse. So much worse. Why had he let those words escape? He had probably scared Eloise off, and she would run right back into the arms of Marc.

His fingers curled into fists at that thought. Marc had been conveniently absent lately. He'd only had a few run-ins with Madeline, but even her torture had subsided. The threats still hung in the air, and the only way to solve this problem would be to keep Eloise safe from them.

Brielle wouldn't lower herself to the level of dating Marc, so she was safe.

The funny thing was that this wasn't simply about keeping Eloise out of Marc's clutches. He'd been completely honest when he'd told her of his feelings—a fact that had shocked him more than he'd anticipated.

He loved her.

It hadn't taken much to figure that out, but he cared about Eloise more than he cared about anyone. She was an amazing listener. She didn't care about his wealth or his status. She spent time with him because she wanted to.

If he were honest with himself, he would have to admit that he hadn't felt like a normal human being for years—not until they'd had their first date.

Shane couldn't focus. The work he had to do mocked him as it sat on his desk. He hadn't heard a peep from Eloise since their date last night, and he knew deep down he'd blown it. There was no coming back from telling a girl he loved her when she wasn't ready to hear it. The worst part was that he couldn't come up with a single plan to fix it.

All he could do was wait and hope that she would eventually be willing to talk to him.

As if that thought alone were enough to summon her, there was a knock at his door. He lifted his head, and the door opened to reveal the one person he wanted to see more than anyone in the world.

Shane rose from his desk, not brave enough to open his mouth and say something he would undoubtedly regret.

Eloise glanced at him, then shut the door and leaned against it. "Hey," she murmured.

His pulse quickened. This was it. The moment of truth. She was going to tell him he was moving too fast and she needed space. As long as that didn't mean they needed to break up, he could manage that, right?

Or maybe he couldn't.

She dropped her gaze and fidgeted. "You have this way of throwing me off balance that I'm not used to. I expect one thing and then, bam, you make a U-turn and I'm stuck here with this whiplash that takes days for me to sort out." Her eyes lifted to him once more. "I don't know that I'm ready to return your feelings yet."

His heart stammered and he took a step toward her but then reined himself in. She didn't need him to suffocate her right now. She needed him to give her the space she'd requested.

This was harder than anything he'd done in the past. All he could do was nod, not trusting his voice. If he uttered even a single word, he would most definitely scare her off indefinitely.

Eloise didn't move from where she stood. She watched him much like he imagined the prey would watch the predator they know is only a few yards away. She was calculating if she had the ability to escape him.

Then he couldn't take it any longer. "You don't have to return my feelings. I shouldn't have confessed—"

"You shouldn't have *confessed*?" She let out a strained laugh. "I don't know if I agree with *that*."

He snapped his mouth shut. If she didn't want to tell him she loved him back, wouldn't that stand to reason that he needed to have kept his feelings to himself?

Eloise took a deep breath and then let it out. She stepped forward and offered him a small smile. "You have to understand that I've been watching all of my sisters fall in love with their soul mates, and they don't seem to have any regrets. They are literally jumping into love with both eyes shut tight and no fear for the future."

"Oh, I'm certain you're mistaken on that."

She gave him a sharp look, and he chuckled.

"Love isn't easy. Frankly, it's *terrifying*," he said. Chills swept down his spine and he moved closer to his desk so that it might steady him. "Confessing that your heart is now vulnerable is the hardest thing a person can do. It doesn't matter if you're telling someone new or someone who has been in your life for ages. To be exposed like that opens you up for all kinds of pain." His thoughts shifted to Madeline. Before he'd moved to Copper Creek, he'd thought all families were like his. But the closer he got to the Callahans, the more he realized that he was wrong. Families did exist where they were willing to do anything for one another. Eloise was fortunate enough to belong to one.

"I suppose you make a good point," she whispered, just loud enough for him to hear. "I came here to tell you that I'm glad you told me. You've pushed me to consider exactly how I feel. I don't know if I'm in love with you... yet." She gave him a strained smile. "But I still want to continue dating." Another deep breath before she moved closer. "Even if that means we need to keep things quiet for a little while longer... then I trust you have a good reason."

Shane couldn't remember a time when he felt more relieved than he did at this very moment. Eloise was giving him the time to figure out the mess he had managed to find himself in—yet another reason for him to care so much about her.

She continued walking toward him, slowly closing the distance between them. When she stopped, she peered up at him with her head cocked to the side. Then she slipped her hands behind his neck and gave him a smile. "Deal's a deal. Our next date is going to be at my place."

He opened his mouth to protest, but she placed her finger on his lips. "I don't know how Brielle found out, but she did."

That wasn't good. Now that Eloise knew about Brielle, his argument for keeping things secret was unraveling. How much had Brielle told her? He prayed that Eloise didn't hear anything regarding his cousins.

Eloise laughed. "Don't look so worried. Somehow, I feel like she's okay with it. I don't know when that happened, but she seems to be on your side."

There was no denying the shock that must have been written all over his face. The last conversation he'd had with Brielle had suggested otherwise. There was no way she was completely on board with him dating her younger sister. If anything, she was tolerating him because she understood that he was the lesser of two evils.

Shane swallowed. "Well then, I suppose I don't have any excuses. We're going riding. Next weekend."

Her face brightened. "Really?"

He enveloped her in a hug, if only to hide his worried expression. Shane buried his face into her hair. "I'd do anything for you."

THE FOLLOWING week went faster than Shane expected. Everything finally felt like it was going to be okay. Still no word from Madeline. He hadn't seen Marc either. The restaurant had become far more popular than he would have dreamed possible.

People were flooding to the country club from out of town, and while Copper Creek was getting a little busier, it wasn't all bad. Even the few locals who complained about the extra activity couldn't deny that it brought in necessary revenue.

Shane was beginning to think he could finally relax. The stress of the last month and a half was coming to a close. Madeline was blowing smoke, and even though she and Marc had purchased the land beside his country club property, even that didn't seem to cause any ripples for Shane or anyone he cared about.

When his work was done, he closed up his office and headed out toward the Callahan property. His life was finally coming together, and the weirdest part was that it wouldn't have happened if his cousins hadn't shown up out of the blue to torture him. If it wasn't for Madeline, he would have never fallen for Eloise.

The closer he got to the Callahan ranch, the more excited he became. He hadn't been riding since they'd taken the horses out at the Keagan property. He couldn't wait for her to show him what made her happy.

Shane parked his car and jogged up the steps. There was an unfamiliar truck parked out front. It was a fire-engine red Chevy that looked like it'd just come right off the lot. His steps slowed and he frowned as he stood at the edge of the porch.

Marc would have bought something like that. Shane glanced at the house, then back to the truck. If Marc was here, then Shane was in bigger trouble than he thought. Eloise hadn't mentioned anything about his cousin since they made everything official. He'd simply assumed that Marc had decided to leave Eloise and her family alone.

He should have known better.

Shane knocked, his thumps sounding far more urgent than he wanted them to. He prayed he was wrong. Please don't be Marc. Please be someone who was interested in dating Brielle.

That was exactly who opened the door.

Brielle stared at him through lidded eyes. "What are you doing here?"

"Eloise invited me."

She lifted a brow, her arms folding as she continued to block the doorway. "Really? Because I feel like she would have said something if that were the case."

He swallowed hard and attempted to peer over her shoulder. "I know we're not really on the best of terms, but I need to get in there and meet with Eloise. She and I are going on a ride this afternoon."

"She's already got a visitor." Brielle snorted. "You really have a hard time following directions, don't you?"

His head reared back. "What is that supposed to mean?"

"Your cousin is here. What was the point of my helping you if you couldn't even keep him from hanging out with my sister?"

And just like that, the rock in his stomach dropped. His whole body sagged with the revelation. "Marc is here?"

She nodded. "He's *been* here regularly. He comes over like three times a week just to chat with Eloise on the back porch."

The worry that started as a small flicker roared to life with a fury that resembled how he'd felt when Marc and Madeline arrived. "He has?"

"Yup. Don't worry. I don't think Eloise has kissed him or anything. But he's been hanging around, and it doesn't matter what I tell her. She won't listen to me. I guess he's here to stay? He bought some place out by the club?"

Shane dragged a hand down his face. "Yeah. He did."

"Well, what are you going to do about it?"

His head snapped up and he stared at her. "Me?"

"Yeah. Didn't you say you were going to handle it? Is that what you call handling it?" She jabbed her finger toward the back porch. "Because I feel like he's only getting closer to her."

Shane brushed past her into the house. "I'm doing my best, Brielle. I don't exactly have control over who you or any of your family members invite over to your home," he muttered.

Brielle's footsteps followed him through the house, and when he turned down a hallway he thought might lead to the back, she chuckled mirthlessly. "On your right, buddy."

He turned on his heel and headed in the direction she told him to go. When he reached the back door, he stopped. Eloise and Marc sat on the edge of the porch. There was at least two feet between them. From the back, their conversation looked completely innocent. He couldn't hear what they were talking about, only their muffled voices.

"You gonna go break them up, or what?" Brielle's quiet voice broke through his reverie, and he glanced at her.

"You said he's been coming here for weeks?"

"Probably since you started dating Eloise."

He turned his focus back to the couple outside. His jaw tightened and he gave her a sharp nod. "I see."

She reached out and touched his arm. "Like I said. They haven't done anything sordid."

"That you know of."

Brielle rolled her eyes. "Come on, Shane. Do you really think Eloise would be capable of something like that? She might not have told you about them meeting—"

"You didn't either."

"Yeah, well, I didn't want you dating her in the first place."

"Point taken."

She heaved a sigh. "I mean, Eloise is allowed to have friends. And if she thinks Marc is good enough to be her friend, then..."

"But he isn't. That's the problem. He's—" Shane caught himself before he said exactly what was on his mind. "He's just not."

"I'd wager that you're not worthy of dating my sister either."

He didn't bother commenting on that. The truth was that he agreed with Brielle wholeheartedly on that topic. Shane sighed, glancing at her once more before he opened the back door. "Thanks," he muttered.

The couple turned toward him, varying degrees of surprise on their faces. Eloise gasped, jumping up from her place on the steps. "Shane. I totally forgot you were going to be on your way." Her eyes darted from him to his cousin. "Marc was just stopping by to visit a bit..." There was an apology in her eyes, but it was quickly overtaken by guilt. He knew that feeling.

Who was he to judge her when he was keeping so much from her as well?

Shane stayed near the door. If he got too close to Marc, he didn't know what he would do. Instead, he shoved his hands into his pockets and rocked back on his heels. "Well, are you ready to go for a ride?"

Her eyes widened. "Actually, I wanted to get those horses saddled before we head out. Give me a few minutes, and I'll be back to get you?" Without waiting for a response, she darted down the steps and around the side of the house.

Shane glowered at his cousin. "I see you're doing your sister's dirty work, huh? Brielle tells me you've been hanging around like an unwanted pest."

Marc slowly got to his feet. He held up both hands and stepped backward until his feet met with the earth. "I know you didn't want me here, and yes, it started out as a way to undermine you, but that's not what I'm doing now."

The fury boiled over and Shane charged toward his cousin. "Oh? Are you suggesting that you've made a change for the better? Have you decided to turn your back on your conniving sister?"

Marc snapped his mouth shut and his eyes flickered with resentment. "You don't know Madeline like I do. I can't just go against what she says. You know that."

"Everyone has a choice, Marc. If you're doing anything to hurt Eloise—"

"I'd never hurt Eloise," he snapped. "I would sooner die."

Shane reared his head back. "What?"

"I like her. She's nice to me."

"Yeah, she's nice to *everyone*."

Marc let out a heavy breath. "I believe that. I just... I don't know... the more time I spent with her, the more I wanted to be around her just because she made me feel... good."

Shane rolled his eyes. "You'd have me believe that you're not here trying to do something to help Madeline's schemes."

Marc lifted a shoulder and dropped it listlessly. "I don't tell

Madeline what we talk about. I don't even tell her every time I come to visit."

"Telling her anything is dangerous, and you know it."

His cousin dropped his focus to his hands. "Yeah." There were notes of defeat in his voice, and when he lifted his gaze back to meet Shane's, it wasn't hard to see the sadness behind it. "You need to be careful, Shane. Madeline doesn't tell me everything, but from the sounds of it, she's about ready to drop something really big on you. I don't want to see Eloise get hurt."

Hearing Marc talk about Eloise in that concerned sounding voice of his made Shane want to slug him right then and there. "Just get out of here Marc. Now."

Marc nodded. "Okay. Don't say I didn't warn you about Madeline."

Shane watched his cousin slink around the side of the house like the vermin he was. If he ever saw Marc here again, he wasn't sure he'd be able to keep his hands to himself.

"Ready?"

Shane jumped, and his eyes found Eloise. She glanced around, then back to him. "Did Marc go?"

"Yeah. He had somewhere he had to be."

She smiled at him. "Well then, let's go for that ride."

20

Eloise

"You didn't tell me you were still seeing Marc." Shane's voice held a bite to it that Eloise had been expecting, and yet she still grimaced when she heard it.

She took a moment to gather her thoughts as their horses plodded along the trail that led to the only natural pond on their property. Her saving grace was that he hadn't yelled at her about it when Marc was there. And from the sound of it, he didn't even do anything to his cousin. Eloise swallowed at the thick lump in her throat. It probably wouldn't help him to know that her guilt had been eating at her far more than anything he could say or do to her.

"Well? Did you just figure I wouldn't care?"

Her head whipped around and she glanced at him. "Of course not."

"Of course you thought I would care?"

She groaned. "I knew you would care, but I figured it would be better for our relationship if you didn't know how close Marc and I have become."

"Close?"

She grimaced. "That's not what I meant. I mean that we're *friends*. He confides in me, and I talk to him about things that are bothering me." She could feel Shane's eyes drilling into her, but she couldn't bring herself to meet his gaze. "I'm sorry," she whispered. "What was I supposed to say when he asked if we could still be friends."

"Tell him *no*," Shane bit out.

This time Eloise did look at him. She shot him a dirty look that he never thought he'd see coming from her. "You're not my father. You can't tell me what to do. And he gave that up a long time ago."

Shane worked his jaw from side to side. He was clearly struggling with this news a lot more than she thought he would. And yet he wasn't demanding anything besides making sure Marc didn't come around anymore. At least that was how it sounded.

She heaved a heavy sigh. "I don't know why you dislike him so much, but he's done nothing to hurt me, and I've enjoyed the talks we've been able to have. I'm not going to stop being friends with him."

"What if I had a good reason?"

"Well, do you?" She gave him a pointed look.

He met her leveled stare with one of his own, and for a moment she thought he wouldn't back down. But then he dropped his gaze. "I don't want to see you get hurt," he said quietly.

"Marc isn't going to hurt me."

"You don't know that. He's... capable of doing a lot of harm."

She let out a laugh. "You sound like you've been through the wringer or something. He's a good guy—"

"No, he isn't. Eloise, listen to me."

She clamped her mouth shut, her eyes finding his. The seriousness of his voice sent a shiver down her spine, and she didn't know what to do with it.

"Marc and Madeline have one common goal. They want what they want, and if they don't get it, they'll step on anyone they have to in order to make that happen."

Eloise shook her head. "He said you might say something like that. He says you've always been jealous of them and a little selfish."

Shane let out a bark of laughter that seemed to echo through the trees they wandered between. A few birds took to flight and the sound of a few furry animals scurrying through the underbrush followed. He shook his head. "Of course he would say that. There's a lot more going on than you could ever know."

"Then *tell* me," she pleaded. "We're dating. You should feel comfortable sharing these things with me."

He stared ahead at the trail. His silence was more painful than she expected. This was what triggered her anxiety. Every time he changed the subject and went quiet, she got that feeling again.

"Fine. You don't have to tell me. But I want you to know that if you chose to talk to me, I'd believe you."

Still nothing.

She pushed aside the ache that had grown in her chest. Shane wasn't intentionally trying to be hurtful. For all she knew, he thought being quiet would help her—keep her safe somehow. She wished she could tell him that he was being ridiculous.

Eloise sighed. She wasn't going to let this pain she held ruin their evening. She had been so excited to show him her favorite place, and she'd be darned if she didn't follow through with it and share a part of herself with him that she hadn't shared with anyone.

They came to a fork in the trail, and she tugged on her reins to turn her horse to the left. Shane stopped behind her. "You're kidding, right?"

She glanced over her shoulder toward him. "What?"

"That trail can't fit a horse."

She let out a soft laugh. "I know it looks like that, but it's not what it appears. I assure you, I've been down this path many times. It's tight for maybe a quarter of a mile, then it opens up."

He gave her a disbelieving look, and she laughed again.

"Just trust me, okay?" Eloise grimaced. "Okay, so I know our trust is a bit on the rocky side right now. But you can trust me on this." She arced her arm around and gestured for him to follow her.

She only watched him for a second to make sure he was behind her, then she urged her horse forward. Just as she promised, the trail opened up after about a quarter of a mile. It led them straight for a pond that was surrounded by several trees so tall they shaded the whole area. The few areas of sunlight that burst through the latticework of branches made the whole place look like a fairytale.

Eloise pulled her horse to a stop and chanced a glance over at her guest. Her sisters knew about this place when they were all younger, but she wasn't sure if any of them had visited since they were little girls. She'd managed to remember only because she made it a point to come after the final frost of spring. That was when all of the flowers were budding and the pond was its clearest.

Shane stared at the scene without blinking. His eyes seemed to drink in everything all at once, and when he finally turned toward her, his expression softened. "This place is amazing."

"I know," she said quietly.

"No. Like *really* amazing. I didn't even know there were places like this in Copper Creek."

"I don't think there are many of them. We're just fortunate to have the forest back up against our property, so it's a bit more wild than other places."

He climbed down from his horse and took the reins in his hand as he led his horse toward the edge of the water. "It's like a scene that painter guy always did on that TV show."

Eloise threw back her head and laughed. "Yeah, I guess it is." She climbed down out of her saddle and then moved closer to her horse's head. Her fingers ran down her steed's neck, and he nuzzled her in show of affection. "This is my most favorite place of all time. When I'm sad or need to feel better, I come here. When I need an escape or when I want a place to just breathe, this is it. Sometimes I even come out here when I'm excited or happy."

"So, you basically live out here."

She chuckled. "Yeah, pretty much." Eloise nuzzled her horse and her voice softened. "This place is my sanctuary. It's where I feel the most... whole." When she looked over at him again, she found him staring at her with an expression she couldn't read. She flushed and looked away. "There are always going to be parts of ourselves that we want to keep hidden. But eventually, I think we will share those parts with the person we feel we can trust the most."

There was no way she could bring herself to look at him again. Not when she probably just said the cheesiest thing she could come up with.

"I'm sorry I didn't tell you about Marc. I would never intentionally hurt you."

She heard him before he came into view. Shane reached out and took one of her hands in his. "I hope you know that I feel the exact same way. I never want to hurt you. The way I feel about you—I think I'd rather jump off a cliff than see you in pain."

Eloise laughed again, though this one was a little more strained. "Please don't do that."

He made a face. "Okay. I won't do that. Just promise me one thing."

"Of course."

"Never forget the way it feels to be with me right here in this moment."

She tilted her head as she studied him. That was a strange thing to say. It was almost like he knew something she didn't. What was she thinking? Of course he knew something she didn't.

Something strange had happened just before Shane had shown up. Marc was talking, and then he cut himself off and looked away before he changed the subject.

Come to think of it, that behavior was very similar to the way Shane reacted when they got into some of their more strained conversations. Perhaps this was a family issue and she'd just have to accept that this was the way the men in her life would behave.

Though something told her it wasn't as clear-cut as she wanted to believe. They were both hiding something. By the way they had reacted to one another from day one, she could tell.

A new feeling squeezed her chest and surprised her so much that she gasped. Shane stepped toward her, concern twisting his features. "Is everything okay?"

Eloise placed a hand to her chest and rubbed at the area above her heart. "Yeah, I think so. That was... weird."

He moved even closer, the back of his knuckle tracing along her jawline. "Are you sure?"

She nodded again, then caught the look in his eye. A spark of something sweet and exhilarating burst where the pain had been, and it took everything in her wheelhouse not to physically react to it.

It wasn't clear at first. In fact, she'd struggled with this feeling for a while now, but now she knew without a doubt what it meant.

She'd fallen for him.

Eloise had allowed the last wall of defense to fall that she had erected around herself. She'd given him the one thing she held most dear when she'd finally brought him here. She'd given him her heart.

21

Shane

When he came into work on Monday, Shane was still reeling from everything that had happened over the weekend.

From finding out that Marc had secretly been spending time with Eloise to having her take him to her special hideaway, his whole soul felt like it had been stuck in a snow globe and shaken viciously. Parts of him were floating up while others floated down. He couldn't find his bearings, and all he could do was try to make sense of what was most important.

And that was Eloise.

He'd already told her he loved her. Now he just had to protect her from Madeline. His cousin had been quiet for far too long, and now he needed to go on the offensive. Marc seemed to think that Madeline was up to something horrendous. The problem was that Marc wouldn't expound on his concerns, so how could Shane trust him or his motives?

Stacks of paperwork were piling up on Shane's desk, a testament to where his head had been since Madeline had shown up. He stared at the pile with disgust. He needed to find a way to get her to leave. Marc appeared to be more benign, so Shane would set his focus on the bigger threat.

"Hello, cousin." Madeline swept into his office without knocking.

Speak of the devil.

Shane watched her float through the room until she ended up at his side. She pushed aside a stack of files that ended up tipping over and perched on the edge of the desk. Madeline traced a manicured fingernail along the mahogany wood before her eyes flitted to meet his. "I'm so glad I caught you."

He didn't dare speak first. He needed as much information as he could get from her without her realizing it. Hopefully she would give him the information he needed to get her to leave.

Madeline pouted, tilting her head as her gaze swept over him. "Oh, you don't look so good. Has work been hard lately?"

"You could say that," he muttered through clenched teeth.

"Well, I've got a proposition for you."

"No."

"But you haven't heard what I'm going to say."

"The answer is still no, Madeline. I don't want anything from you." He shook his head. "No, that's not accurate. I *do* want something from you. I want you to leave Copper Creek and my friends in peace."

He didn't think it was possible, but she puckered her lip out even further. "Oh, you should really play nice, Shane. You don't know what I'm capable of."

Shane knew exactly what she was capable of; that was the problem. "What do you want, Madeline?"

She examined her fingernails, putting on that act she always did when she wanted to pretend she wasn't interested in the conversation. But he knew better. "Like I said, I have a proposition. I came across some interesting information and I thought it might interest you."

He scowled at her. "You're not going to blackmail me."

"Who said anything about blackmailing *you*?"

The blood in his veins went cold and his heart slowed. He couldn't catch his breath no matter how much he tried. His mind immediately went to Eloise. Had Madeline found out something about the woman he loved? She was completely capable of threatening others to get what she wanted. And Eloise was his kryptonite.

Shane swallowed hard as he attempted to keep his expression cool. But the look on Madeline's face was enough to tell him he'd failed.

"Ah. See? I've caught your attention." She stopped examining her fingers and stared at him fully. "Now, before I tell you what I have found, I want you to think really hard about what would happen if certain people discovered secrets in this small town. It's not like where we lived. This place is so close. Everyone has their nose in everyone else's business. It's disgusting, really."

"Then why are you still here?"

Her menacing smile widened, showing off her perfectly white teeth. "Because I want something, and that something is here."

His eyes narrowed. He'd already told her he wasn't going to give her money. Eventually even his money would run out. She had to know that.

Madeline leaned forward so her face was inches from his. "I want to be your business partner. I won't be too greedy. Fifty-fifty should do it."

Something lodged in his throat and he choked. Air refused to pass beyond the obstruction even as he pounded on his chest.

When he finally was able to catch his breath, he gaped at her. "*What?*"

"For heaven's sake, Shane. You heard me perfectly well. And you know how much I hate repeating myself."

"Over my dead body," he ground out, launching to his feet.

She didn't look fazed at all. Rather than confront him, she dug around in her purse until she retrieved a compact mirror and a tube of lipstick. "That's the funny thing, Shane. I know you almost better than you know yourself. You won't have a choice when you finally realize what I have."

"There is nothing that is worth *that*," he shot back.

She glanced at him and then rolled her eyes. "Oh, and did I mention? I want you to break up with your little girlfriend. She'll only get in the way." She returned her attention to her reflection and applied the bright red lipstick to her plump lips. Then she pressed them together before making the smacking sound. "You see, I've thought about this a lot over the last few years. You were never supposed to get any of the fortune Gramps gave you. It wasn't *your* birthright. But I couldn't do a thing to stop him from giving it to you when his will was airtight."

Her eyes swept over him, and she smiled again. "You used his money to make your fortune. Money that should have been mine. So I get access to half of everything that is yours."

"What makes you think I'm going to do anything you say?"

She stared at him, and he could see the cogs in her mind working. She was enjoying this conversation far too much. Finally, she uttered one word. "Brielle."

The brief relief that washed over him when she didn't say Eloise's name was quickly wiped out when he realized that she'd found something so devastating that she thought it would convince him to leave the woman he loved.

His stomach roiled and his extremities went numb. As much

as he tried to tell himself that this wasn't as bad as he thought it would be, he knew better. Madeline never did things halfway. That was one of her strengths. She could look at a problem from all different angles and figure out where the weaknesses stemmed from before attacking.

Deep down, he already knew this was checkmate. If Madeline had something against Brielle, it would not only hurt her, but it could hurt Eloise as well.

He saw the triumph in her eyes before she even said a single word. She cocked her head, and her eyes flashed much like he'd imagine a lioness's would right before she lunged for the jugular. "There he is. There's the man I knew would bend to my wishes. You see, your problem is that what you think your biggest strength is... well, it's actually your biggest weakness. You *care* too much, Shane. You always have. It might have gotten you far, but you can only climb so much before you get knocked off the mountain."

His eye twitched, the stress becoming too great. "How do I know you even have anything you can use for leverage? You could be all talk."

Madeline laughed, and the sound raked against his frayed nerves. "You know better than that, Shane. We've been through this before. I never show up empty-handed." She reached into her purse and pulled out a folded piece of paper. She flung it on the desk in front of him. "Tell me, Shane. What would this town do if they found out one of their beloved cowgirl royals up and got married to some moonlight dancer in Vegas?"

His eyes widened. As far as he knew, Brielle had never left the state. How would she have married someone in Vegas? She was so scared of commitment he couldn't see her getting married to anyone. At least not anytime soon. Shane snatched the paper and opened it to find an official-looking document with Brielle's signature next to some guy named Theodore Brooks. He read over the document several times, then scowled and threw it on the desk. "How do I know this wasn't doctored? I wouldn't hold it past you to do just that."

"You're right," she said simply. "I could have had that document falsified. It might even be real, but she got wise and got divorced. I guess you're just going to have to decide whether or not to call my bluff. Because the second I leave this office, my offer is off the table. I'll spread this information in this sorry excuse for a sweet small town and enjoy watching the dominos fall."

His jaw ached from how tight he clenched it. If Madeline had picked anyone else—literally anyone—to target, he would have thrown the document at her and told her where to shove it. But he couldn't do that. Not to Brielle, not to her family, and not to Eloise.

Shane couldn't help wondering if Eloise knew about this secret past her older sister had. Or supposedly had. Was it something the whole family knew? Or was it something Brielle was keeping all to herself? It wasn't like he could go asking around. He'd have to tread carefully. At any given moment, Madeline could leak this information. Could he risk that it was all a lie? All a bluff?

He crumpled the document and threw it across the room. "Fine."

Madeline lifted a brow. "Fine? Am I correct in assuming that you are willing to accept my terms?"

"No. I'm not going to blindly accept anything until we have something drawn up by my lawyer. I'll not have you holding this over my head every single time you want something else."

She pressed her lips together into a thin line. She was smart enough to know this was how things would turn out. He had no doubt that she would accept what he had to say. Madeline just didn't like being bossed around. She never did. "Okay. We draw up a contract that both of us agree to. But in the meantime, you have to break up with your sweet little girlfriend."

He felt sick to his stomach. Of course that was how this would go. "I don't understand why you don't just demand I give you half of my money. Why drag Eloise into this?"

She rolled her eyes as she got to her feet. "Just do what I said. I want half of everything. Now and in the future. I'm not an idiot, Shane. I've thought through everything. Don't worry your pretty little head about why I want you to break up with her. If you fail to keep your end of the bargain, then I unleash my wrath. And if I—heaven forbid—don't hold up my end, then I don't get a penny... let's just call it mutually assured destruction." She slung her purse over her shoulder and winked at him. "I expect you to break things off by midnight tonight. Don't test my patience, Shane. I've already had to wait long enough." She flipped her dark locks over her shoulder and left the room.

The second the door closed, he lurched from his chair and started pacing the room. He'd spent enough time with Brielle to know that this information would destroy not only her father, but her reputation as well. This town still held onto traditional values, and even a divorce could start unwarranted judgment. On top of that, it wasn't a secret how many men had spent time with the second eldest Callahan daughter—something she shouldn't be involved with if she had a spouse somewhere.

The despair in his heart at the thought of breaking it off with Eloise overwhelmed him. Shane's legs gave way beneath him and he crumpled to the floor. He could feel a sob making its way through his body, but he held it in. He'd brought this on himself. He'd given Madeline everything she needed to manipulate him into giving her everything she'd ever wanted. He wouldn't be surprised if he found out that she'd been planning something like this since the moment the lawyers read their grandfather's will.

He scooted backward until he rested against the wall. His head thunked helplessly there, and he shut his eyes as if doing so would erase everything that had just happened.

Like Madeline said. To fight would be to ensure the destruction of the people he cared about. He couldn't do anything to her. There was no time to find an alternative route. He'd lost.

Shane lost track of how long he sat there on the floor like the fool he was. Thankfully he didn't have any meetings that day, nor did anyone stop by his office. The longer he tried to put off talking to Eloise, the harder it got.

His heart wheezed, unwilling to do the work necessary to get up off the floor. To top it off, at some point he'd gotten a migraine.

Shane couldn't break up with Eloise over the phone, but he also couldn't bring himself to go see her. He knew he'd lose his nerve. Each minute that ticked by was pure torture.

When he could finally think clearly, he pulled out his phone and stared at it.

Impossible.

He couldn't break up with her in person. He'd lose his nerve and tell her he loved her. She'd try to get to the bottom of what he was going through, and that'd put her in danger.

Shane had to become the bad guy so that she would stay safe.

He opened up the last text message he'd sent her. Just thinking about doing this over a message made him feel like he was going to lose the contents of his stomach. Painstakingly, he typed out the only thing he could think of to say that would make him look and sound like the jerk that he was without causing her additional grief.

I have a confession. I've not been honest with you. This isn't your fault, it's mine. It's time I'm honest with myself and come forward. We

*need to break up. There are several reasons, but the most important
one is that I'm not in love with you anymore. I wish you the best.*

It was the longest text message he had ever written, and it still
didn't feel right. Of course it didn't feel right; he'd done the one
thing his body revolted against. He'd made the ultimate sacrifice.

He'd lost Eloise.

22

Eloise

Eloise stared at the message on her screen. She blinked, thinking it would magically disappear or maybe she'd wake up to the sunlight coming in from the windows. It didn't matter how many times she closed the app and then opened it. Nor did it matter how many times she shut her eyes and then opened them. She'd read the same thing again and again.

Shane had broken up with her.

Over text.

She couldn't believe this. It wasn't possible. This had to be a joke. He was messing with her.

Except Shane wasn't a jokester. In all the time she had known him, he didn't prank her or make fun. He was serious—almost too serious. The most laidback she'd seen him be was the time he took her on that date to Texas.

The breeze ruffled her hair, and the sound of birds chirping did nothing to ease the ache she felt as she sat on the back porch steps of her home. Thankfully, no one was home. Everyone had something to do or somewhere better to be. She was alone.

Only now, she felt even more alone than ever.

A hot, fat tear rolled down her cheek and she brushed it away as quick as she could. The last thing she needed was for anyone to notice that she wasn't doing great.

That was the understatement of the year.

Hadn't she just realized she loved him? Hadn't she just told herself to let go and allow her heart to open for him? What was she supposed to do now?

Another tear skidded down her cheek and this time followed the curve until it seeped between the corners of her lips. The salt seeped onto her tongue, causing an almost bitter taste.

"Eloise?"

She jumped, clicking the button on her phone to turn it off before looking up and finding Brielle standing over her.

Brielle frowned. "What happened?"

"Nothing. What makes you think something happened?"

"Is it Shane? It's him, isn't it? I *knew* he was going to do something stupid." She let out a groan and threw her hands into the air. "I should have never—" She snapped her mouth shut as her eyes found Eloise's. "Hand me the phone," she demanded.

"What? No. Why?"

"Eloise," she warned. "Give me your phone. You're clearly upset, and the only one who could do that kind of damage is a boyfriend."

"*No*," Eloise protested. "Friends can..."

The look on Brielle's face made it clear she wasn't about to let Eloise talk her out of getting what she wanted. And Brielle was smart enough to see right through her.

Eloise sighed and held the phone out to her sister without meeting her gaze. "Fine. I don't care anyway." Her voice broke on the last word and another tear leaked from her eyes. She did not like her emotional state right now. She'd always known there was a reason her sister didn't seriously date anyone, and this must be the reason. It was so much easier to keep her distance when she didn't get attached.

Well, she'd royally messed that up.

Brielle let out a string of expletives, and Eloise's eyes widened as she stared up at her sister. "I don't *believe* this!" She took off pacing as she shook her head. The color of her face would have put a poinsettia to shame. "Who does he think he is? He can't just dump you like that. It's not right. We're going over there right now."

"What?" Eloise squeaked. "No, we're not. I don't want to see him. At least not right now. I'm still processing—"

"He owes you an explanation." Brielle gestured toward the phone in her hand. "Didn't you read this? He broke up with you over text because he didn't want to face you. He's a coward, Eloise. He needs to own up to what he did, and he needs to be a man about it."

Eloise stared at her hands and shrugged. "Maybe I don't want to see him right now because I don't think I would be able to stop myself from crying." Her voice was soft and broken. Right then, it felt like her heart had broken in two and she didn't have anything left. "Maybe that will change, but right now, I would rather not see him."

Brielle groaned. "Come on, Eloise. You deserve better than this."

"Maybe I don't."

"*What*?" She seethed.

Eloise peeked at her sister. "He told me he loved me."

Her sister's face contorted with even more surprise and fury. "He didn't."

"Yeah, he did. And I didn't say it back. I didn't give him any indication that I was in this for the long haul. Maybe he just got tired of waiting." That was it. That confession lifted the flood-gates and the tears spilled down her cheeks. The more she thought about it, the more she had to admit that this definitely felt like it was her fault.

When Shane confessed his love for her, she should have given him something—*anything* to show him that his feelings weren't one-sided. She could have prevented this if he'd only known where she stood.

The step creaked beside her as Brielle settled onto the old wood plank. "It's *not* your fault."

Eloise shrugged.

"I mean it. Guys like this are trash. They don't deserve women like us. We're like diamonds."

She could tell Brielle was trying to help, but at this point Eloise didn't know if there was anything that could.

"Because, you know, diamonds take years and years of pres-sure to get to their fullest potential. *Years*, Eloise. If Shane cared about you like you think he did, then he would have waited as long as it took until he could have you on your terms. He's just a jerk."

"No, he's not. There's more to him than you realize, Brielle. He's a good man."

Brielle snorted. "He's a liar. He said so himself. What do you think Dad would do if he found out about this?"

Eloise stiffened. She sucked in sharply and stared wide-eyed at her sister. "Don't tell Dad a single thing. He doesn't need to know."

"I *know* that," Brielle muttered. "But based on the way you just reacted, you can't deny that I have a point. If Dad wouldn't like what happened, then you shouldn't put up with it either."

"Dad doesn't know Shane like I do. He wouldn't understand." Eloise snatched her phone away from Brielle. Her fingers itched to message Shane back and ask to see him. She wanted to talk to him and find out what was going on. There had to be a reasonable explanation.

Unfortunately, a seed of doubt had been planted. Not only from Brielle but from those strange gut instincts she'd been feeling when she was around Shane. He'd been hiding something from her. Was his losing interest in her part of that?

"I think I'm going to be sick." Eloise got up from the step and hurried inside. She needed a drink of water and maybe a sleep aide so she could go to bed early and come back to this with a clearer head.

Brielle followed her. "If you decide you want to go see him, I'll go with you."

Eloise stopped. She faced her sister and gave her a firm stare. "I'm only going to say this once. Leave him alone. I don't need you meddling. If everything is the way it appears, then I'm going to cut my losses."

"What is that supposed to mean? *If* everything is the way it appears? He broke up with you, Eloise. There is nothing to interpret."

"Yeah, maybe." She spun around and headed for the kitchen. *Maybe.*

"I can't believe this. I've tried calling him four times and I've sent him three text messages asking him to see me. What is wrong with him?" Eloise paced out in the pasture where she'd been exercising her horse.

Marc leaned against the corral and shrugged. "Sometimes guys have to put their tails between their legs and just let the consequences of their actions take place."

She stopped and stared at him. "What is that even supposed to mean?"

He glanced away. "I don't know. I think I was just trying to say I agree with you." He rubbed the back of his neck and then peeked at her again. "It's like when you make a mistake and you have to own up to it. You do it in the way you can handle. Maybe Shane knew he wouldn't be able to see you face-to-face without it breaking him."

"*I'm* broken. *He* broke *me!*" She resumed her pacing. "We were in a relationship, but the only people who knew were you and my sister. I can't even talk about this with anyone else because no one would believe me, or they'd say Shane was a terrible human being."

Marc didn't say anything. His lack of response caught her off guard, but she shoved the concern aside.

She continued, "Shane isn't a bad guy. He's the nicest person I know. He's helped so many people."

"Nice people can be bad boyfriends, you know," Marc said quietly.

"That's just it. I don't feel like he was a bad boyfriend either. Shane was thoughtful, and he made me laugh. He opened up to me." Her voice grew softer with each thing she said. "I think I loved him, Marc."

Heat filled her face and the tears started again, only this time they were embarrassed tears. She covered her face with her hands and let out a groan. "I can't believe I let this happen."

"You didn't let anything happen, Eloise."

"You sound just like my sister," she said. "And I didn't let her talk me out of this either. I know I should have done more. I should have gone straight to his work and talked to him that day when he messaged me. Now he's got his office locked, and he's got his secretary screening his calls and personal appointments." The tears increased. Each time she blinked another one spilled down her cheek.

Marc moved toward her, crossing the dirt to pull her into his arms. She resisted at first, unwilling or unable to allow herself any comfort her heart longed for. But Marc persisted. His arms were secure around her, holding her tight. He didn't say anything, but he didn't have to.

Simply being there was enough to stop the tears from falling.

She lost track of how long they stood like that. Eventually, when she pulled away from him, he allowed her to have her space. Eloise let out a watery laugh. "I'm sorry, you probably have zero interest in hearing about my love life."

"It's fine. Like I told you before. Your friendship is important to me. I'm gonna be here in whatever capacity you need me to be."

Eloise waved off his hand and laughed again as she wiped her own face. "I'm such a mess right now. I can't imagine anyone would want to be my friend at the moment."

"Well, that's where you're wrong. I'd be your friend if you were covered in mud like those pigs at the barn."

She laughed again, and this time it sounded more genuine. "I'd wager their company would be preferable to mine."

Marc shook his head. "Not a chance. You are worthy of love."

Her eyes widened, unsure of how to react to that.

"You are. Just because one guy messed up doesn't mean that you aren't allowed to find it again. You are the most amazing woman I know. And I need you to believe that."

Chills rolled off her as she stared into his eyes. What was she supposed to say to that? Was he hitting on her? No. They'd talked about it before, and he knew how much she loved Shane. She couldn't even think about opening her heart again after what Shane had done.

Her heart still belonged to him, but for how long, she didn't know. At this point she couldn't see a reality where she would ever stop loving Shane. He was the one she wanted to be with for the rest of her life.

Eloise looked at Marc. "I want you to know that I appreciate you. Just listening to me today has been really nice."

"Sorry I couldn't be more help."

Eloise snorted. "What more could you do? It's not like you know what's going through Shane's head, right?"

Something flashed across his face. It was short, but she could have sworn she saw an emotion that might have given her some information if she'd been more diligent. Her eyes narrowed as she studied him, wondering if it would appear again. But then Marc looked away. He took a few steps back and then turned away from her. "I don't know Shane nearly as well as I would like. He barely tolerates my sister and me."

She recalled Shane had mentioned something to that effect. Marc was capable of nefarious stuff. Still, she couldn't see it. Marc had been nothing but sweet and supportive.

Perhaps she needed to accept that not everything was as it appeared. There were still things that she would never understand or figure out.

And Shane's relationship with his cousins was one of those things.

23

The country club was filled to the brim with locals and people that Madeline had insisted Shane invite for a soiree. She'd pulled out all the stops, hiring an out-of-town caterer as well as a country music group. She'd insisted this was her way of introducing herself to Copper Creek.

Whatever kept her busy was fine by him. He just wanted her out of his hair while he tried to come up with everything he needed to put in his part of their contract.

"You look absolutely terrible."

Shane turned toward the person speaking, but he already knew that voice. Brielle was dressed in a black dress that clung to her frame and accentuated it perfectly. He had been waiting for this to happen. He knew better than to believe Eloise would keep this from the only sister who knew about their relationship. "Thanks," he muttered.

"No, seriously. I have never seen you look so... like you've been hit by a train."

He sighed.

"Make that fifty trains," she added.

"I get it, Brielle. You don't have to rub it in."

She reached for a glass of champagne from a tray that floated by on a waiter's hand. "Um, that's where you're wrong. Don't you understand? You broke my sister's heart. For that fact alone, I will do everything in my power to make your life miserable."

He glanced at her, no energy to utter a single argument. He was already miserable and he deserved every second of it. He was taking this cosmic punishment with as much grace as he could muster.

"What? Cat got your tongue? What is *wrong* with you? I *told* you not to fall in love with her. I *told* you to leave her alone after you got Marc away from her. But I guess the joke's on me because Marc is still hanging around like a bad cough."

Shane stiffened. His pulse quickened as he let this realization wash over him. Marc was supposed to leave Eloise alone. Madeline had assured him that they wouldn't have anything to do with the Callahans after he'd agreed to give her half of everything. He worked his jaw, his eyes scanning the room until they landed on Madeline.

His future business partner stood in a group of prominent ranchers, laughing and visiting like she belonged here. That vile woman was the symbol of everything he hated, and if Eloise wasn't caught up in the crossfire, he would have gone all scorched earth on her.

"Shane. I'm *speaking* to you."

"I'm sorry, Brielle, but I'm not in the mood." He raked a hand through his already mussed hair, praying he wouldn't run into Eloise at this event. Everyone, including the Callahans, was invited. Brielle was the first he'd seen of the lot.

Even while he prayed Eloise wasn't in attendance, he searched for her. His gaze scanned the entire ballroom, and a mixture of relief and anguish filled his stomach when he didn't find her.

Good. If she wasn't here, then she wouldn't have to deal with Madeline. He wouldn't be surprised if she had something up her sleeve when it came to messing with the woman he loved. Brielle could hold her own. It was Eloise he was worried for.

He moved through the crowd, darting in and out of groups, avoiding speaking to anyone. Brielle was right. He hadn't gotten any sleep since he'd sent that text message to Eloise, and that was two weeks ago.

On top of his terrible sleeping habits, he had lost his appetite and had already dropped ten pounds. His only saving grace was that his businesses were practically running themselves. He had hired excellent people who were great at running the basic operations.

Shane found a quiet, dark corner where he could nurse a drink with a slightly higher alcohol content than the champagne that everyone else was enjoying. He swirled the two fingers' worth of whiskey, staring at the liquid for a moment before glancing around the room again. On the one hand, he wanted to drown his sorrows. He needed more than something that would just take the edge off. He needed sleep. And he needed to drown his sorrows.

Yet again, Madeline was the problem. She wouldn't hesitate a single second to take advantage of him if he were to become inebriated. He could ask himself if there was anything more she could take from him, but he knew the answer to that question already.

She could always take more. That was Madeline's specialty.

"Mind if I join you?"

Shane's narrowed eyes landed on Marc, and he sneered at

him. "What? Are you here to rub it in? Let me guess. You've come to gloat about Madeline getting what she always wanted and now you can swoop in and take Eloise. Well, she's smarter than that. She's—"

"I know."

He snapped his mouth shut. What did Marc mean by that?

Marc eyed his glass. "Can I have one of those?"

Shane glanced down at the whiskey in his hand and then shoved it toward his cousin. "I probably shouldn't be drinking anyway."

Marc lifted the tumbler before taking a swig. "Eloise *is* something else. She's more of a person than I will ever deserve to have as a friend."

Shane scoffed. "She's more of a person than any of us deserve."

"No argument there."

"Then why aren't you leaving her alone?"

Marc was quiet for longer than Shane anticipated. The more seconds that ticked by, the more antsy he became. He itched to grab his cousin and throw him to the ground. That would be just the thing to get some of the fury out of his system. Only he couldn't do that. This was his business. It had his name on it. He couldn't exactly start a brawl where everyone would see and inevitably wonder if they should continue to support him.

Shane shook his head. "Forget it. You're just like your sister."

"I'm nothing like her!"

He snorted. "You're more like her than you might want to admit." Shane moved to walk away in search of yet another place where he could hide, but Marc's hand on his shoulder stopped him.

"I'm *not* like Madeline," he repeated. "She's..." He shook his head. Conflicting emotions crossed over Marc's face. Anger, sadness, and fear. "Maybe you're right." His voice sounded so disheartened that Shane nearly felt bad for him.

That was ridiculous. The only thing that made sense was that Marc was *in* on this whole thing. He was *part* of the problem. "I don't have the energy to fight you, Marc. If you're here to spy on me, you can tell Madeline—"

"I'm not."

Once again, Shane didn't know what to say.

"I'm just... maybe I'm tired of Madeline's shenanigans too."

"I doubt that," Shane huffed.

"You don't have to believe me. I wouldn't expect you to. I'm... I'm sorry that I played a part in any of this."

Shane moved out from under his cousin's grasp. "Enjoy your drink." He turned around and blindly made his way toward his office. He couldn't stand being in here pretending that everything was going well when he felt his life crumbling around him.

He collided with someone, and instinctively his hands shot out to grab onto her to prevent her from falling backward.

Big mistake.

Eloise peered up at him, surprise and pain emanating from her eyes. If he could have been struck down by some invisible force, he would have chosen this exact moment to pray it would happen.

"Eloise..."

She held up a hand, shaking her head. "I don't want to hear it. I don't even know why I came. Brielle convinced me I should, and this... this was a big mistake."

He grasped her wrist, tugging it down so he could get a better view of her face. "Eloise, I want to explain."

"You had plenty of time to do that before tonight. Do you know how many times I tried reaching out to you? To call you? To see you?" Her voice shook. "I had *wanted* you to explain yourself. I thought I would have been okay with whatever you might have said, but I was wrong."

"It's not what you think," he pleaded. "I did it to save you from—"

"You wanted to *save* me?" Eloise's bark of laughter drew the attention of some of his guests. A few of them even noticed the way he was still holding her wrist in his grasp. Already, he could predict the sort of things they might whisper when they thought he wasn't paying attention. "If you wanted to save me, you wouldn't have made me fall in—"

"Attention, everyone!" Madeline clinked her champagne flute with a spoon, and the whole room grew eerily quiet. Her eyes met Shane's for just a second, but that was all it took. This was it. There was no going back once Madeline made the announcement.

Shane reached for both of Eloise's hands. "I need you to come with me. Now."

"I'd like to take this moment to thank each and every one of you for coming tonight. As you might have guessed, this isn't an ordinary party."

Eloise's eyes were locked on his cousin, much like every single guest in that room. It wouldn't matter if he got her to listen to him. He wouldn't be able to get her out of that room before Madeline did whatever it was she planned on doing.

"Shane. Please come here." She reached her hand toward him, and he froze. Eloise locked her eyes with his, confusion the only clear thing he could read from her. He gave a subtle shake of his head, and Madeline laughed. "It would appear our host is a little shy tonight. No matter, I'd like to take this time to share a little story with you. My aunt and uncle were unable to conceive, though they truly wanted a child of their own. Luckily, they were able to find a lovely young woman who needed to put her baby up for adoption. That baby was Shane. He was lucky enough to be welcomed into our family, and no one is more grateful than I am." Her dark gaze seemed to latch onto him, locking him in place. "Because after all these years, we have found that we have a mutual interest."

Shane released Eloise's hands and took a step toward Madeline, but he was too late.

"Shane? What's going on?" Eloise said quietly beside him.

Madeline let her gaze sweep through the room. "You have all been so welcoming to Shane. He's found a new family here. And I hope to be part of that family as well when we become business partners as soon as the paperwork is signed."

He waited for the moment when the room would ripple with gasps of shock or stone-cold silence, but it didn't come. Instead, those around him clapped politely. A few even raised their glasses toward him.

He spun around to find Eloise, but she had disappeared. Shane stood tall, still searching for the woman he needed to speak to most. Eloise needed to know what had really happened. He didn't know if she'd listen to him or even forgive him, but he had to try.

A strong hand wrapped around his forearm, dragging him backward through the crowd. It wasn't until they had slipped away from the waves of people that Shane got a good look at who had rescued him.

Tristan scowled at him, his arms crossed. "What have you done?"

"What have *I* done?" Shane jabbed a finger toward the way they'd come. "Do you honestly think I had anything to do with that? She has me over a barrel."

His friend didn't look convinced. "The last time we spoke, you said you had a plan. What happened to that?"

Shane paced through the quiet hallway, raking both hands through his hair. "I don't know. Things just got away from me."

"You *think*? Geez, Shane. You and I both knew how far Madeline could take this—"

"Really?" Shane shot back. "You think I could have predicted *this*? She's gone completely mad. And I don't have any choice but to let it happen."

Tristan stared at him, mouth gaping. "What do you mean you don't have a choice. She doesn't have a loaded gun to your head, does she?"

Shane slowed, turning to face Tristan. His wife would soon be caught up in this fiasco as well. There was so much at stake here. The only option he could see would be to sell everything and move away, taking Madeline as far as he could from Copper Creek. Deep down, he knew that Madeline wouldn't stop with him. She'd do whatever it took to get her hands on everything. She'd be the next corrupt politician running the town if she had her way.

"I can't stay here," he said as he brushed past his best friend. "I need to make arrangements so that I can leave here and take her with me."

"You're not making any sense, Shane. You can't just leave."

"Why not?" Shane spun to face him again. "She's here because of me. She wants my money and power. I'm not going to let her control this place and bleed it dry like I know she is fully capable of doing. I refuse to be the cause of this town's destruction."

Tristan grabbed his arm again, stopping him from storming off. "Then what? She'll just do what she does in the next town and the next. What does she even have over you?"

Shane glowered at Tristan. "Let go."

"Not until you tell me what's going on."

"It's not my secret to tell. Madeline is just lucky she found someone to threaten that I also cared about enough to protect.

She's not going to stop. Now, let go so I can find Eloise. I need to tell her I'm sorry."

Tristan released him, holding both of his hands up. "You don't want to do that."

"Why not? Has she said something to Dianna?"

"No. But from the sounds of it, you made a clean break. Why hurt her even more by stretching this out?" Tristan made a good point. There was only one problem.

Even if Shane couldn't explain everything, he needed to at least tell her goodbye. He couldn't leave without apologizing for how he ended things. At this point, he figured she probably wouldn't want to see him anyway. This was a last-ditch effort. Soon he'd be gone, and he knew he wouldn't be able to live with himself if he didn't at least try to mend a few bridges before he left.

24

Eloise

Eloise climbed out of her father's truck and slammed the door a little too hard before storming toward the house. She was an emotional wreck. This wasn't how everything was supposed to go. When her father had relinquished his hold on their dating lives, they were all supposed to find the men who would be there for them until the end.

She'd naively thought that person was Shane.

Eloise couldn't have been more wrong.

Shane was just as terrible as Brielle had said he was, and Eloise had been a fool for thinking otherwise. She should have never gone to that party. It was a stupid decision that had been misguided from the beginning. It was too hard seeing Shane again.

Of course she was going to run into Shane. He owned the place. She slipped down onto the porch step and buried her face in her hands.

All this rational thought did nothing to ease the pain she felt inside. She just wanted to go up to her bed, form a cocoon and wait for her feelings for Shane to be over with before she emerged again.

Headlights flashed up the hill, and she let out a sigh. Brielle had likely left early because of her. Now she was ruining the night for people she cared about.

Maybe if she could muster the energy to go inside before Brielle parked, she wouldn't have to listen to her sister tell her that she'd dodged a bullet.

Because that was the last thing she wanted to hear in this very moment.

Her eyes narrowed and she got to her feet. That wasn't Brielle's truck. It was Shane's.

Nope.

She wasn't going to do this tonight. She'd already had to handle the party. She wasn't about to put herself through additional torture in order to alleviate the guilt Shane was probably drowning in. Or maybe he had zero guilt, and he was just coming to tell her this was her fault.

That thought gave her a fresh surge of energy, and rather than head inside, she stormed toward his car as he put it into park. She didn't know what she was going to say or do, but that didn't matter. Her whole body hummed with an energy that needed to be released, and if she didn't do it soon, she could combust.

Shane stepped out of the car and closed the door. He hovered there, not moving, and she came to a halt about six feet away from him. "Eloise, I—"

"No. I don't want to hear it," she rasped. "It's my turn now. You've had your chance to explain."

He closed his mouth with resignation. They were bathed in the light from the porch as the evening grew darker, but she could still see that he was hurting. She couldn't for the life of her understand why he might be so upset other than the fact that his reputation was at stake. If she really wanted to, she could spread some nasty rumors about his heartbreaking ways.

Eloise crossed her arms tight over her chest, hating how much she wanted to throw herself into his arms and feel his warm body against hers. She still craved him—his comfort, his strength, all of him.

Hot tears threatened to escape from behind her eyes, but she refused to let them come. Shutting them tight, she gathered her thoughts. "Is it true?"

"Eloise..." his voice broke.

"Is it true?" she demanded again. "You don't love me anymore?"

The way he set his jaw as he looked away gave her everything she needed. With that reaction alone, her heart crumbled. She'd barely been able to hold it together for the last few weeks. This was the thing that finally broke her.

Eloise's voice filled with despair. "This was what you were hiding from me." She scowled through her pain.

Shane opened his mouth, but she held up a hand. "It makes a lot of sense—the way you were acting. You didn't want anyone to know of our relationship. You did everything you could think of to keep it quiet. You were just competing for my attention against Marc."

"It's not what you think—"

Her lips curled into a sneer. "I don't know whether or not to hate you or him more."

Shane's head snapped up as she stopped directly in front of him. She attempted to read him, to see if he would give her anything that might make this situation better.

Those eyes she'd fallen in love with remained guarded. The set of his jaw was hard, and his body tense.

"Did you ever love me?" She didn't think it was possible, but Shane's whole body tensed even more. The muscles in his face twitched. "Well? Don't just stand there. Spit it out. Tell me exactly what it was you came here to say." Her voice shook with the emotion that had made a sudden return.

"Eloise," he murmured, "I wish I could tell you—"

"Oh no, you don't. We're not doing that. I asked you a question, and I deserve an honest answer. Either tell me what I need to know or get back in your car and run away like the coward you are."

His eyes darkened, consumed by a haze of something she didn't recognize. "You want to know the truth? I'll tell you the truth." Shane stepped within inches of her, his eyes piercing into hers so she couldn't make an escape if she wanted to. His voice dropped to a whisper. "Life isn't perfect, Eloise. There is no cut-and-dried way to deal with the stuff that it dishes out. You might think you know where your decisions will take you, and then you're knocked to the ground with something you didn't expect."

Eloise glowered at him. "That's a lot of talk when all I wanted was a simple answer."

Silence hung in the air between them, sending chills down her spine until she couldn't take it any longer. "That's what I thought," she snapped. "You're nothing but a coward." Eloise spun from him and stalked toward the house.

"Eloise," he called out.

The despair in his voice was so strong that she turned around.

"I didn't want it to end like this. I didn't want us to end at all."

The last bit of her heart shattered, taking with it any decorum she had left. How could he say that if he wasn't in love with her? Instead of running toward the house, Eloise made her escape to the barn. She needed to get out of there—somewhere Shane wouldn't come after her.

"Eloise! Wait!"

Tears streamed down her cheeks, but she ignored them, setting to work saddling her horse. It was late, but she knew this place like the back of her hand. There was a hunting cabin not too far past the fields where the animals grazed. She'd be able to lick her wounds there.

Eloise saddled her horse faster than she'd ever done in her life, and in no time she was flying down the trails that would take her to her sanctuary. Branches clawed at her, tugging at the dress she hadn't changed out of yet. Her hair fell from the style where she'd pinned it and now flew freely around her face. The only light guiding her was that of the full moon, but it was more than enough.

By the time she made it to the small cabin, her tears had stopped falling, but the skin on her face felt tight and itchy. It wouldn't have been possible to cry a single drop more. She'd shed the last tear she ever would over Shane Owens.

Eloise slipped from her horse and tied the mare up to a post in front of the cabin. She hunted around for the hide-a-key and eventually got inside the building. Then she collapsed on the sofa and stared with a daze toward the dark, cold fireplace.

She thought she might just curl up and fall asleep when there was a knock on the door. Immediately, her heart raced. No one knew she was out here. Shane was good with horses, but even he wouldn't dare follow her out here, would he?

Slowly, she got up from the couch and inched toward the door. Right beside it hung a repeating rifle on the wall. Someone who wanted to do her harm probably wouldn't bother with knocking, but she'd been taught better than to believe everyone was on the right side of things.

Eloise grabbed the gun, checked to see if it was loaded, then leaned up against the wall beside the door. "Who is it?"

"Marc."

"What in the world—" She pried open the door and stared at Marc, dumbfounded. "How did you find me? Why are you here?" She shook her head. "Were you *spying* on me?"

"What? No, of course not."

She glanced over his shoulder and spotted an ATV. How had she not heard him coming?

"What are you doing here?" she asked.

Marc rubbed the back of his neck, then shifted so he could peer inside. "Could I come in? I'll explain everything."

She stepped aside, allowing him entrance, then shut the door. "How did you even know about this place?"

He chuckled. "After buying that property out by the country club, I thought it might be a good idea to learn how to handle a hunting rifle." His focus shifted to the one she held. "Your father was willing to show me a thing or two, and we came out here once."

"My fath—" She shook her head. "No. My dad wouldn't have done that."

"Maybe not for free. But he was willing to take a pretty penny from me." He gestured toward the couch. "Mind if I sit?"

She nodded, then returned the gun to the wall.

"Anyway, I showed up just as you were leaving, and Shane—"

Eloise scowled at him. "I don't want to hear anything you have to say about Shane. He's shown his true colors, and I just want him out of my life."

"You really shouldn't be so hard on him," Marc said.

"Oh? Why's that?" Eloise remained standing, unwilling to allow Marc to talk her out of how she was feeling. She needed to let the fury burn through her—to scorch everything bad that had happened so the way she felt about Shane didn't come back even stronger.

"Because it's not his fault." Marc sighed. "It's really hard to talk to you about this when you're over there. Can you just... I really shouldn't even be talking about this at all." Marc jumped to his feet and paced in front of the couch. "If Madeline knew—" He snapped his mouth shut and then stared at her, pain emanating from his gaze. "Madeline is manipulating Shane. She found out something about your family—I'm not sure what—and threatened to tell everyone. It's gotta be pretty bad because Shane agreed to give Madeline fifty percent of his business and break up with you, even though he can't stand her."

He stopped his pacing and blew out a long breath.

Eloise couldn't move. She had so many questions, and at the same time, she didn't want to believe a single word he'd said. Her heart fluttered and heat rushed to her face. "What are you saying?"

"I'm saying that Shane is only trying to protect you from my sister. I'm really sorry."

"Why are you telling me this? I thought you and your sister were close." It was so much harder to find her voice than she thought. Each word took great effort to produce.

Marc moved closer to her, small step by small step. "Because I realized that I don't want to enable her anymore. She's not the kind of person I want to be around." He rubbed one arm and looked away. "It's like I said. I admire you, Eloise. You're a good person. I'm not willing to let Madeline hurt you like this. You deserved to know."

She shook her head vehemently. "No. That's not good enough. You can't just come here and drop a bomb like that. We can't let her get away with this. Shane doesn't deserve this either."

Marc's expression faltered. "You don't know her like I do. She's not going to go down easy."

"You've got to know something that could help. We can't just sit around and do nothing."

He glanced at her once more, and she was taken aback by the anguish she read in his eyes. "You're right. I think I know what I have to do."

25

Shane

A full week and Shane hadn't heard from Eloise or anyone in her family. He had half-expected Zeke Callahan to come by his office and demand to know what was going on. But then he reminded himself that the man likely had no clue about their relationship.

The relief from knowing he wouldn't be getting a visit from the most intimidating man in town was overshadowed by everything else he had to deal with.

He sat in his office chair, trying to focus on his work, but that was proving impossible with Madeline pacing while speaking to someone on her Bluetooth device.

"I don't care how you do it. You're going to make it happen." She glanced in his direction. Oh, how he wished he could wipe that smug smile off her face.

It didn't matter how many times he ran the scenarios in his head; they always came out wrong. He wasn't going to be able to stop Madeline. She'd started this train and had it going full steam ahead. Any feet-dragging on his end would prove disastrous.

Madeline got off the phone and pulled the Bluetooth from her ear. "Can you believe it? These people are acting like we can't completely destroy them with a snap of our fingers. They need to get it in their heads that money is power."

He pinched the bridge of his nose and took a calming breath. "I'm not going to help you ruin anyone, Madeline. You can't just expect people to fall in line because you wave a wad of cash in their faces."

She pouted, wandering toward him, around his desk, then sitting on it beside him. Her fingertip trailed along the desk and tapped a few times. Her fingernails were like the talons of the birds of prey he saw on those nature documentaries as a kid.

Shane flinched from the closeness, and she leaned down closer to his ear. "You'll do everything I say or suffer the consequences." She pulled back as she let out a laugh. "When are you going to understand that I own you? And all because you don't want your precious little friends to have their feelings hurt."

He pushed out his chair, shooting to his feet. His mind went blank. Anything he might have said would only rile her up more. All he could do was glower at her as he took his jacket from the hook and stormed toward the door.

"Where are you going, Shane? You can't run from me," she called after him. "I know this place pretty well now. You can't hide either."

Oh yes, he could. He might not be able to find sanctuary on his own property or with the woman he loved, but he could clear his head at one ranch where Madeline wouldn't find him.

∽

SHANE PULLED up to the Keagan property and shut off his car. He stared at the house that still looked like it needed a lot of work done. Brielle had done so much already, and it was definitely improving, but it would be another while yet before it was brought back to its former glory.

After Madeline had made her announcement at that party, most of the people in town appeared uncomfortable around him. They didn't seem angry. It was more like confusion as to why he would bring in another stranger to Copper Creek. They had just started to accept *him*.

Whatever. He'd lost the most important thing in his life already. And going forward, he'd make sure he didn't spend time with the folks in town so he could keep them shielded from Madeline's devious nature.

Wade was one person he hadn't seen at the party. That didn't mean he hadn't heard the news. In fact, Shane was positive everyone in this town and the surrounding ones knew about the local billionaire and his over-the-top new business partner. More importantly, had Brielle told Wade that he'd broken up with Eloise? Shane just couldn't be sure how Wade would react. If he walked up to that front door and asked to borrow a horse, it could go one of several different ways.

The man might laugh at him or treat him with his usual barely veiled disdain. Either way, it was going to be better than having to sit in the same building as Madeline.

Shane climbed out of his car, shutting the door behind him before heading for the house. The property was quieter than he'd expected. The Keagan family had twelve children. Normally, he would have expected to see at least a few of them wandering the property. The older ones were supposedly working the ranch, but it wasn't unusual to see children as young as eight pulling their own weight.

The front door of the house banged open, and Shane got his

first good look at the wrong side of a shotgun. He stumbled back a few steps, but his shoe caught on a rock and he fell onto his backside. Wade held the gun up to his face, his eyes flashing with fury.

"I didn't think you'd be stupid enough to show up here after what you did to that poor Callahan girl."

Shane held up his hands. "I didn't do anything to her."

Wade snorted. "You city folk are all the same. You think you can toy with people and get away with it."

"I wasn't *using* her. This wasn't how any of it was supposed to go."

Folks thought Zeke Callahan was scary, but they hadn't come face-to-face with Wade Keagan. This was a man everyone should think twice about crossing. Shane couldn't wrap his head around how Wade was acting. It wasn't like he'd been dating Eloise. He'd been interested in Brielle last Shane had heard.

Shane scrambled backward so he could get to his feet and move away from the madman with a gun. "I swear, the only reason this is happening is because I'm trying to protect her. No one knows just how bad Madeline can be."

Confusion blended with the fury in Wade's eyes. "If she's so bad, then why are you making her your business partner?"

Wasn't it obvious? Madeline equaled bad. She was forcing his hand. Shane cleared his throat and gestured toward the gun that was still pointed at him. "Do you mind?"

"Yeah, I do."

He raked a hand through his hair. "It doesn't matter. The point is, I don't want her here any more than anyone else does. But she's got me over a barrel—sorta like you." He nodded toward the gun again. "I'm stuck. She's got... information."

"So spill it before she does. It takes away her power."

Shane swallowed hard. "It's not that easy. She's got information about—" He caught himself before he gave away too much information. He couldn't share Brielle's secret, especially not with Wade. He wasn't afraid that Wade would gossip about it. It was more of a concern regarding the relationship that might be growing between the two.

It wasn't his secret to spill.

Wade gave him a pointed look. "She's got information about what?"

Clearing his throat did nothing to release the bulge lodged there. "Madeline has stuff on the Callahans."

Wade's brows shot up like a rocket. The neutral color of his skin burst with color and his eyes darkened. "That little..." His eyes darted to Shane, and he lowered his gun. "So what are you gonna do about it?"

Shane shrugged. "What can I do? If I don't make her my partner and keep away from Eloise, she's going to spill every detail she has."

"You need leverage."

"Don't you think I've thought of that?" Shane said. He leaned against his car and folded his arms. "I've gone over everything in my head more than once. I can't sleep. I can't eat. I'm stuck in my own personal purgatory with no way out."

Wade moved toward him. "Well, you can't just let her hold that over your head. What happens if one day she decides she doesn't care anymore and she spills everything out of spite."

Shane shook his head. "She wouldn't do that. I've got it built into our contract. If she does, she's liable for millions. It's mutually assured destruction. I'm the ball and chain she's attaching herself to, and if she hurts the people I care about, she's going to drown, too."

"You really must love her."

Shane's head snapped up. "I *despise* her."

"No, *Eloise*. For you to sacrifice your own happiness just to keep this information private..." He let out a sigh. "Sheesh, man. Does she know?"

"What? Of course not. I couldn't tell her that. First of all, Eloise isn't your typical woman. She wouldn't want me to sacrifice anything for her. It's not in her nature. Secondly, she's not talking to me. So, it doesn't matter anyway."

Although clad in dusty jeans and a ripped T-shirt, this man probably had the most profound thing to say. "You can't do that to her. Not telling her is just as bad as stepping aside and letting your cousin destroy lives. You're not just sacrificing your happiness, but you're sacrificing hers too."

Shane snorted. "Somehow, I don't—"

"Shut up for a second and listen to me."

He snapped his mouth shut.

"I might not know much about your relationship other than what I was able to observe when you demanded my help. But even I could see that she cared about you. Whether or not you go through with the deal—which is a load of bull, by the way—you need to tell Eloise. You're at a fork in the road. If you keep this from her, you'll forever wonder *what if*. Perhaps it's not a secret you could tell, but it might be one she could bring to light and take all the power away from Madeline. It's worth a shot, right?"

Chills coursed through Shane's body. While Wade's point was a good one, it wouldn't be up to Eloise to come forward. And it wasn't Shane's place to talk to Brielle about any of this. He'd made his bed, and he was prepared to lie in it.

He just needed to try once more to tell Eloise goodbye.

THE FIRST CAR Shane noticed on the Callahan property was his cousin's. Marc was there. The anguish that had been ruminating in his stomach roiled and churned until it was poisoned by rage.

How dare Marc come here, to this home, and pretend everything was okay?

Shane shot out of his car and charged toward the house. He might not have been willing to beat his cousin to a bloody pulp before all of this had happened, but he was ready now. He'd break every bone in his hands if he had to in order to get his point across.

Before he got to the door, it opened and three people materialized on the porch. Shane's focus immediately zoned in on Marc despite him being flanked by Brielle and Eloise.

The only thing that surprised him was that he couldn't see any animosity in his cousin's eyes. If anything, he read pure contriteness.

Shane slowed as he reached the bottom of the steps and then came to a complete stop. His eyes bounced from Marc to Brielle and finally to Eloise.

The anger he'd expected to see reflected in the girls' eyes was absent. Neither one of them seemed prepared to tear out his throat like they had been the last time he saw them. Something had changed. Did they know? Had Marc come clean?

He couldn't dare hope. It wasn't in Marc's nature to turn his back on his sister. "What's going on?" Shane said. "Why are you here, Marc?"

The three exchanged nervous glances then Eloise stepped forward. "Marc told us everything."

Shane's eyes darted to Brielle. "Everything?"

"Everything I know," Marc offered. "Madeline is still keeping some stuff from me, but I get the gist of it. She forced you to break up with Eloise to keep you in a weakened state so that it would be easier for her to force you to become her business partner. Plus she's threatening to spill secrets of people in town—specifically the Callahans."

Actually, it was strictly about Brielle.

Unless it wasn't. It could be more people.

For Pete's sake. Now he had to worry about more than the one family he cared about.

"It's really sweet of you to be willing to help, but you don't need—" Eloise started.

Brielle shook her head. "Don't say that. We need to know what we're up against. We have to know the secret so we can decide how to move forward." Her eyes locked with Shane's. She didn't seem terribly nervous. Was it possible that she thought the blackmail was regarding someone else?

"*Brielle*," Eloise admonished. "We talked about this. If Shane hasn't come to us about it, then it must not be about us. What if it's about Dad and his business dealings?"

"That's the point," Brielle said. "I don't know about you, but I would rather not be surprised in the future if something comes out that could destroy our family business." Her eyes found Shane's again. "I don't want to risk losing something my family has worked years to attain."

Shane shook his head. "It's not something that would ruin your ranch."

"So what is it?" she demanded.

"Brielle, seriously! Curiosity killed the cat. We're not going to have Shane tell us because we've got a plan," Eloise said.

"You do?" Shane blurted.

26

Eloise

Eloise smiled softly at the man she knew without a doubt that she loved. This was a man who had been willing to offer up his happiness and his freedom to save her family from whatever gossip Madeline had dug up.

It didn't matter *what* the secret was. If Madeline and Shane thought it was enough to put the Callahans in a sticky situation, then she trusted that Shane had made the decision that would best keep them safe. She made it to the bottom step so her eyes were level with Shane's. Placing her hand against his cheek, she tilted her head. "When Marc told me about what you had done, I knew we couldn't just let Madeline get away with it. We needed to come up with something that would bring her down once and for all."

Shane shifted so he could look behind her, presumably at his cousin. "I've already tried coming up with something. I've racked my brain for anything that would be enough to blackmail her with, just to level the playing field. There's nothing."

Brielle sighed. "We're not gonna blackmail her. That just assumes that she wouldn't go to the authorities and claim we planted stuff on her."

He brought his gaze back to Marc. "So you actually have stuff you can plant on her?" There was no hiding the hope he had in his voice. Eloise could easily have imagined that he'd been so resigned to losing everything he cared about that even the smallest prospect of being able to fix this had bolstered him somehow.

Marc looked down at his feet, and Eloise felt a small degree of pain for him. He'd been through a lot with his sister. It wasn't really fair for him to have to do what it would take to bring her down.

Eloise framed Shane's face in her hands and forced him to look at her. "Marc is going to tell you some things, and you have to keep an open mind." She took a deep, shuddering breath, still unable to imagine the courage it was going to take on Marc's side to do what they had discussed. Then she glanced over her shoulder toward him. "Go ahead, Marc. Tell Shane."

Marc shifted his weight from one foot to the other. His right fist bounced against his right leg. All eyes were on him, and for a moment, she didn't know if he would have the courage to go through with it. But then he lifted his head and met Shane's gaze. "Madeline is a criminal."

Shane snorted, and Eloise shot a warning look at him. If this was going to work, they'd need Shane's help.

Marc swallowed hard. "If she finds out—"

"It's okay, Marc. Shane isn't going to turn you in."

Shane glanced at her with surprise but then swiveled his focus back to his cousin.

"We all know Madeline has an enormous amount of greed. She's never been happy with just getting what she wants. She does things without thinking most of the time, only caring about how it will get her more money or more power. There's a lot of stuff we could pin on her, but I've only got proof of the tax evasion and money laundering."

Eloise could sense Shane stiffening beside her more than she could see it.

"You've got actual proof?"

Marc nodded. "Emails. A paper trail. We only got the ranch because she needed a way to launder money she was getting from some politicians in DC."

Shane sucked in sharply and made a move to step forward, but Eloise blocked him. He peered over her shoulder. "And you're just now telling me this?"

"Shane," she said. "This was Marc's idea. Let him finish." The anger had returned to Shane's eyes, and she wasn't sure he would be on board with what Marc wanted to do.

Marc's expression crumpled. "If I come forward to out her, I'm going to be arrested, too. I'm not completely innocent in any of this."

"You *think*?" Shane snapped. "You're just as guilty as she is. I have zero empathy for you."

His cousin flinched.

"*Shane!*" This time it was both Brielle and Eloise who scolded him.

Eloise blocked his view of Marc. "We don't have a plan without Marc. And we wouldn't even have a chance at getting rid of Madeline if Marc wasn't willing to come forward. If we want this to work, we need your help too."

His brows creased. "What do you need *me* to do? Sounds like you have all the information you need to go to the police."

Marc shook his head. "If Madeline gets even a whiff of this

happening, she'll be in the wind. We need the top dogs. Didn't you go to college with some lady who is in the FBI?"

Shane didn't move for what felt like an eternity. "You're serious," he finally said.

"Yeah," Marc said. "I'm serious. Madeline needs to know she can't mess with Eloise." Marc glanced toward her and offered her a sad smile. "We all need to get out from under her influence." He really was a sweetheart. It was just too bad that he'd been wrapped up in all of this.

Shane's jaw tightened, and his hand reached out to grasp Eloise's. She looked down at where he held her, and her latent feelings came back to life with a vengeance. The sparks of electricity, the shivers, the desire. He brought her hand to his lips, his eyes locking with hers before he turned toward Marc. "Yeah, I have a friend in the FBI."

"Do you think she would be willing to help us out? Get Madeline out of our hair?" Eloise asked.

Shane glanced from one person to the next. "I think we could figure something out. I'll have to make a few calls."

Relief washed over her like the first rainfall in summer, warm and refreshing. She finally allowed herself to regain the hope she'd been so desperately needing since he'd broken up with her.

Shane moved up the steps toward Marc and Brielle. "You're really willing to throw yourself under the bus if it means getting Madeline arrested? That doesn't sound like you at all. What's the catch?"

Eloise nearly slugged him. She could understand to a degree why he wasn't willing to trust Marc easily, but he'd already given a lot of information. He'd already risked a lot by just telling Shane. Before she could point any of that out, Marc stepped forward.

He lifted his chin and stared Shane in the eyes. "All my life, I've been stuck in Madeline's shadow. Doing whatever she says.

Then I met Eloise, who's the first person to see something potentially good in me. She's the first real friend I've ever had. I can't let her life of happiness with you be threatened."

Marc avoided looking directly at her as he continued. "If that means I have to go to prison because I was involved with some of my sister's dealings, then so be it."

Shane shifted, and Eloise squeezed his hand reassuringly. He glanced at her, a hint of a smile touching his lips. "I'll make a few phone calls and see what we can do. I can't make any promises, but even if Madeline decides to go on the run, then the worst thing that would happen is that she spills those secrets. I suppose we could figure out what to do with that when the time comes."

"Thanks, Shane," Marc said. "I know we haven't been on the best terms, but I appreciate it."

"Hey, I'm not the one going to prison."

Marc grimaced. "I guess that's true." He glanced at Eloise. "I'll see you tomorrow?"

Shane's hand tightened on hers almost painfully, but he didn't say anything.

Eloise nodded. "I'll see you tomorrow."

He moved past them and headed for his car. Once he was out of sight, Brielle sighed. "Weird how things work themselves out, huh?" She thumbed at the house over her shoulder. "I'm gonna get some lunch. You two want anything?"

Eloise shook her head.

"I'm good." Shane tugged on Eloise's hand, pulling her close enough that her side brushed against his. "I think we're just gonna hang out here and chat for a little bit if that's okay."

Brielle's eyes met Eloise's. "I'll be just inside if you need me."

"I'll be fine," Eloise assured her, though her insides begged to differ. She didn't know what Shane was going to want to chat about, but she had a feeling it wasn't going to be an easy conversation. It was times like these that she really wished they could move past the nitty gritty stuff and pretend it didn't happen. But she knew better.

They had to air out the events of the last several weeks. They needed closure.

Once they were alone, Shane guided her over to the porch swing. He didn't release her hand for even a second as they took their seats.

The chains creaked with the weight of their bodies, but besides that, the property was quiet—peaceful. She closed her eyes and rested her head back against the swing. Before she could even start to scold him for not telling her what he'd been dealing with, he started.

"I'm sorry."

She didn't open her eyes. Already the emotion threatened to spill. She'd been on a rollercoaster from the beginning of this relationship, and even now, she didn't have any regrets. That couldn't have been normal.

"I should have told you about my cousins when they arrived. I should have told you what they were capable of when Marc was trying to date you. I should have—"

Her eyes flew open, and she placed a finger against his lips. "You're right. You should have." She heard Shane groan. "But we can't live our lives thinking about what we should have done differently. It happened. It *hurt*. More than I ever could have imagined. But it's starting to move into the past."

Shane still looked so heartbroken. "I don't think I'll ever be able to forgive myself for the pain I caused you."

Her heart ached for him in that moment. He'd been through the wringer more than just at Madeline's hand. He'd had to deal with more pressure than she'd realized. "I love you, Shane."

His eyes widened. "You do?"

She laughed. "Of course I do. I've never stopped loving you. Once you stole my heart, I was done for." Even though she'd tried to keep the emotion locked away, a tear still slipped down her cheek. "It all makes sense now. The things you said, the way you acted, it was all to keep me safe. And while I don't condone any of it, I can understand it a little better."

He took both of her hands in his and brought them to his lips. "You are so amazing."

She shook her head. "I'm not all that *amazing*."

"But you are. Even after everything I did—everything I said—you still wanted to help me."

"I guess that's what people do when they're in love."

"I guess so." He cocked his head to the side. "Does that mean you're gonna give me a second chance?"

"I don't know." Her eyes danced with amusement. "I've been told it's a huge red flag to date someone who broke up with you."

He flinched. "I'm never going to live that down, am I?"

Eloise laughed. "Never."

"Then I guess you're just going to have to let me make it up to you for the rest of our lives."

She grinned. "I think I can handle that."

27

Shane

"I don't know where you've been for the last couple of days, but it's time you start acting like the partner you are and get that contract in my hands." Madeline was draped over the loveseat in Shane's office.

He still hadn't given her access to his house, a point she grumbled about constantly. He was surprised she hadn't pushed the issue more, but he was grateful she was preoccupied enough to let it go for now.

Shane looked up from a report he had in his hand, finding Madeline staring at him. He put the folder down and crossed his arms. The wire beneath his shirt was giving him anxiety. At any moment Madeline could bound toward him like the vulture she was and discover it. Then all would be lost.

According to Janice, they had a good amount of evidence to put Madeline away, but it would also mean that Marc would get just as heavy of a sentence. Their little group had figured on

Madeline rolling over on Marc the first second she got if she were to be arrested. They needed something irrefutable if they wanted to take her down and help Marc in the process.

The whole situation felt like they were diffusing a bomb. One wrong move and Madeline would figure out that they were up to something. It was a miracle she hadn't done so already.

Madeline's eyes narrowed. "What are *you* looking at?"

"You looked at me first."

She rolled her eyes as she reached for one of the decorating magazines on the table nearby. The pages fluttered in the room, being flipped with clear contempt.

Shane released his pent-up breath and returned his eyes to the report, though not really seeing it. Get through today. That's all he had to do. If he could get something on tape, then they could use it to their advantage.

"I think we need to remodel this office so it suits my tastes better."

He glanced up, finding her staring at him.

"Are you even listening to me?"

Slowly, he rose. Placing his hands on the desk, he glowered at her. "This is your last chance to back out of this and walk away."

Madeline's eyes didn't leave his face. For a moment he thought he'd finally gotten through to her. But then she threw her head back and let out a laugh. "Where is *this* coming from?" Madeline tossed her magazine to the table and got up from her seat. "Suddenly you're all big and tough?" She stalked across the office like the predator she was and came right up beside him. Her voice lowered and she purred next to his ear. "You will *never* be free of me. I'm too close to getting what I want. There is no way I'd walk away from that. You think this blackmail is bad? I've done so much worse."

"I know," he muttered.

She pulled back, briefly stunned. "What?"

"Yeah. Marc told me everything."

Madeline laughed again, her cackle echoing through the office. "Marc doesn't know anything."

"He knows enough to get you put away in prison."

Her eyes narrowed and she paused, seeming to understand where this was going. "It doesn't matter what Marc knows. If he were to snitch, he would go away too. Everything I've done has both our names all over it. And you won't do anything because you *care* too much." She pouted. "Poor little Shane, always thinking of others instead of himself." She poked him in the chest. "Don't ever change, buddy."

Madeline laughed again, moving across the room back to her seat.

Shane glowered at her, wishing he could wipe that smug expression off her face. "You must think you're one of the smartest people in the world."

"Yup," she said without looking up from her magazine. "I got everything I wanted, and all I had to do was blackmail my rich cousin and a few politicians." She snickered. "Once I clean that money, I'll be set for life."

He stared at her, his eyes wide. When she looked up at him, she sneered. "What? You can't do anything about it without hurting other people. And what about Brielle? You don't want me to spread that stuff either. So you're stuck."

His heart hammered. He got exactly what he needed on the tape. It would open up an investigation, and she'd get arrested. But she'd made one really good point. Her leverage was how he felt about the Callahans. She could share her secret with anyone. "You know, I have connections at the FBI."

Her eyes cut to his. "Is that a *threat*?"

Shane cleared his throat, shaking his head briefly. "Just something to think about. You might want to consider being nicer to me. If you ever found yourself in a tight spot, I would be the one to pull some strings and help you out. Might want to hold onto that trump card of yours."

The way Madeline's eyes drilled into him made him itch. He didn't want anything to do with the woman who looked at him with such a calculating stare. The sooner she was out of his hair, the better. He only hoped that Janice was listening on the other end of this wire and would acknowledge that she'd come through for *him* when Madeline inevitably got arrested. It was only a matter of time now.

SHANE STOOD TOO QUICKLY and bumped his head on the surveillance van. He winced, rubbing the tender spot.

"You're sure she's going to be there?" Janice demanded. She pushed her glasses up farther onto her nose. "Because if we did all of this and she ends up disappearing, there's nothing I'm gonna be able to do for Marc."

He nodded as she adjusted the camera she'd attached to his collar. "Madeline won't miss this because it's her party. She planned everything right down to the design on the cutlery."

"How does she even know that many people?"

"She doesn't. She's just inviting the whole town, and the folks here are coming because they're *good* people."

Janice lifted a brow. "I'll never understand why you had to come all the way out here. Then again, I guess the reason is inside that country club all dolled up and about to be arrested. With her gone, are you gonna consider moving back to the city?"

Shane shook his head, an easy smile spreading across his face. "This place is my home now. I love it here."

"Mmm-hmm. I think it's a some*one* that's keeping you here."

His thoughts shifted to Eloise and his grin widened. "Maybe you're right." During this whole planning period, he'd had to remain as far away as he could from her. As much as it pained him, he had to let Marc keep an eye on her. Thankfully, Madeline had agreed that Marc swooping in to comfort Eloise was a great plan, and as far as she was concerned, everything was status quo.

Shane stepped back as soon as Janice was done with her work. He needed to confirm something before he went inside. "About Madeline..."

Janice glanced at him. Just by the expression on her face, he could tell she knew where this was headed and didn't want to participate.

"I need leverage."

"You know I can't go to my boss unless I have something concrete. You're the one who refused to tell me what she was blackmailing you with. For all I know, the stuff she's holding over your head isn't worth cutting her a deal. I don't think my boss is going to go for it."

"It's not just that, and you know it. She tracked me down here, and she was willing to wreak havoc on any innocent victim she could use to her advantage. I wager she would have targeted the Callahans even if I hadn't stepped in. I'm not saying give her a lesser sentence. But maybe don't put her in the worst prison? We need to give her a reason to keep her secrets about the Callahans—hold something over her head, like not going to the worst prison. Is that something you would have control over?"

She glanced at her watch. "I can't say. What I can tell you is the sooner we get her into custody, the better for everyone."

"And what about Marc? You said you'd figure something out for him. A shorter sentence or a fine?"

Janice sighed as she faced him. "I can't make any promises at this time. I told you I'd do what I could, but that's all. He was a willing partner in a lot of what Madeline was involved with. Marc worked with her for years."

"But he's put a lot on the line. Madeline could hurt him just as much as anyone here."

She rested her hand on his shoulder. "Let's get tonight over with first." Janice's expression sobered. "You know, there's one thing I don't understand. You said Madeline dug up some stuff on the Callahan family that would hurt *their* reputation. There aren't many who would willingly throw away their own happiness to save another."

"That doesn't sound like a question."

She chuckled. "You're right. It isn't. I guess what I'm getting at is that I'm impressed."

"So you don't think I'm crazy?"

"Oh, you're definitely crazy. I don't know a man in your position who would let anyone yank him around like that. You must really care about these folks."

"I really do."

Janice stopped fumbling with whatever she was working on and glanced at him. Her smile widened, and he could see her coming to the same conclusion he had when he arrived in Copper Creek. "Then I suppose it's all going to work out. Get in there and let's make this happen. All we need is a clear shot and we can send our guys in to grab her and Marc."

Shane stepped from the van, straightened his suit jacket, then headed inside. The club was already full of people. Immediately, he was overcome with an undeniable feeling that he belonged there. The people came out to support *him*. They *cared* about him.

If nothing else, he couldn't let Madeline stay for that one reason alone. She poisoned everything she touched.

There was only one exception.

Marc.

Shane's cousin had been under his sister's thumb for his entire life, and now he was making the right decisions in spite of his sister's influence. It was hard not to be proud of how far Marc had come.

He let his gaze sweep through the club. It didn't appear that Madeline had made her grand entrance yet. She had to be lurking somewhere. Someone tapped on his shoulder, and he turned to find Marc. His cousin shifted nervously, his eyes darting to and fro.

"Have you seen Madeline yet?"

Shane shook his head. "I thought you would have come together."

Marc glanced toward him. "I came with Eloise."

Immediately, Shane's heart took off.

"Is everyone in position?"

His focus landed on Marc, and he forced himself to calm his racing heart. Here was a man who was willingly going into the fire. Shane wasn't even sure he'd be willing to do the same if he were in that position. Willingly giving up the love of his life to save her was one thing, but to throw his whole life away to put someone he cared about in prison was an entirely different matter.

Shane placed his hand on his cousin's shoulder. "I don't think I've gotten a chance to tell you this, but I'm impressed by this new you."

Marc met his gaze, and if Shane wasn't mistaken, there was a degree of embarrassment that came from his compliment. "Thanks."

"If you don't mind my asking... what changed?"

Looking away, Marc squinted at nothing in particular. He took a deep breath and exhaled. "I guess you could say my friendship with Eloise."

"You barely know her." It was hard not to let the jealousy sneak up on him. Eloise had said they spent quite a bit of time together, but Shane hadn't thought it was enough to cause this kind of change.

"I know. But there's just something about how nice she is. Or maybe it's this place. I don't want to see any of them hurt." He gestured around them. "Copper Creek is a special place. Unlike any other place I've experienced."

Shane chuckled. "That's what I've been saying all along."

Finally, Marc met his eyes again. "I know when they arrest me, they're going to take everything. And when I get out, I'm going to need a new place to start over and—"

"You'll always have a place here."

Marc worked his jaw. It wasn't hard to see the way Shane's statement had hit home with him. He nodded and shoved his hands into his pockets. "Thanks. I won't let you down."

"I know you won't." Shane glanced around at the guests once more. "Where are Eloise and Brielle?"

"I think they went to the kitchen or something." Marc tilted his head, a smile touching his lips. "What's up with Brielle? Is she—"

"Don't even think about it." Shane's voice was sharper than he'd intended it, but Marc didn't seem to notice.

"Yeah, I figured you wouldn't want me dating your ex."

"I'm pretty sure you wouldn't be up for the challenge anyway. She's more complicated than even you can handle."

Marc scoffed. "I'll have you know—"

"There's Madeline." Shane nodded to the other side of the room, where Madeline swept through the crowd. Her eyes immediately landed on Shane, and she smiled in that wicked way she had perfected. "Don't give anything away. They're gonna come inside within the next few minutes," Shane muttered through his teeth. "Don't forget to be respectful and go willingly. Janice will notice." Before he could say anything else, Madeline reached him.

She stood right next to him, reveling in what she thought was her victory. He glanced at Marc out of the corner of his eye, only half-surprised to find him still there.

This was really happening. They were going to get rid of Madeline once and for all.

Madeline pulled away from him, then turned to her brother, disdain clear in her eyes. "Where have you been? You were supposed to come with me."

"We talked about it. You said I could escort the Callahans."

Her eyes narrowed, and her lips curled into a derisive sneer. "Well, I don't *see* them. I want to make sure they all get a front-row seat to my conquest of Copper Creek."

"You're not conquering anything or anyone, Madeline. You might be putting on this show for everyone else, but I'm not going to play along."

She rolled her eyes, slipping her hand around his elbow and digging her fingers into the muscle there. "You'll do what I say, or I'll make your life miserable. I don't care what the agreement might say. I'll find more dirt on more people, and you'll be stuck with me forever because you're just that gullible."

He pried her hand from his arm and placed it at her side. "You only have so much leverage, Madeline. I'd be careful how you use it." Where was the crew? Weren't they supposed to be storming the castle by now? He needed this to be over. They all did.

Madeline opened her mouth, probably preparing to throw the gauntlet down, when the doors burst open and half a dozen agents strode into the room. Janice led the fray, coming right to them. She held up a document.

"Madeline Owens, we have a warrant for your arrest. You have the right to remain silent. Anything you say can and will be held against you in a court of law..."

His cousin's eyes flew wide, and she darted behind Shane,

screeching his name and demanding to have her lawyer present, but he moved to give the agents access to her. Madeline swore obscenities at him, then her eyes narrowed. "Do you realize what you've just done? You've orchestrated your own destruction. I can still spill everything I learned about these people and—"

Janice yanked on her arm once her wrists were handcuffed together. "I'd be careful what you say next. You wouldn't want to add defamation to the growing list of charges." She glanced at Shane, her smile more strained than anything else.

"It's not defamation if it's true."

Shane stepped toward her, his voice lowering so only she could hear. "With the evidence we have, you're going to be locked away for a long time. You might want to start making friends now while you still have a chance. This is my college *friend*, Agent Murphey. You'll recall I have a few friends in high places."

Madeline swore at him, her glare shooting sparks of fury. "You'll be sorry you did this, Shane. Mark my words."

Another agent approached Marc, but he held his hands up. "I'm coming peacefully."

"I'm sorry. It's policy." The agent glanced at Shane, then slipped the cuffs around Marc's wrists. "I'll take them off once we get into the car."

"I'm going to get you a lawyer. We'll do what we can to get you out of this," Shane promised.

Marc offered a wan smile. "I'll be fine. Just don't go back on your promise, okay?"

"I wouldn't dream of it."

As Marc was being guided toward the door, Eloise rushed past Shane. She threw her arms around Marc and gave him an awkward hug. Her lips moved, but Shane couldn't tell what she was saying to him. Marc nodded, and the agent nudged him forward.

Shane approached Eloise's side. He didn't dare ask what

she'd said—he didn't think he could handle it. Instead, he draped his arm around her shoulders, and she leaned into him.

"I guess it would be a good idea to make an announcement, huh?"

Eloise let out a sad laugh. "Probably. It's not every day that folks around here get to see a billionaire's cousin, who's also the hostess of the party, get hauled off in cuffs. They might have a few questions."

28

Eloise

Surprisingly, not much happened in the days or even weeks following Madeline's arrest. Eloise couldn't believe how easy it was for the town to accept what had been going on under their noses. It wasn't like they had much of a choice, but even the known gossipers turned to something else rather quickly.

Maybe there was something to be said about that.

Rather than discuss Shane's strange and failed business partnership with his cousin, the ladies shifted their focus to his newest interest.

They wandered along a trail, side by side, as they led their horses behind them. Today was a day to relax and be grateful that their plan hadn't backfired. There was still no indication that Madeline would use her trump card against them. Last they'd heard, she was due for her court appearance and had been on her best behavior.

Eloise leaned into Shane, a contented sigh escaping her lips. "This is nice."

He turned and pressed a kiss to the crown of her head. "Yeah, it is."

"You know, we could have been doing this a lot sooner if you had been more open about what Madeline was up to."

The warm chuckle that reverberated out of his chest gave her pleasant shivers. "And how do you suppose that would have gone? Would you have even believed me?"

She scoffed, stopping so he was forced to do the same and face her. "I would have believed you."

He arched a brow, though a smile tugged at his lips. "Really? Because I'm pretty sure that you ignored my recommendations to stay away from Marc."

Eloise made that sound again as she poked Shane firmly in the chest. "Well, maybe that was meant to be. He seems to have grown because of it. And, to be fair, Marc turned out to be a better ally than you expected."

"Yeah, that was a... surprise."

"Why is it so hard to accept that he's a good guy?"

Shane shrugged. "He wasn't always a *good guy*. But I will say that he seems to be reformed. I guess I never got over how he was pursuing you. You probably would have started dating him if everything had gone according to Madeline's plans."

Eloise cocked her head to the side, studying him. This was a side of him that he rarely showed her. He was usually so closed off—unwilling to open his heart to her. Lately, he'd made great strides in making those connections that had been so hard at first. He told her about growing up without his parents and what had happened when his grandfather passed. It would have been easy to hate Madeline even more after what he'd told her, but she didn't. If it weren't for Madeline and Marc, he might not have ended up in Copper Creek. Everything he'd experienced had brought him to her.

Which only made his statement about Marc that much sweeter. If she hadn't gone on those few dates with the man Shane despised, then they wouldn't have ended up together.

Eloise reached up to touch his face, tracing his jawline with her fingers. "Well, even if he hadn't gone to prison, you still wouldn't have to worry about me dating him. Because I'm in love with *you*."

Shane wrapped his hand around her fingers and brought them to his lips. He brushed a soft kiss to her fingertips, sending fresh waves of electricity through her body. "Good. Because I have something to talk to you about."

He stepped back and pointed east. "Do you know what's out that way, just over the crest of the hill?"

She laughed. "I don't think I've explored that much of your property. I mean, has anyone at the club even gone riding out this far? The trail looks like it's barely been used."

Shane pulled her close, one arm around her waist as he leaned his face closer to her ear. "Just over that hill is a ranch property that I bought."

Eloise's brows pulled together. "The country club already sits on the biggest piece of land other than my father's ranch. Why are you expanding?"

"You want to go see it?"

"I guess. But what does this have to do with our discussion?"

"You'll see." His arm still around her waist, he guided her back to their horses and helped her into the saddle.

She stared down at him as he double-checked the straps for the saddle bags they'd filled for their picnic. His hands made quick and sure work of his task. They weren't large or calloused like her father's hands, nor like the hands of any ranch hand that resided in Copper Creek. But they were his, and they fit perfectly with her own. Those were the hands that could set her on fire with a single touch. They were the hands of a man she loved.

He glanced up at her and grinned. "I can't wait for you to see it. I have a feeling you're gonna like it."

"I'm sure I will."

"No. *Really* like it."

She laughed. "Okay, I get it. Now let's get going so we can have our picnic and head back to my ranch. Faye asked me to do some of her chores, so I have to get back sooner rather than later."

"I have a feeling you're going to want to take your time when I show you what I've got going on."

This right here was one of the reasons she loved Shane so much. He was always thinking about other people. She couldn't think of a single person who did that more. Shane was a good man, and he'd become one despite those around him that wanted to drag him down. At times, it was hard to accept that out of anyone in the world, he'd chosen *her*.

He climbed into the saddle and nodded toward the trail that would take them to the property he was talking about. The ride was a lot shorter than she'd expected. They must have gotten pretty far from the club for them to come up against the fence that divided the ranch from Shane's first property.

She glanced up and down the fence line that stretched for miles in either direction. "There isn't a gate. How are we supposed to get the horses on the other side?"

He climbed down and offered her his hand. "We walk. I'll grab the food. There's a perfect spot for our picnic."

"Yeah? Is there a pond or a creek? Or maybe there's a clearing surrounded by flowers?"

"You'll see." He gave her a quick peck on the lips, then took her hand in his. "I'm not going to ruin the surprise, so you're just going to have to be patient." He dipped low to climb through the fence, then rose on the other side. His eyes flashed with excitement as he jerked his chin in the direction they'd be headed.

All this secrecy only added to the fun. Her chest filled with flutters as she followed the path he'd taken. His hand slipped easily into hers, and they were off.

Her thoughts shifted to Marc. While they'd gotten a lot of updates on Madeline's progress through the judicial system, she'd heard next to nothing about Marc. She didn't know if they were going to cut him a decent deal or if he'd end up serving a full sentence.

"Have you heard from Marc?"

He glanced at her out of the corner of his eye. "Why do you ask?"

Eloise shrugged. "I guess I miss him. I sorta wish he hadn't needed to do what he did—though I get it. I just think it shouldn't have gone down like that."

"To be fair, he was involved in his share of criminal acts."

"I know, but people change. Even you have to admit that."

He sighed. "Yeah. You're completely right on that front. Marc changed for the better." His hand squeezed hers, drawing her focus to his face. "He told me the reason for that, you know."

"He did?"

Shane nodded, bringing her hand to his lips again. She almost sensed a nervousness about him, as strange as that was. He tore his gaze from hers, letting his focus sweep over the landscape. "He said it was because of your friendship."

She laughed, which earned her a surprised look from Shane. "I'm sorry. It's not *funny*. I just don't believe that something like that happens."

He stopped and faced her. "It *does*. And it did for me, too. You changed something in me. You made me want more out of life—more for myself. Before you, I was willing to continue doing everything I could to help others. It was my way of making sense of the gifts I'd been given. I was lucky, Eloise. I was taken in by a loving couple and then again by a man who didn't have to. My family gave me a second chance at life—one I still don't feel like I deserve."

"How can you say that? You do so much for so many people."

"That's what I'm saying. I do it to maintain this... balance." He peered at her, moving closer. "But you helped me see that I deserve to find my own kind of happiness. And I found it with you. I've finally been able to give myself permission to do something for myself."

His words hit with more force than she was anticipating. She held back the emotion that threatened to overflow. Shane had just taught her it wasn't enough just to be a good person for everyone else, but to value oneself, too. She bit her lips together and nodded. "I get it."

He waited for another moment, then motioned again in the direction they were headed. "It's just over the crest of that hill."

Her eyes followed his gesture, and together they hiked to the top. An adorable farmhouse was situated in the middle of nowhere with a barn and a small corral. The ranch looked to only be big enough for crop production. She hated to think that this cute place would be torn down to be added to Shane's growing empire.

Eloise glanced at Shane and smiled. "It's *lovely*."

"I sense a 'but' coming."

She bit back a smile. "*But* I think you should leave it as it is. I'm sure some small family would love living here."

"I'm sure you're right. That's why it isn't for the club."

Her eyes darted to meet his just before the sound of a wooden storm door echoed across the field in front of them. Her focus returned to the house. She squinted, then her eyes flew wide and she spun to face Shane with a gasp. She put her hands on her hips, her tone accusatory. "Why didn't you tell me Marc is here? How long—"

He placed a finger on her lips. "He got a deal. He's going to be under house arrest for a year, and then for the next four years, he'll be confined to Copper Creek. The judge agreed to have him work for me when it gets to that point."

Even from here, she could tell Marc was smiling as he leaned against the column holding the house's porch awning up. "You did it," she whispered. "You came through for him."

"Yes…" he drawled, "but I did it for you, too. I know how close you two got over the last few months. I figured it would be good for him if you remained a positive influence in his life."

She threw her arms around his neck and her lips crashed over his. This had to be the most selfless act Shane had ever done, and he'd done it for her.

Their kiss was thwarted when his lips curled into a smile. Eloise pulled back to give him a strange look.

"I almost wondered if you wouldn't approve."

Her expression pinched as she glanced over toward the house and Marc. "Why wouldn't I approve."

He chuckled. "Because I had to spend a great deal of money to make this work. Getting the ranch back from the auction alone was—"

This time she put her finger to his lips. "I guess sometimes it's okay to use your money to impress a girl. Especially if it means helping family."

"We can definitely agree on that." He pulled her close again, brushing her hair from her face. "I love you, Eloise. And I want to spend the rest of my life with you."

Any attempt to quell the flutters inside her was futile. She tilted her head, keeping her tone light. "You're not proposing to me. Are you?"

"Would that be a problem?"

She shrugged.

"Well, I *did* have this whole thing planned where we could fly out to that lake in Texas and recreate our first date... but I suppose here is just as good."

Her eyes flew wide and she stumbled back from him. "You're not serious."

"Oh, I assure you. One day I will ask you to marry me. And you will say yes."

She blinked, her heart thundering so hard she was sure he could hear it. "Is that so?"

"Yep." Shane closed the distance between them once more. "Be ready, Miss Callahan. I fully intend on sweeping you off your feet."

Eloise crossed her arms and let out a laugh. "How are you going to do that if you don't even know how to dance?"

"You know how to make a guy work for it, you know?"

She couldn't help herself. There was no more need to play, flirt, or otherwise string him along. Eloise slipped her arms around his neck and stood on her toes so her face was inches from his. "Haven't you figured it out by now? I'm already yours."

EPILOGUE

Shane

"This isn't going to work," Shane said in exasperation.

"Relax. You're doing great." Brielle placed her hand on his shoulder. "Come on. One more dance and then you can get out there and make Eloise the happiest woman in the world."

He remained stiff, finding it difficult to allow her to help him. Brielle was the only one who had been willing and available to teach him how to dance. In hindsight, he should have just been patient and gone to the city for professional classes. But that ring had been burning a hole in his pocket since the day he surprised Eloise with Marc's return. One month later, and he knew he couldn't hold onto it one day more.

Eloise would be his, and he would be hers.

"Don't watch your feet," Brielle admonished. "She's going to think you're trying to look down her dress."

He shot her a dark look which only caused her to laugh.

"Come on, I'm allowed. You asked your *ex* to teach you how to dance so you could impress her *sister* and ask her to marry you. I'm never not going to push your buttons."

Shane rolled his eyes. She still had no idea that he knew about her past. And she never would. That little tidbit of information would remain hidden until she was ready to deal with it in her own way.

The music stopped and she pulled away almost too quickly. She crossed her arms and then jerked her head toward the door of his office. "Okay, go on then. Ask her to dance, and then you can make it official." The look on her face hinted at a pain she had buried beneath the surface, and all he wanted to do was assure her it would be okay.

Nope. He wasn't going to do that. She wasn't his responsibility —not in the same way Eloise was. And Brielle wasn't the type to accept help, no matter how good of a place it came from. He swallowed and nodded. "Thank you, Brielle."

She stepped aside. "Just don't break her heart."

"Never," he said as he slipped past her.

The club was filled to the brim. But that was typical for the weekends. The second he stepped into the ballroom, his eyes found her. Eloise chatted with one of her friends who worked in the restaurant. They laughed, and Eloise's eyes moved across the room until they landed on him. She said something more to her friend, then strode toward him.

Her hands remained behind her back, and she rocked forward onto her toes and back again. "Hey."

"Hey."

"I thought you'd never get done with your work. It's nice to see you out of the office."

He reached for her hand and ran his thumb over her knuckles. "I want to ask you something."

She cocked her head to the side and her smile lit up her whole face. "I have an idea of what that might be."

Shane shook his head. "I don't think you do."

"It's like I told you, Shane. I'm already yours—"

"Dance with me."

Her brows shot up and she let out a little laugh, then sobered just as quickly. "You're serious?"

He nodded as he took her hand and led her to the dance floor. The music changed, and she gave him a surprised look. "You've been planning this."

"I had a little help." He glanced over to where the DJ stood and found Brielle standing beside him.

Eloise's focus followed the movement and she gasped. "You're kidding. Brielle?"

He chuckled. "Don't let her find out you know. She wasn't too thrilled about helping me in the first place." Shane led Eloise into a few moves, pleasantly surprised it wasn't as difficult as he thought it would be.

"She just needs to get off her high horse and accept that Wade is crazy about her," she said.

"You noticed too, huh?"

Eloise laughed. "Everyone has noticed. Those two have been doing the 'will-they, won't they' dance for far too long. Brielle should stop pushing him away."

"Maybe she has a good reason."

She shook her head. "Brielle has been around the block long enough. She knows what she wants. She's just not willing to take the plunge."

"Maybe she would if she wasn't already married."

Eloise planted her feet and her mouth dropped open. "She's *what*?"

He grimaced. Shoot. That wasn't supposed to come out. That

was what he got for trying to focus on his footwork instead of their conversation. Shane slipped his hand into hers and tugged her toward the doors. "I only found out because Madeline told me." It wasn't hard to see that Eloise was connecting the dots on that tidbit of information. This was the secret he'd been trying to keep quiet.

"Who?"

Shane shook his head. "I didn't recognize the name on the paper, and I don't remember who it was. It's not someone who lives here." It would definitely be best to keep out the fact that the guy was a dancer in Vegas. "It doesn't matter anyway. Madeline never said whether or not Brielle had filed for divorce. I just didn't want it getting out. Your father—"

"Oh, he'd blow a fuse if he found out." Eloise glanced over her shoulder toward Brielle. "That explains so much, though."

"You can't say anything."

She whipped her head around and gave him a flat look. "I'm not going to rat out my sister. I just feel bad for her."

He made a face. "Somehow I don't think she'd like that either."

"You're probably right." Eloise sighed. "Well, then I might actually be the last to get married out of all of us."

They made it out to the veranda, and Shane grew still. She rested her forearms on the railing, glancing at him before giving him a nervous smile. "What? You can't be *that* worried I'll spill the beans. I kept our relationship a secret—"

"Eloise, I have everything I could ever want in the world."

She snickered. "You don't have to rub it in."

"No. What I'm trying to say is that I don't want anything else. Well, except for one thing."

Eloise sobered, facing him as she leaned her hip against the rail. "Yeah?"

"Yeah," he whispered, moving closer. He brushed the back of his knuckles against her cheek. "I never realized just how empty my life was without someone to share it with. And I've finally found her. You can say you're already mine until you're blue in the face, but the truth is, you'll never be truly mine until you..." He stepped back, dug the ring out of his pocket and sank to one knee. "...until you say yes."

She stared at the ring, her expression not changing. "Are you sure?"

His insides churned. That wasn't the reaction he'd been expecting. "I wouldn't be on my knee if I wasn't."

"It's just that you were so worried about making our relationship public and—"

"Eloise," he said, his heart practically splitting. "It's an easy yes or no answer."

Her eyes flew to meet his as she cut herself off. They stared at each other for what felt like an eternity. Time slowed, noises from the club faded. A breeze tugged at her dress. And then she said the one word that gave him more joy than he would ever deserve.

"Yes," she whispered.

~

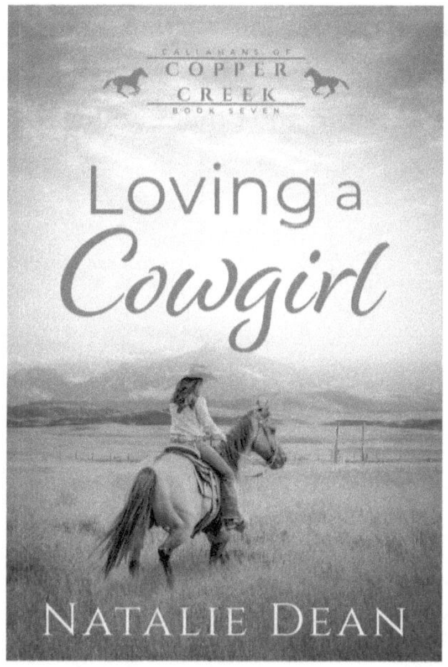

Hello reader,

Did you enjoy Eloise and Shane's love story? Then you won't want to miss what's next with the Callahans...

Brielle Callahan has a secret she's kept for ten years—one that could ruin her family's reputation if it ever came out. When her estranged husband from a reckless Vegas wedding suddenly shows up in Copper Creek, she's forced to face her past.

Wade Keagan has loved Brielle for years and isn't about to let her go without a fight. But to help her save face and protect her heart, he agrees to a crazy plan that tests every bit of his patience—and his love.

Will Brielle see the truth about the man who's always stood by her side, or will her past destroy her chance at happiness?

Don't miss the drama, heart, and second chances in *Loving a Cowgirl, Callahans of Copper Creek Book 7!* Look for the paperback at **nataliedeanbooks.com** and other retailers.

ABOUT THE AUTHOR

Born and raised in a small coastal town in the south, I was raised to treasure family and love the Lord. I'm a dedicated home-schooling mom who loves to travel and spend time with my growing-up-too-fast son.

When I'm not busy writing or running my business, you can find me cleaning house, cooking dinner, feeding our three rescue cats, trying to make learning fun and coaxing my son to pick up his toys. On less busy days, you may also find me paddling down a spring run in Florida, hiking a mountain trail in Georgia (on the rare vacation to the mountains), or enjoying a book.

If you love Natalie Dean books, you can be notified of new

releases by signing up to my newsletter at nataliedeanau thor.com, where you will also receive two free short stories for signing up. Just click on the "Free Books" tab at the top and you'll be on your way!

Also, as previously mentioned, I've opened my own online bookstore and I'd love your support! As of June 2024, I'm selling my ebooks at Natalie Dean Books. By late summer or fall 2024, I should have audiobooks, regular paperbacks, large print paper- backs, dyslexic print paperbacks and signed paperbacks all avail- able. At the request of my loyal readers, I'll also be adding merchandise, such as glasses, cups, magnets and more. So come check out my small mom-owned author business at nataliedean books.com.

You can also scan the QR code below to be taken to the home page of Natalie Dean Books.

facebook.com/nataliedeanromance